Swear

ADRIANA LOCKE

Swear
Copyright © 2017 Adriana Locke
All rights reserved

Cover Design:
Kari March Designs

Photograph:
Adobe Stock

Editing:
Adept Edits

Interior Design & Formatting:
Christine Borgford, Type A Formatting

Also by

ADRIANA LOCKE

To everyone that struggles to find their place in the world.

And to *Susan*. Thank you for being you.

Ford

BLIND DATES WOULD WORK OUT so much better if you were actually blind. And deaf. And maybe a hundred miles away.

My head pounds with the remnants of Blind Date, and final date, Number Three's ridiculous giggle last night.

Each candidate hand-selected by my brother Graham's secretary-turned-girlfriend-turned-pain-in-my-ass seemed decent at first. All were pretty, fairly intelligent, and each of them were memorable . . . just for the wrong reasons. It is possible that maybe, just maybe, I just hold them to an impossible standard set by a woman a long time ago. Either way, it is what it is.

"Mr. Landry?" My secretary's voice chirps through the Bluetooth. "Are you there?"

I take the exit for the freeway and sigh, coming back to reality. "Yeah. I'm sorry, Hoda. I got distracted. What were you saying?"

"I was saying that Graham stopped in a little while ago. He said your cell must be dead because you aren't answering. He asked me to have you call him as soon as possible."

"It's a ploy," I tease. "He's just seeing if you're scared of him."

She laughs. "I'm pretty sure he already knows that, Sir."

"He's a big baby. The whole asshole thing he has going on is just a front." Graham's name blinks across the dash. "And now he's calling me."

"Please answer it."

Chuckling, I hover my finger over the call button. "I'll be back in the office in a few. Talk to you then."

I click over and don't get a chance to greet him. He just talks.

"Hey, Ford, I was looking over the numbers and—"

"I hear you've been terrorizing my employees again. Can you knock it off? I'm not fucking mine. She might quit."

"I'm not fucking mine either. I fired her and then moved her in with me. Remember?"

"Gee, that's right. She—"

"Hi, Ford," Mallory singsongs into the phone, clearly loving catching me off-guard.

"A little warning would've been nice, Graham."

The Georgia sun is hot and high in the sky, blazing through the windshield of my truck. I've been out of the office in meetings with potential clients all morning. I'm desperate to get back to my to-do list, a glass of tea, and some uninterrupted hours of work.

Landry Security is my baby and we're just getting off the ground. After a couple of tours of duty in the military, something I never expected to be a career, this is my first foray into something all my own. Something I'm in charge of, my brainchild. Although Graham, the CEO of our family's business, Landry Holdings, was instrumental in putting it together, it's now all mine. And I love it.

"Before you guys go talking shop, how'd the date go last night?" Mallory asks. "Neither of you called me, so I was hoping that meant it went well."

"She spent fifteen minutes giving me a dissertation on nail polish, Mal. A quarter of an hour discussing the way the light bounces off reds differently than pinks. And although she volunteered to wrap her legs around my face and let me do my own little experimentation, the conversation was mind-numbing."

"But," Graham interjects, "did you do the experimenting?"

"Damn right I did."

"Just stop it, both of you," Mallory sighs. "Let's focus on what matters: you didn't hit it off?"

"No, we didn't hit it off. I mean, I hit it and got off, but . . ."

"I'm starting to wonder whether you really want to find someone or not," Mallory groans.

I can't help but laugh. "I told you from the beginning I don't. I only went along with this blind date BS because you made it a requirement to borrow your yoga studio to train my security guys. Otherwise, I'd be—"

"Hooking up with women with 'KARMA' tattooed across the top of their butt cracks," she deadpans.

Graham's laugh booms through the truck speakers, making me wince.

"I'm never telling Lincoln anything again. Our brother has no loyalty," I say, trying not to laugh too. "And for the record, there were butterflies along with the lettering."

"Oh, that makes it better," Mallory says, sarcasm thick in her tone.

Graham's laugh breaks through our banter again. "Sometimes I listen to you two and wonder if you're the siblings and I'm the outsider."

"Oh, no, G. You brought her into this family. That honor is all yours."

"Damn right it's an honor," Mallory teases.

I unscrew a water bottle with one hand and bring it to my lips, keeping my eyes on the road as my brother and his girlfriend banter back and forth.

Moments like this remind me of how different things are from what I expected when I was discharged and moved back to Savannah.

My brothers, all three of them, are settling down. Graham has Mallory. Our oldest brother, Barrett, the newly minted Governor of Georgia, has Alison, and Lincoln, the youngest, walked away from a major league contract to marry Danielle.

At least my baby twin sisters, Camilla and Sienna, are as confused about their lives as me.

Mallory clears her throat. "So . . . how do you feel about one more blind date?"

"I feel like that's the most ridiculous question I've ever heard. My debt is paid. Move along."

"But I saved the best for last," she promises as I swerve through traffic and let loose a slew of profanities.

"Hey! Where are you?" my brother asks.

I check the overhead signs and relay the information. "Why?"

"Great! This is perfect. Can you do me a favor?"

"Depends on what it is."

Sliding my truck between two semi's, I get rewarded with a loud honk from the one behind me. I give him a little wave. He doesn't know I've driven heavy machinery in the middle of gunfire in a war zone. Twice. I do the honorable thing and ignore him flipping me the bird.

"I need you to swing by a place not far from you," Graham says. "I'll text you the address."

"I'm going there for what?"

"To check it out," he says blankly. "I told them we'd swing by and give them a security plan and estimate."

"By 'we' you mean me."

"Semantics."

The text comes across the screen and I see I'm not far at all from where he needs me to go. Still, I need to get back to the office and have little interest in picking up a small job on the side.

"I don't really have time for this," I sigh. "What kind of thing is it? We talking personal security? Business? What?"

He takes a deep breath that worries me. Something about the way he does it causes the hair on the back of my neck to rise, but before I can call him out on it, he replies. "I'm not sure. I just had a quick conversation about it and am doing it as a personal favor to a close friend."

"I suppose I could send Mike." I start to mentally go through the schedule and remember where he's working today and if he can make it to this side of town before the end of the day.

"This is a personal favor, Ford. I need you to go. Not Mike."

I can't tell him no. Graham does everything for our family and keeps the businesses running like the well-oiled machines they are. There's nothing I could ask of him that he would deny. Even though I have no interest in this little mission, I have to do it, and he knows I will.

"Fine," I groan. "Just check it out and provide some kind of plan?"

"Yeah. Just go and see what you think. I have confidence you'll work it out when you get there."

"You owe me, asshole."

We say our goodbyes as I take the exit I need. Before the country song on the radio is over, I'm pulling up in front of the location.

"He's got to be kidding me."

I parallel park my truck across from a row of storefronts. Glancing at my phone, I read the address on Graham's text again. Then I look back at the numbers just below the mint green awning with the word "Halcyon" spelled out in bright pink letters. The numbers match.

I can't believe what I'm seeing. Why in the world would Graham send me here? He knows my business plan and the types of customers I want to attract. This is not it. This is almost disrespectful.

With a groan, I grab my phone and call my brother back and mince no words.

"Are you fucking joking?" I ask. "You sent me to some little shop called Halcyon?"

He tries not to laugh. "I take it you made it."

"Graham, for fuck's sake! I'm trying to run a reputable business here and you send me to provide security for a little . . . whatever this is. A department store? No, it's not even that."

"It's a boutique," Graham supplies.

"Well, you can call that *boutique* and tell them Landry Security is booked. I'm not providing some rent-a-cop service."

"You are going inside and doing a visit because the contract has been signed," he says carefully.

"I haven't signed shit."

"No, but I have."

I almost come out of my seat. "You can't do that!"

"I already did."

"Graham, what the hell?" I say, my blood starting to boil. "Why would you do this? You can't do this. I'm the CEO of Landry Security."

He sighs, his irritation as thick as mine. "And I'm the CEO of Landry Holdings, which owns Landry Security. So, in a way, I'm your boss."

"Apologize to Mallory for me."

"Why?"

"And Mom. Tell her I'm sorry."

"What the hell are you talking about?"

"I'm going to kick your ass."

He laughs. I don't.

"There's already been a deposit paid. Just do the review and then if you really don't want to do it, I'll figure it out. But I need you to do this for me."

I glance at the building again. There is black paper hung so you can't see in, but white Christmas lights outline the windows from the inside. Next to the door, there's a sign with "CLOSED" written in red.

"Graham, this is such a waste of my time."

"Maybe. Possibly. Probably," he chuckles. "But I've committed and I need you to follow through."

"You need committed," I mutter.

"Just do it for heaven's sake."

"Fine," I growl, opening the door of my truck and stepping out on the street. Locking up behind me, I stride through the two lanes of traffic to the sidewalk in front of Halcyon.

The bakery next door has its door propped open and the smell of cinnamon rolls takes away some, but not all, of my irritation.

"I'm here," I let him know. "And when I'm done, I'm coming for you."

"I'll be waiting."

"You should run. It's gonna hurt, brother."

"I'll try to prepare myself."

Rolling my eyes, I end the call and slip the phone back into my pocket. My palm pressed on the bright white door, I give it a gentle shove.

Ellie

"DO WE WANT A POP-UP when someone logs onto the website? Or just a tab at the bottom for them to sign up for the newsletter?" Violet Schaffer looks at me over the top of her computer, playing with the tail of her long, red braid. "I prefer the tab. The pop-ups stress me out, although research says they're effective."

"Research also suggests that anti-aging creams reduce fine lines and wrinkles," I point out. "I still have crow's feet."

"You do not," she laughs.

"Oh, I do too. But it's fine. I'll just continue to wear bright lipstick and low cut shirts to divert attention away from my eyes."

"Speaking of your cleavage, did the guy from the bistro call you last night?"

"Yup," I say cheerfully, examining some sunglasses we just got in. "I hit the trusty FU button. Right to voicemail he went."

Violet hangs her head, her braid swishing on the tabletop. "Why?"

"Meh," I shrug.

"Meh?" She looks up at me and rolls her eyes. "What more could you possibly want? He was very good-looking, had a good job from what we could overhear, smelled fantastic, and I so kindly gave him *your* number and not mine."

"Only because you have had two good weeks of screwing Jonas."

"Your point?"

"That doesn't make Bistro Guy any less meh to me."

She flashes me another look, one that says I'm too picky, but I ignore it. We've been over this too many times to count and it always ends up the same way—her confused and me frustrated.

So what if I have a laundry list of stipulations a man must meet to even spark my interest? That doesn't make me a bad person. It doesn't even make me difficult. It makes me smart.

It's not me that keeps getting burned by men over and over. Yes, I got roasted once. Hurt so badly that I didn't think I'd survive . . . but I did. And like all the songs say, I'm stronger for it. I'm even thankful for it. There's no way I'd be the me I am without having had my heart smashed from the start.

"Maybe all those things don't add up to the homerun you think they do," I suggest.

"Maybe you'll never know if you FU him." A grin dances across her lips. "I'd have FU'd him in a much more gymnastic way."

"I'm sure you would've," I laugh.

We go back to the tasks at hand, Violet working on Halcyon's website and me sorting through shipments of inventory for our new shop. Vi is the brains behind the operation with her business degree. I'm the sales specialist with my major in marketing. Our store is a little shop of affordable, stylish, and practical items for women. It's not just clothes, but accessories, lifestyle items, and fun trinkets. The best part about our business model is that a percentage of every purchase goes to local charities, including Shelters for Savannah, the one closest to my heart.

The grin on my face that's ever-present when I'm inside this building is pasted on my lips. I've never had something that makes me want to get up in the morning and just get after it before now. This isn't just a job to me. It's the start of a new life, one that I worked my tail off for.

After working my way through college in Florida, waiting tables and cleaning office buildings, I worked in marketing at an online company for a few years. I paid my dues, strategized, saved, and made my way.

And here we are.

The door chimes in the front and Violet looks at me with a furrowed brow. "You expecting someone?" she asks.

"Nope."

"Could be Mr. FU," she teases.

"Oh," I say with mock excitement. "Hold me back."

"You're such a jerk," she laughs. "I'll see who it is. I need to grab my water bottle anyway." She takes off through the doorway towards what will be the sales floor. Her footsteps trail off under the hip-hop music she has playing from her phone through the sound system.

It's a few minutes before I hear her clear her throat. Glancing up, she's standing at the doorway with a huge smile on her face. She wiggles her eyebrows.

"What's that all about?" I laugh.

"I hope he has a brother," she giggles, walking towards me.

"Who?"

"The security guy. Holy hell, Ellie."

Tossing a checkered blouse back in a bin, I face her. "He's cute, I take it?"

"Cute? Ha! He's tall, but not dark, and so, so handsome. Like, *so handsome*," she exaggerates, one hand lying dramatically over her heart. "Did I mention he's wearing a suit? I just want to rip it off with my teeth—"

"Down girl," I laugh, shoving her playfully. "Are you going to show him around or what?"

"Do you seriously want to leave that to me? It could be an insurance liability before we ever even open our doors."

Laughing, I see her point. "I'm not sure what the end goal here is, really. I get we aren't in the ritzy part of town, but I'm not sold on the idea we need to pay for security."

"I'd pay for that."

"Violet!"

"Hey, a girl's gotta do what a girl's gotta do."

"Lord, help me," I mumble. "Okay. I'll show him around and then we can kindly tell him we don't need his services. Sound like a plan?"

"You are so not fun," she pouts.

"Hey, tell Mallory you need security at your house," I joke. "Have her send him to you there where you can really *do business*, if you get my drift."

She points at me. "You're a genius."

"It's been said." I glance down at my blouse, now a little worse for wear from moving boxes and cleaning shelves. "Do I look decent? I don't have dirt anywhere or cookie crumbs on my shirt, right?"

"No, but check between your boobs," she teases.

"He's not going to be seeing between my boobs."

"Not with that attitude."

Shaking my head, I leave the back room. As I enter the front, my feet stutter-step.

This only happens to me every once in a while, maybe twice a year now, when I'm in a crowded restaurant or a movie theater. Every time, when I think I smell his cologne, my breath catches in my throat. Without fail, I'm taken back to warm summer nights, cheap strawberry wine, and the sound of crickets chirping as the sun goes down. My heart flip-flops and I have to remind myself of the rest of that story to settle myself back down again.

I round a stack of boxes, a couple of cans of paint we're testing on the walls, and a few racks that need assembled. The mess distracts me, especially the swatch of paint on the far wall. It's more of a lime green than a mint one and I hate it. Making a mental note to talk to Vi about it, my head whips to the side and I see a large body standing near the front windows.

"Hi, I'm . . ." My voice drifts away, shoved aside by the sheer incredulity of the moment. "I . . ."

I've often wondered as I've taken a seat in that restaurant or movie theater what would happen if I turned around and the cologne *was* coming from Ford Landry. Now I know.

My hand trembles as it flies to my mouth as my brown eyes nearly bug out of my head. The organ inside my chest responsible for loving this man betrays the years of telling it I don't anymore. It throbs so wildly I think I'm going to pass out.

The man I haven't seen in so long that I almost convinced myself he never existed is here, in Halcyon, like he just wandered in off the street.

"Oh, my God," I stutter, reaching blindly for something to grab on to.

His head is down, pointed to the floor, as he crouches and examines a box of hats. The hard line of his jaw is angled to my benefit, the expanse of his shoulders and chest awe-worthy. He fills out the pricey black suit stretched over his body like it was made just for him.

His hair is lighter now and there are little lines he didn't used to have at his temple. He still carries the regal-ness that the Landry's are known for. Somehow, in all that, he's maintained the sense of approachability that I always loved about him.

Simply put, he isn't the boy I used to know. He's an amplified, all-male version that has me gasping for breath.

The fog in my brain starts to lift as he stands. Panic creeps into my belly, along with a heavy sense of dread. I've managed to avoid the little ice cream shop on the east side of town where we used to go get milk-shakes. It hasn't been that hard driving to the movie theater in the town next door so I don't have to remember making out with him in the back of ours. But as he starts to turn his head my way, I realize: there is no ignoring him now.

I turn to head to the back when my shoulder bumps a stack of boxes and knocks them off balance. They topple to the floor. Ford whirls right around.

To face me.

For the first time in almost ten years.

His eyes widen, his head twisting to the side like he's as surprised to see me as I am him. I take a step back, needing every bit of space between us as my emotions struggle to get in line.

"Ellie?"

The richness of his tone, the way my name sounds rolling off his tongue, sends a shock wave through me. I don't answer him. I don't trust my voice. Not yet.

"My God, Ellie. Is that you?"

This can't be happening.

I watch his face transform from curious and confused to confident and assessing. He takes me in from head to toe, the weight of his gaze washing over me like a warm blanket.

I lift my chin. "How are you, Ford?"

I'm impressed at how smooth I sound. It gives away nothing—not at how much he hurt me or how much I've managed to hate him or how surprised I am that he's here. It's completely devoid of any shits given. It's perfect.

"I . . ." He stammers, still wrapping his brain around the situation. He runs a hand through his hair, the way he does when he's nervous or thrown for a loop. "Wow. I didn't expect to see you here."

"I'll bet."

"I didn't mean it like that," he says hurriedly. He takes a step, then stops. "I . . . How are you? How have you been?"

"Great." I give him the sweetest smile I can manage, but he notices the sarcasm. "And why are you here?"

"To do a security assessment, actually." He looks around the room. "Is this place yours?"

"Yes."

"Were you expecting me?" He gives me a hopeful look, one that I have to look away from. I don't want to see anything in his features, hear anything in his voice, that will make me feel anything but the detachment I've managed to hone when it comes to him.

Or that I think I've honed for him. The way my hands are shaking, I'm not sure I have it as mastered as I may have believed.

"If I'd known you were coming, I would've cancelled the appointment."

"Ellie," he breathes, "I just want to say—"

"It's okay. You don't need to say anything," I say simply. "I didn't know it was you coming as much as you didn't know it was me you were coming to. No harm, no foul."

We stand in the middle of Halcyon, watching each other from opposite sides of a trench dug deeply between us so long ago. There are so many landmines scattered around us, things ready to explode, and I know he feels it too. It's best we just end this now.

"We don't have a need for security," I say, clearing my throat. "I'll thank Mallory and tell her we decided it wasn't necessary."

"Wait. Mallory? As in Mallory Sims?"

I nod.

He looks at the ceiling and laughs. "I'm gonna fucking kill her."

"Me too," I mutter under my breath. "How do you know Mallory?"

"She's dating my brother, Graham. They're living together, actually."

"Oh," I say, pulling my brows together. "That's so odd. She couldn't have known that you and I, um . . ."

There's no easy way to say what we were to each other. The fact of the matter is, I'm not even sure myself. I'm not about to open up that can of worms and let all of that mess out in the middle of the store. Not with Violet around. Not after all these years.

It's done. I loved him. I needed him. He left me. Done.

His lips press together as he struggles with how to respond. Finally, he shrugs. "I know it seems odd, but with Mallory in the mix, it just got a whole lot less random. How do you know her?"

"I just started taking yoga at her studio. This security thing was a 'token of friendship,' she called it, for Violet and I. But, as we can see, it's totally unnecessary."

Turning on my heel, I take precisely one step before he speaks.

"I'm happy to draw up a security plan," he offers. There's something hidden in those words, an emotion I'm not interested in picking apart. Instead, I face him.

"We don't need you. Thank you though."

"I didn't say you needed me."

We exchange a look, mine verging on a glare, his something else entirely.

"Look, Ellie, I—"

Silencing him with a shake of my head, I half-laugh. "I don't know what you're going to say, but I don't want to hear it."

His face falls a bit. "What if I wanted to say I'm sorry?"

"I would try not to laugh."

"Ellie—"

"If you're sorry for what you should be, you're about a decade too late."

"I know."

For a split second, I look at him objectively. There's a hint of sadness behind those baby blue eyes, and if I looked deep enough, I would remember the Ford I used to know. A look of vulnerability. A glimpse of uncertainty. Not the fine-as-hell man in front of me, but the boy that wasn't sure how he fit in the world around him.

It's a good thing I don't look too hard because it makes it that much easier to remember everything else.

"What's been going on with you?" He leans against the wall, finding his footing. The hesitation has cleared from his eyes and he's watching me now, looking for a weakness.

He's my weakness. It's a good thing he doesn't know that.

"I don't have time for small talk," I scoff, feeling my determination to resist him begin to wane. "I have a million things to do."

"As do I," he grins. "But my day was scheduled prior to knowing you were in town." He shoves off the wall, towering over me with his six-foot-three frame. "It's been a long time, Ellie."

"Not long enough."

Instead of backing him down, my words seem to only rile him up. He grins. The asshole grins at me.

My eyes involuntarily roll in my head. "Some things never change."

"You're right. Some things don't." His head cocks to the side, his smile deepening. "And some things do."

"I'm not playing words games with you," I huff. "Why don't you see yourself out?"

"Why don't you go to dinner with me?"

"What part of this conversation are you not understanding?" I take a step towards him, my eyes narrowed. "I don't want you in my building, and I sure as hell don't want to go to dinner with you."

It's only when I'm standing directly in front of him, head tilted back to look into his face, close enough to be able to lean my head against his chest and have him wrap his powerful arms around me, do I realize what a bad idea this was.

Our breathing quickens, his eyes growing stormy. A chill tears through me as he accidentally-on-purpose brushes his arm against mine. It's like muscle memory, my body remembering exactly what to do around his.

My knees dip, my mouth waters, and I fight the ache in between my thighs as he looks down at me like it's *me* he wants for dinner.

"What if I throw breakfast in afterwards?" he prods. "Does that make me, I mean it, more appetizing?"

That's all it takes, that one little hint of arrogance, that brings me back to reality.

I flip him a smile. "It makes it less, actually."

His own smile wavers. "I get that you might dislike me."

"Dislike you? Try again. It's much more than that."

I'm not sure that's true—I don't know how to put into words how I feel about him. I just know that right now isn't the time to try.

"I want the chance to explain," he says. "Give me the chance to sit down and talk to you."

"You have the same chances of getting the chance to explain as I do of getting what every woman wants."

"What's that?"

I lean in, like I'm going to tell him a secret. "Being able to eat all the pizza and not gain an ounce."

I start to head to the back as his chuckle fills the room. "That was good. I'll give you that."

I shrug and keep walking.

"You can at least let me apologize."

The authority in his tone, like I owe him something, stops me in my tracks. I whirl around to face him. "You don't deserve a chance to apologize to me."

"I didn't say I deserved it," he says earnestly. "But I would love the opportunity to do so." He forces a swallow, my eyes glued to his lips. "I would appreciate the chance to get to see you again."

The snicker that comes from me is unexpected by both of us. "So charming. I forgot how good you are with words."

"Does that mean that's a yes?"

"That means that's a no," I smile. "That means I'm not about to let you come in here and look at me with those bright blue eyes and make me forget what it felt like to have you rip my heart out."

"I didn't mean to do that, Ellie."

"Don't act surprised," I laugh angrily. "There's no way you thought I just went on with my life after you left. I dated you for four years, Ford. And after what we went through . . ."

It's me gulping now, the anger so palpable that I almost have tears in my eyes. My hands shake as I remember the fight that ensued after he told me he was enlisting.

"You left me," I repeat, shaking my head. "So leave me again. There's the door. Should I hold it open for you this time?"

I motion behind him, my eyes trained on his.

He takes me in for a long moment, a lifetime of memories washing over his features. With one final smile and an ease in his shoulders, he heads to the door. I sigh a breath of relief.

"What time should I swing by next week?" he asks.

"What are you talking about? Was I not perfectly clear?"

"You were," he says simply. "So do you get in around eight? Nine?"

A rustle breaks out behind me, surprising us both. Vi approaches with an amused look in her eye. "Am I interrupting something?" she asks sweetly.

"Not at all," Ford chirps, deliberately looking over my head. "You can actually help."

"I'd love to," she says all too happily.

"Can you tell me what time you usually start in the mornings?"

"Vi . . ." I warn.

She ignores me, her eyes dead-set on the hunk of man candy in front of her. "I'm usually here by nine, but I think you mean what time Ellie will be here."

"Violet."

She ignores me. "Ellie is usually here by nine-thirty, depending on the line for vanilla lattes at Frank's."

"Great. I will see you next week then," he says.

"No, you won't," I command. As he opens the door, ignoring me completely, a stream of fear and anger roars through my veins. "We don't want you here, Ford."

He turns on his heel. Bending down so we're at almost eye-level, his breath is hot against my skin. "Go to dinner with me."

"No."

"Fine. I'll see you around nine-thirty," he grins.

"No, you will not!"

He leans against the door frame. "You can't expect me to know you're here and not want to see you."

"I absolutely can expect that and I do."

"Oh, just let him come back," Violet almost begs. "I mean, look at him, Ellie."

"Stay out of this, Violet," I groan.

Ford chuckles, but doesn't take his eyes off mine.

"This isn't funny, Ford. I have a business to run—"

"Me too, and mine has a contract with yours."

"No, you don't," I state matter-of-factly.

He looks at Violet with a smirk that almost melts me. "You seem like a reasonable woman. Isn't it prudent to have some sort of security plan in place to protect your assets? Why do all this work and leave it open to unnecessary risk?"

I roll my eyes. "Seriously?"

Ford ignores me and keeps his focus on my helpless friend. "I'd love to come back and put together a plan for you. And, if price is an issue, I have a crazy deal this week that we could throw in."

"Ellie did mention the budget," Violet offers.

"How does this work for your budget?" he turns to me. "It's free."

I look at the ceiling, words escaping me, as Violet begins to laugh.

"I'll be here in the next few days to get started," he grins.

"Ford, please," I stutter, trying to figure out a way to stop this before he disappears. "This isn't necessary."

"I'm not just going to walk away from you again that easily." He lets his gaze linger on me for a moment longer than necessary. Then he looks behind me. "Nice to meet you, Violet."

The sunlight seems to swallow him as he jogs across the street, his suit jacket trailing behind him.

Ellie

MY FEET ARE FROZEN IN place as I stare at the spot he just occupied. I can still feel Ford in the room, smell his cologne, sense his energy. Violet comes up behind me and presses the door shut, the sound barely registering in my daze.

I'm stunned. Downright, absolutely dumbfounded.

"You know he's totally coming back, right?" Violet laughs, shaking me out of my reverie.

Words don't come. There aren't enough syllables in the English language to string together a coherent summary of my thoughts.

"And if you hadn't been so hateful, you could've been coming right now too," she adds.

"Really, Violet?" I sigh.

"Yeah, really. He looked at you like he wanted to eat you!"

As I make my way into the back room and towards the mini-fridge with the small bottles of cheap wine, she just keeps talking.

"And you can't pull that 'I'm so not interested in this hot guy' act again because *that* was no run-of-the-mill hot guy!" She wedges herself between me and the fridge. "Don't even tell me he doesn't check off every single one your silly little boxes."

"What boxes are those?" I tap my chin in faux-thought. "The ones with all the characteristics of a man I actually want? Yeah, no," I say, rolling my eyes. "He doesn't."

"What could he possibly be lacking? And don't tell me if he has a small dick because that would just ruin so many dreams I just had."

Glaring at her, I move her out of my way and extract a bottle of vino. "He's handsome. I'll give you that. He's intelligent, or he was when I knew him, anyway. He's sexy as hell and he's good with his tongue." I open the bottle and grin salaciously. "I'll let you consider in how many ways."

"Oh, God," she almost moans.

"He most likely has a good work ethic and definitely has a good family name. The Landry's are definitely good people." I begin to tip back a drink but stop. "And his cock is huge."

Violet falls dramatically onto the pink couch in the corner, one hand falling across her forehead.

The wine goes down effortlessly, the alcohol no match for my amped up state. I wipe my mouth with the back of my hand.

"There's no shame in your game," Violet says with a touch of disgust on her face. "I feel like I should join you, but I have a suspicion you aren't celebrating."

"What would I be celebrating, Vi?"

"Call me crazy, but if any female I know, other than you was asked out to dinner by a man looking half that good, they'd be celebrating."

"Most women have no idea the destruction a man looking half that good can cause."

The look I give her works. She frowns, holding up her hands as if she's surrendering.

I'm grateful that the ribbing stops. My head is going too many directions and her jabs just keep spinning me around. Flopping down next to her, I take a deep breath, glad I no longer smell eau de Landry.

"This is not what I had planned for today," I say on a sigh. "Or ever for that matter."

"How long has it been since you saw him?"

"Almost ten years."

"Wow."

I rest my head on her shoulder. "I started dating him when I was almost fifteen. We were together all throughout high school. I went to public and he went to Providence, a private school across town. We spent almost every evening and all our weekends together from the day we met until the day he left."

"Oh," she draws out, putting things together. "He's the one . . ."

"Yes. He's the one that, after the worst few weeks of my life, signed up for the military and took off."

The look of pity is the exact one I've tried to avoid. That's why I never delved into the ins and outs of my relationship with Ford. It's the same reason I've never even really said his name.

I don't want pity because I don't want to seem pitiful. While he may have decimated me in the past, I am where I am because of that. Because of him.

"I'm so sorry, El. Had I known that was him, I wouldn't have been so ga-ga."

"Yes, you would've," I laugh.

"Well, probably," she giggles. "But I wouldn't've been as nice. How's that?"

"That's fair." Raising my head, I manage a real smile. "I know you look at him and think one thing. I don't blame you. But don't blame me for not being in that same boat."

She grins. "I don't blame you for not being in the same boat. I blame you for not being in his bed."

"You are a crappy friend," I laugh, standing and heading back to the fridge. "A good friend would have my back right now."

"What must've he done to you?" She gasps. "Did he cheat on you? If he cheated on you, that's it. He just fell from an eleven to a seven."

"Just a seven?" I pull out another bottle of wine.

"I just can't go below a seven and not lie."

"Well, he didn't cheat. I don't think he would cheat, actually. It's not in his makeup."

"Good. I'll bump him to a nine until I hear the offense."

Violet might be my best friend in the entire world, but there are reasons I haven't told her the details. I haven't told anyone. I don't know if I ever will. It's too embarrassing and makes me sound too weak, too much like a lovestruck teenager.

"You aren't going to tell me, are you?" she asks.

I slump back into the sofa beside her.

Finally, she looks at me and smiles. "Maybe this is the universe's way of putting you two back together."

"Maybe this is Mallory's way of being a busybody," I counter. "Or the universe telling me I did fine without him."

Violet's inner romantic is dying over this. She's plotting out our romance novel already. She's nearly bouncing on the balls of her feet.

"This isn't like you and Luca," I warn her. "There isn't going to be some whirlwind reunion like the two of you have every year."

"But it could be," she insists "You've been in love with that guy, rightfully so, since the day I met you."

My heart breaks a little. I won't admit that and I won't deny it either. Neither would make a difference.

"Love isn't always enough," I say. "Besides, I'm not sold on the idea that I loved him anyway. Maybe I loved the idea of him or it was some first-love thing that I haven't gotten over. That's normal, I think."

Violet just looks at me unconvinced.

"He didn't come here to see me, Vi. He came here to do business."

"You could've been his business, methinks."

"Burn me once, shame on you," I say, standing up. "Burn me twice, shame on me."

"Burn me three times, he must be really hot," Violet winks.

She wraps her arm around me and says the first thing she's said today that makes sense. "Let's grab that other bottle of wine and get back to work."

Ford

THE SOUND OF THE DOOR shutting echoes through the foyer of Graham's house. I march through the marbled hallway towards the lights in the back. The house smells like cilantro and pepper and it makes my stomach rumble. After the shock of the afternoon, I forgot to have lunch.

I've held myself back from calling Graham about Ellie today for three reasons. One, I needed to wrap my brain at least halfway around it before I faced their—meaning Mallory's—onslaught. Two, I know they expected a call and it would drive them crazy not knowing what I was thinking. Three, I wanted to do this in person.

My self-restraint was worth it. The looks on their faces as I waltz into the kitchen is everything I imagined it would be. Shock. Anticipation. Maybe even a little fear.

So worth it.

Graham is standing behind the island, facing me, a large knife in one hand and a cutting board filled with vegetables in front of him. Mallory is at the stove, but quickly turns away from me like whatever she's cooking is the most important thing in the world.

"How was your day?" I ask. Swiping a piece of cauliflower off the board, I head to the dine-in table. I don't sit. I'm entirely too keyed up to relax.

My blood pulses through my veins at a heart-attack tempo. It's not that I'm mad, because I'm not. Ellie is the reason I accomplished not even a piece of paper's worth of work once I got back to the office. She's why Hoda got to go home early today. It's because I saw her that I feel like I'm walking on air and my brain is firing on all cylinders.

I set my gaze on my brother.

"I had a fine day," Graham says carefully. "What about you?"

"My day was peachy." I motion towards Mallory. "What about you, Mal? How did your day go?"

"It was good." She tries to sound chipper, but I hear the stress in her tone. I almost laugh.

"I thought you would've called me today," Graham says, looking at the green pepper in his hand.

"Why would you think that?"

"Oh, just . . . you know . . ."

"What you pulled today deserves way more than a phone call. This deserves a personal visit."

Graham makes a face as he slices the pepper. He's still trying to figure out how to play his hand, and I'm not giving him anything to go on. He's frustrated—that's clear. Curious, too. But I'm not about to make this any easier on him. It's too much fun watching him squirm.

I start to speak again when we hear footsteps and it's just a few seconds before Camilla comes in.

"Do any of you knock?" Graham asks, looking between Cam and I.

"You don't at my house," I point out.

"Or mine," Cam says, also helping herself to the veggies in front of our brother. "I don't even have the ability to go on a date without a series of questions. So, yeah, I think walking into your house is acceptable." She crunches on a carrot. "How are you, Mallory?"

She looks over her shoulder at my sister before accidentally meeting my gaze. She turns back quickly to the stove. "Good," she mumbles.

"Why don't you have a seat, Swink?" I ask, using the family nickname for Camilla.

"Sure. But why?"

"I'll be the one asking questions." I stand tall and look at my brother. "I'd like to blame this on you, G, but I have a feeling the guilt lies . . . elsewhere."

Mallory rolls her shoulders up and down but still doesn't turn around. A grin tickles the corner of my lips, but I fight it. I don't want to give them something to go on quite yet.

You could hear a pin drop as they await my next move.

"How's yoga going, Cam?" I ask, knowing it's only going to drive Graham even crazier. "Have you been attending classes regularly? Really working on your flexibility?"

"Yeah. I've been working on my Handstand Scorpion," she offers. "Why all the interest?"

"No reason. What about you, Mal? How have your classes been going?"

"Great. Enrollment is up. It's going well."

Graham drops the knife with a sigh. "I can't take this. Cut the shit. How'd it go with Ellie, Ford?"

"Oh, crap," Camilla mumbles, leaning away from me like I might explode.

"Did you know about this?" I ask her.

"Um . . . kind of?"

"Let me ask you all, since you're co-conspirators from what I can gather: What on the face of the Earth made you think it was a good idea to send me to see her with no warning?"

They all start to talk at once, Mal's hands flying through the air, Camilla bouncing off her chair, Graham holding his hands out in defense. I whistle as loud as I can and they stop mid-sentence.

"Mallory? You're up," I say, flashing her a look.

"I put two and two together a couple of days ago."

"How? Did she say something about me?"

"Not exactly," she admits. "She mentioned being from here and said just enough about a guy that she never named that matched with things Graham or you have told me. I couldn't help it, Ford. I didn't think you'd be mad."

Leaning back against the table, I blow out a breath. "This isn't a blind date. Ellie and I know each other. There's a history there and that makes it entirely more complicated than a blind date. And you," I say, turning to Camilla. "You were in on this?"

"I wouldn't say I was in on it," she winces.

"Oh, you were too!" Mallory cries. "You helped me get the plan together."

"And you went along with it." I look at Graham. "Fuckin' A, G. I didn't expect this out of you. Don't you have enough shit to do than worry about what or who I'm doing?"

"I'll have you know I was against this at first," he says, popping a cherry tomato in his mouth. "But when I realized it was Ellie, I thought these two were on to something for once. Maybe you needed to see her and get some closure or whatever it is you need."

Mallory steps towards me with a look of determination on her face. "I didn't think this was overstepping, but maybe it was. I just want you to be happy, Ford."

"Maybe my happy doesn't look like your happy," I suggest.

She moseys up to Graham's side and wraps her arms around him. "Don't lie to me. You want what we have so bad you can taste it."

"I can taste it all I want and not have the responsibility," I wink.

"You—" The ringing of her phone cuts her off. She looks at the screen sitting on the counter and then at me. "It's Ellie."

"Answer it."

"But—"

"Mallory . . ." I warn.

She scoops it up and holds it in the air. "Fine. But I'm talking to her in the living room." I hear her greet Ellie, and I find myself holding my breath. Graham is watching me and so is Camilla, but I'm mentally walking into the other room with Mal.

I wonder what Ellie is saying and if she's angry or amused or upset. I had to fight myself all day from going back to Halcyon or digging up her phone number and calling her. But why would I call? To apologize? I wouldn't for showing up today. That was a gift I'll thank Mallory for later after I've managed to screw with her some.

I don't know what I'll do if Mallory comes back in here and tells me Ellie is adamant I don't show up again, if she decides she really doesn't want to see me again after our encounter today. There's no way in hell I can go about my life and pretend I don't know she's living and working in Savannah. This is something I've not even had the courage to hope for over the last few years and here I am—in the same city with her. Both of us unattached from what I can tell. And we both feel the connection we've always had. I know that to be a fact.

Camilla's hand hits my bicep. "You okay?"

"Yeah."

"These two came to me with this idea—" Graham begins before Camilla interjects.

"Easy on the blame game there, G."

"I told them to stop getting in your business," he continues. "But then I thought about it and realized they're right."

"Thank you!" Cam says. "I went to the late class rather than the morning one like I usually do when Mallory called me asking about Ellie and I realized it might really be her. Sure enough, it was. I had Joy do all the dirty work of finding out if she was dating anyone or seemed like she'd gone off the deep end since I saw her last. I did my homework, Ford."

"They kind of made me proud when they came to me with a plan in place," Graham almost beams.

"Watch it or I'll be taking your job," Camilla laughs.

They banter back and forth, and I struggle to hear Mallory's end of the conversation. Her voice trickles into the kitchen, but not loud enough to make out words. I'm relieved when she appears in the doorway. Her phone is at her side. My eyes are glued to it, hoping that maybe Ellie is still on there and wants to talk to me. But when I look back at Mal's face, I know it's not true.

"What did she say?" I ask, a hint of nerves in my tone.

"Not much . . ." She continues her pace across the room until she's standing at Graham's side. "She's a little angry, I think. Maybe it's more just shock. I'm not really sure."

"Did she say anything about me specifically?"

She considers this. "Yes. Of course. But . . ."

"But you aren't going to tell me, are you?"

"I can't," she sighs.

"You did this," I point out, flashing Graham a quick look too. "I should be a hell of a lot more pissed off than I am because I'm still reeling from it. Ellie's just not another girl, and you two," I say, motioning to my siblings, "know that."

My chest rises and falls beneath my white dress shirt. Suddenly, I feel like I can't breathe deeply enough. I work to undo the top two buttons, but my fingers fumble. Camilla takes pity on me and reaches up and helps me out.

"Answer me this: are you sure she isn't in a relationship?" I ask.

"She's not," Cam replies. "She told Joy she hasn't been in a serious one in a long time."

My brain roars to life, processing a thousand memories, a million ideas, in a few short minutes. "Is she going to have a serious problem when I show up there again?"

"You're really going to go?" Mallory asks with a wide smile. "She said you mentioned it, but she thought you were just kind of blowing off at the mouth."

"Do I ever do that?"

"Yes," Camilla says at the same time Mallory says, "No."

"You three should've handled this differently." I look pointedly at Graham. "For how smart you are, you can be really fucking stupid."

"But . . ." Mallory goads.

"But I can't worry about that right now because I have to figure out how to make her not throw me out of Halcyon when I show back up there."

Camilla squeals, clapping her hands. "It worked!"

"It didn't work yet," Mallory warns, her grin slipping. "Ford may have his work cut out for him."

"I guess it's a good thing I'm a working man then, huh?" I wink. Walking by the island, I snag another piece of cauliflower. "We will revisit this subject later."

"Hey, Ford!" Mallory calls.

I turn to look at her.

"I told you I saved the best for last," she winks. "Does this mean I'm right?"

"No," I say, heading to the door. "It means you stepped in shit and just happened to come out smelling like a rose."

Ellie

I SLEPT LIKE CRAP IF I even slept at all.

All night, I was buzzing around like I'd drained a pot of coffee. I cleaned the kitchen cabinets, scrubbed the bathroom floors, and found and matched up all the socks strewn around the laundry room. Basically, I did all the chores I put off because I couldn't sit still.

My emotions went in waves.

Phase One: excitement would rustle in the pit of my stomach as a vision of Ford's grin or a whisper of his scent would strike my memory.

Phase Two: I'd be planning our future, complete with a dog and a complete set of matching pots and pans from an online wedding registry.

Phase Three: Images of us with a baby would begin to flicker through my mind and the excitement would sour. Almost instantly, I'd be scrubbing with extra vigor fueled by an anger I've known for a long time.

"Ford?" I say his name with a hesitation, with a fear that I can taste. My chest heaves as I try to stick to the plan I made up last night after I found out. "I need to tell you something."

"What is it?" He brushes my hair off my face as I look up at him. My head is on his lap as we lie in the back of his truck. It's so peaceful, the sun so warm, I want to close my eyes and pretend all of this isn't real.

Tears kiss my eyes. He looks at me with a slight grin, like he's waiting on me to tell him I gave my lunch away again today to a kid that didn't have one or that one of the girls in chemistry was mean to me again. Instead, I rock his entire world.

"I think I'm pregnant."

"Earth to Ellie," Violet singsongs. "I know you're all dolled up today, but you could pretend to be a worker bee like me."

"Sorry." I point to the blue card in her hand, trying to shake away the hollowness the memory left behind. "I like that one. Red is too bold."

"Blue it is," she sighs. "Do you need another coffee or something? You're out in la-la land today."

"I know. I'm sorry. I'm just exhausted."

She twists her lips. "Anything you want to tell me?"

"I'm tired because I didn't sleep because I was cleaning the house last night." I stand from the table. "Is that what you wanted to hear?"

"Nope. I wanted to hear you didn't sleep because you were—"

"Don't say it."

"You don't even know what I was going to say!"

"Yes, I do," I laugh.

"Then tell me."

"I'm not saying his name."

"Whose name?"

"Stop it, Violet."

"You mean . . . Ford's name?"

The look I give her isn't friendly. She doesn't care. She laughs and continues filling out the form in front of her. "The mascara and lip gloss, while not quite makeup-makeup, were quite a shock this morning."

"Huh." I know where she's going with this and I knew she'd head that direction. As I added a third layer of black-brown to my eyelashes, I could hear Violet chiding me.

I don't wear makeup. A lip balm to keep me from biting my lips, sometimes a colored one if it tastes like cherries or strawberries, is the beginning and end of my regular cosmetic routine. So what if I added a little gloss and mascara? Does it matter?

When I look at Violet, she's grinning. "Hoping for a certain someone to drop by today?"

"Hoping for it? No. Preparing for it in case of the super small percentage that it actually happens? Yes."

"The makeup bit coupled with the tight black shirt and the strategically ripped jeans—don't worry. He'll definitely forgive you for being incorrigible yesterday."

"I don't want his forgiveness," I huff. "I hope he forgets I exist and I never see him again."

So she doesn't call me out on that, I stand and begin to make my way into the front.

"You lie. You lie and you're terrible at it." Violet's voice follows me as I turn the corner.

The front of the store is still a mess, and although I've put off sorting through the contents for days, it's better than listening to Violet. Organizing physical things typically helps me sort my mind when it's also a mess, so I hope it's a two-for-one kind of day.

Four tall boxes are emptied, their content scattered around me, when Violet appears. She lets me know she has to run to the bank and offers to pick up a blueberry muffin from the bakery next door. It's her way of offering a peace treaty.

I work easily through the inventory, picking through the items and putting them into boxes in combinations that make sense. Lifting a stack of scarves handmade in Peru, one of them catches my eye. I slip it out and place it on top.

It's a turquoise sea with a golden sun hanging high in the sky. The water almost shimmers, luring you into the scene.

When the chimes ring, alerting me that Violet's already back, I don't bother to look up. "I'm not mad at you," I tell her. "Just go do what you have to do and bring me back carbs."

"Good to know."

The scarf drops out of my hands and falls to the floor.

Ford's grin is stretched ear-to-ear. One hand is stuck in the pocket of dark denim jeans and a black button-up shirt hangs untucked off his frame. He's carrying a cup of coffee.

It takes me a bit longer than I care to admit to find my voice.

"Oh, it's you." Looking up from my spot on the floor, I try not to let him notice how shaky my breathing has just become.

"So, French Toast or chocolate chip pancakes?" he asks.

"What are you talking about?"

"You said you wanted carbs. If we hurry, we can get to Hillary's House before they switch to lunch."

"You are unbelievable," I mutter, getting to my feet. "Why are you here?"

"Well, I brought you a vanilla latte from Frank's."

It's impossible not to smile that he remembered my drink of choice. It's also hopeless to pretend that the boyish grin he's flipping me doesn't melt away some of the ice around my heart.

Still, I don't want to play nice.

"I already had coffee today. But thank you," I say politely.

"No offense, but you are kind of irritable this morning. Maybe you could use another shot of caffeine."

"You think I'm irritable now? Keep it up."

"You never were a morning person," he laughs. "Some things never change."

"And some things do," I point out, giving him a look. "Seriously, why are you here?"

"I have business with Violet. Remember?"

"That's bullshit anyway, but she's not here. You'll have to come back later."

"Is that an invitation?" he laughs.

"Did it sound like one?" My arms cross over my chest and I'm aware it makes my boobs look bigger. As his eyes drop and catch the top of my cleavage, his gaze burns a trail on the ascent back up to my eyes.

Satisfaction paints a smug look on my face and desire burns in the apex of my thighs. As discreetly as possible, I clench my legs together to quell a bit of the ache that's beginning to throb under his observation.

When our gazes meet, his is crackling. He lifts a single brow. "I damn sure hope that's an offer to come. If it's not, we have a problem on our hands."

"No, *you* have a problem on your hands," I say, shrugging. "It has nothing to do with me."

"It could."

I'm smart enough to know that at times like this, it's not always my brain that gets to my mouth first. Logic sometimes isn't quite as quick as my libido. Knowing that, I don't respond and instead drop back to my knees and finish picking up the inventory.

Much to my surprise, Ford joins me on the floor. His arm muscles bulge under the sleeves of his shirt as he stretches and reaches for the stacks I created a few minutes ago. I try not to stare, make every effort not to accidentally brush against him or make any sort of physical contact at all. I might combust on the spot.

His next question catches me off guard. "How's your dad?"

I pause, holding the last few scarves in my hand. "He's good." I force a swallow. "Hanging in there."

"You know, every time I go fishing, I think of that man." He leans back on his arms, stretching his long legs out in front of him. "Remember when we went out to Longs Chapel Road and he got that huge fishing lure stuck in his hand?"

"I forgot about that," I laugh. "It was so gross. I panicked, do you remember? I was crying and trying to get you to drive him to the emergency room."

Ford's laugh melds with mine. "Yeah, and your dad was like, 'Take me to my brother's house.' Your Uncle Larry cut it out with a knife."

We wince at the same time, remembering the pseudo-operation performed on my uncle's bathroom countertop.

"He's lucky he didn't lose a hand over that," I point out.

"He took it like a champ. With only a mouthful of whiskey and he didn't even flinch."

"I did," I chuckle.

We look at each other over a spread of boxes, a warmth settling over the room. For a moment, I don't hate him. For a second in time, we are the kids that fell in love on a random Sunday afternoon at a lake in the middle of the woods. But that is over.

I move to the side to stand up, to put some distance between us, when my hand covers something sharp. Pulling back, I yelp like I've been burned. The tip of my middle finger is cherry-red and a little purple dot is in the center.

Ford has my hand in his before I can object. "What did you do?" he asks, twisting my palm in his and examining the offending digit.

"I don't know . . ." I stammer.

His hand is nearly twice the size of mine. It's rough, calloused, and I wonder what work he's been doing to get them that way. As he holds mine in his, I feel my heart drop.

He's gentle, rubbing his thumb across the injury. It should hurt, should make me jump, but his touch has some kind of calming effect.

"This did it." Still holding my hand in his, he reaches next to me. His arm brushes against my side, barely slipping against the top of my breast. My nipples peak under my shirt, my core pulling so tightly it's a struggle to breathe. "See?"

He holds up a pin that was attaching an information sheet to some of the products. I look at it, then back to our interlocked hands.

"We fit like a glove," he says, twisting them back and forth.

"Your grip is a little weak." I slip out of his grasp and clear my throat. "I need to get back to work."

Instead of giving me some space or pretending to heed anything about what I just said, he leans closer. "I think you need something else."

His lips curl in a suppressed smirk, the lines around his eyes deepening.

"I need a lot of things, none of which you can supply," I toss back.

"Maybe you've forgotten how versatile I am," he teases, bending even closer. "I can supply tons of different things. You name it and I'll make it happen, sweetheart."

"You are entirely too self-interested to give me what I need," I say as assuredly as I can.

"That's not nice." His lips get closer to my cheek, nearly brushing against it. I wouldn't even have to fully turn my head to capture his mouth with mine. Just a small, slight movement would be all it takes . . . Would it be that bad?

Sucking in a breath, I feel him move towards my mouth. I hold it, wait for it, only to have him pull away just before contact is made.

The breath comes out in a loud, frustrated huff. As sense and sensibility come barreling back to my brain, I realize I've been toyed with.

The self-righteous asshole grins.

"You are such a selfish bastard," I say, springing to my feet.

"Oh, did you . . ." he begins casually as he stands. "Did you think I was going to kiss you?"

"Be glad you didn't if you didn't want punched in the junk." We both know what just happened, but that doesn't mean I'm going to admit it.

"My junk would've been happy with any contact," he chuckles.

"I'm sure you can find someone willing. That can't be hard for you."

"So, is this your way of saying you wanted me to kiss you?" he asks, feigning surprise.

"Hardly." Lifting a box, I move it along the back wall. I'm faintly annoyed when he follows suit.

It's a struggle not to watch his body move, not to wait for his shirt to slip when he bends over and reveals the snippet of skin at the small of his back. I fight to get his cologne, now stronger because of his activity, out of my senses. Focusing on the task at hand and not on the man beside me is a nightmare.

We move the rest of them without saying a word. By the time the last one is in place, I've managed to get myself together.

"Thank you," I tell him. "I actually have a lunch meeting in a few with Heath."

"Who's Heath?"

It's my turn to smirk. "A friend that's helping me with a few things around here."

His eyes narrow. "I just told you I'm helpful."

"I just told you I need to get back to work."

He nods, running a hand through his short blond hair. "I do too, actually. I have an appointment I took on Barrett's behalf in a little bit."

"I'll let Violet know you were here," I offer.

He heads towards the door, but turns around with his hand on the knob. "Dinner? Tonight?"

"I have plans."

"Tomorrow night?"

"No, Ford."

He twists the handle. Sunlight pours into the room and I squint. Still, I don't miss the look on his face.

"Tell Heath to keep his hands to himself," he demands.

"Why would I do that?"

"He may not know I'm in town."

"Why would he care?"

"Because this thing between us started a long time ago. We might've thought it was over . . ." A soft smile plays on his lips. "But it's not. Have a good day, sweetheart."

He leaves me standing in the middle of the room wondering what in the hell just happened.

Ellie

"HEY, DADDY!"

I pull open the screen door and see my father sitting at the table in his kitchen. A little television is propped on one end. He refuses to get a new one. There's a large flat-screen in the living room, but he spends most of his time in here. He always has.

Growing up, I figured he just stayed in the kitchen because that's where most of the action happened. Besides, he was the one at home—a stay-at-home Dad before those were a thing. He was ten years older than my mother to start with, but after an injury that got him discharged from the Army and then a career with the railroad, he retired when I was still little. That was fine with me. We'd spend nearly every day from spring to fall outside gardening, walking the woods and empty fields, and fishing. He was the coolest guy I knew.

Then Mom died when I was nineteen, shortly after Ford left, and Dad withdrew into himself. Stopped hanging out with his one friend. Declared himself too old to do the things we used to do. He'd just sit at his table and watch old Western re-runs over and over again.

"Hey, pumpkin." He leans his cheek out so I can give it a kiss, which I do before sliding into the empty chair between the table and refrigerator. "You look pretty."

"Thanks. I thought I'd put a little effort in now that I'm a business-woman," I say, instead of telling him I didn't want Ford to see me at my worst.

"How's the store coming?"

"Good! You should come by and see it sometime."

He shrugs, his eyes going back to the cowboy on the screen. His cheeks tell the tale of a man that's lived a hard life, his skin now seeming to hint at a yellow that makes me a little edgy. His hair has receded rapidly over the last few years and the once black strands are now a silvery grey. There are sunspots and moles and I wonder how so much changed in him in what seems like such little time. It makes the guilt inside me soar.

"You need to get out of this house," I insist. "When is the last time you left this room?"

"I don't sleep in here."

"Okay. When's the last time you saw John? Or went to Kenny's," I say, talking about his lone friend and the pool hall four streets over that he used to frequent.

"What are you? My keeper?" he grins. "I'm fine, Ellie. Don't worry about me."

"Of course I worry about you! You're my daddy."

This makes him smile. "That I am."

Glancing around the room, I notice all the dust and cobwebs covering everything not used daily. My mom's owl collection lacks its usual luster because of all the grime. The once-white walls are starting to peel in places, and the ceiling looks like it had a leak in it at one time.

"I'm going to come over here and clean this place up," I tell him. "We need to wash stuff down, paint a little."

"You have your hands full downtown."

"But I will always make time for you."

"Don't bother with it," he says, leaning back in his chair and wincing as he stretches his arms over his head. "I'll get around to that stuff."

"Sure you will."

"Stop needling me and tell me what's happening with you. How's the shop coming together?"

"We're aiming to open soon," I say. "Maybe a month or so. It's taking a little longer than I thought it would."

"I warned you."

"I know," I sigh. "You've warned me about a lot of things in my life."

The words tumble from my lips before I can stop them. Taking a deep breath to try to settle the little flutter in my belly as my brain demands to replay Ford's smile from earlier today, I look at Dad. Of course he notices my hesitation.

"What's this all about?" he asks.

I could lie to him. Or, more accurately, I could try to lie to him. He'd know though. He always does.

Sucking in a breath, I go for it. "Ford is back in town."

His features remain passive, but I see the sparkle in his eye. "He is, huh?"

"He came by Halcyon."

"How's he doing?"

"I don't know," I say as casually as I can.

He scoffs, leaning forward so his elbows rest on the table. "Don't be like that, Ellie."

"Don't be like what?"

A low chuckle rumbles from his chest, but he's not amused. It's more irritation, a frustrated huff that his baby girl is a little more like him than he cares to admit.

"Life's too short for this," he warns.

"Life's too short to not want to have an in-depth conversation with someone that broke your heart?"

"You were both young."

"I. Don't. Care," I bristle, knowing he'd take my side in a second if he knew the truth. But I have never told him, and if I'm honest with myself, a part of the reason is I don't want him to be mad at Ford. I don't know why I don't. I just don't. "I know you've always liked him, but you could at least pretend to like me more."

His laugh this time is genuine and I almost return it.

"He's a good man. I know you—"

"Daddy, don't start on this now."

"Ellie Dawn, listen to your old man for a second," he says in the way that lets me know I'm about to get an earful. "You are the only person in this world that I love. The only reason why I'm not lying beside your mama right now," he tells me. "I only want the best for you. I want you to have a full, happy life."

"I know that."

He sighs. "I have one regret and that's raising you to be too much like me."

"What's that supposed to mean?"

"You're just like me," he says with a hint of pride. "You're as stubborn as a mule and ready to argue for the sake of it."

"It's served me well."

"But once you get to be my age, you realize it's the setup for a lonely life."

My heart constricts in my chest as I watch a flutter of memories flicker across his face. I reach out and take his hand, speckled with dark spots and calluses from a life of hard work.

"Are you lonely?"

"Not really," he lies. "I got my Westerns here."

Words escape me as I hold his hand, his skin not as warm as it used to be, nor is it as strong as I remember it being when I was young.

"Look at me," he says finally. "What have I become? Your mama passed away and I just sit here, day after day, wasting my life away. Hell, I'll die one of these days, and I don't even have six friends to carry my casket."

"Don't talk about that," I say, blinking back tears. "You aren't going to die for a very long time."

He smiles at me in a way that makes me wonder what he's thinking and feeling. But I don't ask. I can't. I'll start crying and that's something he can't handle.

Slipping his hand out from mine, he pats the top of my knuckles. When he speaks, I can hear the lump in his throat. "Why don't you go on now? My show is coming back on."

I stand and kiss his cheek, ruffling his hair with my fingers. "I want you to come see Halcyon this week, okay?"

He just nods.

"I love you, Daddy."

He nods again and points to his television. I squeeze his shoulder as I head to my car, my heart both heavier and lighter than it was when I walked in.

Ford

THE LATE-MORNING AIR IS A little chilly, the golf green still a little wet with dew. There's an energy to the day though and it's not just me. My brothers feel it too.

The day started off with a dream about Ellie, something that is becoming increasingly common since Mallory's matchmaking attempt.

"I do find it amusing that Dani kicked you out of the house." Graham grins at Lincoln over the hood of the golf cart.

"She didn't kick me out. Not exactly."

"No, she just called me and said, 'Hey, Ford. Come get your brother for the day before he doesn't make it to see his newborn child,'" I shrug. "Call it what you want." I slide my driver out of my golf bag and level up to the tee. My brothers pay no attention to golf etiquette and keep talking behind me as I pull my club back and wallop the ball. It goes sailing.

An easy breeze flows around me, the air smelling like pine on a beautiful Saturday morning.

When I turn around, Lincoln is in the driver's seat typing away on his phone while Graham watches with a smirk.

"Whatcha doing, Linc?" I ask, exchanging a grin with Graham.

"Just checking on Dani."

"Mallory is with her," I laugh. "She'll be fine."

His head whips to me with a look of bewilderment on his face. "She's nine months pregnant, Ford. The baby can come anytime. She needs me. She can't be doing—"

"She can't be driven crazy by you," I tell him. "Seriously, brother. Relax a little bit. Enjoy the time outside, breathing in the fresh air. Once the baby comes . . ."

"We'll never see you again," Graham finishes for me. He tugs Lincoln's hat over his eyes, making it impossible for him to see the phone screen.

"Hey!" Lincoln moans. "Fuck you, G."

Graham and I chuckle as we climb back on the golf cart, a new fancy ride with four seats. Graham takes the driver's seat from Lincoln and we make our way to the cart path that leads down the green.

"This is the most nerve-wracking situation of my life," Linc says, not so much to us, just out loud. "I keep thinking of all the wrong ways this can go. I read a book about delivery and shit and if one little thing goes wrong . . ." He pales.

"Look, Linc. That one thing *can* go wrong," I say, trying not to keep a straight face as he looks like he's going to vomit. "But you know what? The majority of the time everything goes perfectly fine. You need to concentrate on the good that's going to come out of this."

"That's hard to think about right now."

"Okay," Graham says, looking at Linc as he pilots the cart around a hole. "Let's talk about the baby. Are you ready for a son or a daughter?"

"I wish I knew what it was going to be, but Dani wouldn't find out. That just makes it worse."

"It'll be fun," I say, bumping him with my shoulder before climbing out at the next hole. "What are you naming it?"

"If it's a girl, she's naming it. If it's a boy, I get to name it."

"She trusts you that much?" I joke.

"Yeah, she does."

"What's the short list?" Graham asks, trying to distract him.

Lincoln shrugs. "I just want to hold the thing in one arm and Dani in the other and be done with this shit. No more kids for us. I can't do this again."

"You realize you're doing none of the work, right?" Graham laughs. "It's her that's going to be split in two—"

Lincoln drops his club, making Graham and I burst out laughing. "I hate you two."

He gets his ball balanced on the tee after four tries. Instead of hitting it, he stands there fidgeting.

"You think he's going to be okay?" Graham asks me quietly. "I've never really seen him like this."

"He'll be fine. He's just not used to giving a shit about anyone or being serious about anything. I mean, he has you for the serious stuff."

"Very funny."

"I wasn't being funny," I yawn.

Graham furrows his brows. "Not sleeping well?"

"You're really going to ask me that?"

"It's a fair question."

"No, asshole, I'm not sleeping well thanks to you."

"Thanks to me?"

"Yeah, you. Do you know how hard it is to want her so bad I can taste it, and, yet, I can't have her." I think for a half-second. "Yet. I can't have her yet."

He grins. "I like your optimism."

"Yeah, well . . ." I look out over the course. "I like her."

Graham adjusts in his seat and gets comfortable. "So, have you been working all night then? That's what I do when I can't sleep."

"Some. I also did a couple of hundred push-ups, a couple of hundred sit-ups because I'm not a pussy."

Graham's hand clamps down on my shoulder and he gives it a little squeeze. "About the whole Ellie thing—I really am sorry for that."

"You're a fucking liar."

"You're right. I'm not sorry I went through with it. But you should know, if you haven't considered it, that I do nothing without thinking it through—this included."

I turn to face him. He's a little shorter and a lot darker than I am. Still, it's obvious we're brothers. And when he smiles, the edges of my lips turn up too because I know he's right. He did think this through. He wouldn't have thrown me into this without being absolutely sure it was the right decision.

Lincoln breaks the moment with a string of profanities. He swings and misses the ball then proceeds to call it every name under the sun. It's all we can do not to laugh.

"You know," I say, "Mallory is usually a giant pain in the ass. But I woke up today kind of appreciating that little fact about her."

"I bet you did." He rocks back on his heels. "Have you given any thought how you are going to go about this? Mal said Ellie wasn't exactly jumping for joy over this whole thing."

"It's all I think about," I respond honestly. "I've spent years wondering what happened to her and wishing I'd handled things differently back then. And now—here she is standing in front of me, looking more beautiful than ever, and you know what? When I look in her eyes, I feel exactly the same way as I did then."

"Wow."

"Just don't let me turn into that," I crack, motioning towards Lincoln.

Graham laughs. "We need to make a pact. If either one of us breaks that hard, we just throw them in the car and toss them in the sea."

"Deal."

We watch Linc lean on his golf club, his phone back in his hand. He's typing away furiously, his forehead marred with lines.

"This was your first time seeing Ellie in all these years? You never saw her on leave or anything?" Graham asks.

"No. I left and did boot camp and . . ." I remember the feeling of her not answering my calls and then the conversation when she did. "I called her a couple of times and she wasn't home. Then I did get through to her once and it didn't go well. She was just so pissed off and hurt, and I just figured she was better off if I let her be," I shrug. "I heard she went off to college and that was that. I didn't hear from her again."

I watch Lincoln stand at the tee and tuck his phone back in his pocket. "I love her, G. I've always loved her. When I walked in there and saw her in Halcyon, it was like reality just smacked me in the face and said, 'Wake up, asshole. This is what you've been looking for.' Does that sound stupid?"

"I get it," he says softly. "I could never love anyone but Mallory. Not now, not after having with her what I do. Even if something happened and she left me, if I saw her again in ten years, I'd still feel this way. You can't wipe away what we have or," he says, lifting a brow, "what you and Ellie have, maybe."

We exchange a look that only brothers can, a look that doesn't need words to describe it. He gets it. I'm not crazy, although I certainly feel that way.

We quiet down as Lincoln reaches back and smacks the ball with his club. The ball goes wildly off course, hits a tree, and lands in a sand trap.

"Fuck this game," Lincoln huffs, marching passed us.

"Lincoln," I say as Graham pulls his phone from his pocket and answers it. "You need a drink or something?" I follow him to the cart and sit next to him. He looks at me with a somber face.

"Ford, I'm going to be brutally honest with you."

"Okay."

He takes a deep breath. "I'm scared shitless."

"I get that. You're going to be responsible for another human life, one that's defenseless and vulnerable. You—"

"Not. Helping," he groans. "So you don't think I'm a lunatic?"

"No," I snicker. "I don't think you're a lunatic. You're going to be a dad, man. That's a big thing."

I gaze off across the golf course, the greens of the trees and grasses, the blues of the sky shining back at me. I imagine myself in his situation, waiting to have a child with my wife. Two things are clear: One, it's the best feeling I've ever felt, and two, it's only Ellie I can see that with.

I force a swallow as my heart squeezes. "You're on the cusp of having a family. *A family*. That's an awesome thing, Linc."

He doesn't answer. I give him a few minutes and when he fails to say anything, I finally turn my head to look at him.

"You know what sucks?" he asks.

"What?"

"None of you are having a family too. I always thought our kids would all play together, you know? Like we did growing up. I figured they'd grow up causing havoc, sneaking out together, lying to us to cover for the other," he chuckles. "And out of the six of us, I'm not sure who the closest is to being next."

I look at Graham as he paces back and forth near the tee. "My money is on him. Barrett is too busy politician-ing. Speaking of which, has he talked to you about maybe running for the Presidency?"

"Not really. He made quick mention of it, but I think he knows I'm a little preoccupied right now." He watches Graham grow frustrated over something on his phone. "Can you imagine Graham as a dad? That would be something to see."

"Right? Imagine what he'd do when he'd realize he can't put it on his schedule," I laugh. "He'd have a complete breakdown when there are toys strung out everywhere and baby puke on his ties."

We laugh, the sound catching Graham's attention. He flashes us a look but I wave him off.

"What about you?" Lincoln asks, his voice quiet. "You think you'll settle down soon?"

My chest rumbles as I feel the seriousness of the question.

"Right," he says, sparing me from having to answer. He scoots up in his chair as Graham marches towards us. G looks at me and then at our brother.

"That was Mallory," Graham says too carefully. "We need to *calmly* and *rationally* head back to the clubhouse."

"Why?" Lincoln barks, his eyes going wide.

He takes a deep breath. "Your wife is in labor."

"Oh, dear God," Lincoln says, turning white. He pops the golf cart in drive and takes off, Graham leaping onto the back in the nick of time.

"Slow down!" Graham laughs, climbing into a seat. "Labor can take hours, Lincoln. We don't need to drive like a bat out of hell."

"She's in labor," Lincoln nearly shouts. "And I'm not there." He looks at me. "Screw you, Ford, for making me come today. I will never forgive you for this."

He continues on a tirade, cutting through the greens and getting shouts from other golfers for interrupting their game as we head back to the clubhouse.

Lincoln doesn't even have the thing stopped before he jumps off and makes a mad dash to Graham's SUV.

"You're driving," I tell Graham as we follow our brother. "I need to be free in case he needs restrained."

Graham elbows me as we watch Lincoln pace back and forth, his arms thrown up in the air. "Maybe just knock him out now. It'll make for a more peaceful ride to the hospital."

Ford

"THERE'S UNCLE FORD." LINCOLN'S WHISPER is barely heard over
the beeping of the machine hooked up to Danielle. Mom said they were
giving her some fluids. Even though the delivery went quick and fairly
easy, she still lost a lot of blood and they want to keep an eye on her.

I close the door softly behind me. Danielle is lying in the bed, her
eyes closed. Lincoln sits in the plastic blue chair beside her bed looking
into the nest of blankets in his arms, whispering things to his newborn
son that I can't hear. I stand just inside the doorway and take it all in.

The feeling in the room is the most peaceful thing I've ever felt.
There's so much love floating around among the baskets of flowers on
the windowsill that you can almost reach out and touch it.

Lincoln and I have had our fair share of arguments over the years.
The two youngest of the boys in the Landry family, the two most athletic
and physical out of the bunch, we've had moments where we've really
butted heads. But to see this—my baby brother, the All-Star pro-baseball
player with shoulders as broad as a barn, holding this little baby in his
giant hands with the tenderness of a parent—is incredible.

Something has changed in Lincoln since I saw him a few hours ago.
He's somehow more ferocious than I've ever seen him, yet, at the same
time, the gentlest he's ever been.

He looks up as I wipe the side of my eye. With a grin, he simply nods his head. That's all he really needs to say.

"How ya holding up?" I ask, clearing my throat of the emotion that's started to build.

"He's perfect, Ford. Absolutely perfect." He lifts the baby's hand from beneath a blanket. "Look at this—centerfielder hands if I've ever seen them."

I laugh softly, reaching out and touching his little palm. His fingers wrap around mine, not long enough to close around it completely. I look up at Lincoln and he beams.

"With that grip, he may be a better hitter than his dad," I whisper. Lincoln chuckles.

"What did you name him?" I ask.

Linc looks briefly at Danielle as she begins to stir. He forces a swallow as he watches her intently until she settles down.

"I can go. She probably needs to rest."

"Ford," she says, her lashes fluttering open. She sends me a sleepy smile. "Did you meet our new man yet?"

"I'm getting ready to." I release my finger from the baby's grip and walk to the side of her bed. "I can go if you're tired. Or bring you guys back some dinner?"

She smiles. "Not until you meet Ryan."

Turning, I see Lincoln standing with the bundle of blankets tucked under his chin. "Wanna hold him?"

"Absolutely." A few seconds later, Ryan is placed in my arms. He whimpers for a split second before nestling against my chest and falling right back to sleep.

I've never felt anything like this in my entire life. My entire heart feels like it's going to burst. This little thing cuddled up against me pulls at pieces of me I didn't know could be tugged.

"His name is Ryan Lincoln Landry," Lincoln says softly as he pulls the blankets down from his face, revealing a slightly up-turned nose and full lips. "Ryan after his beautiful mother and Lincoln after his awesome father."

"Don't worry, Ryan," I say. "His conceit isn't genetic. You'll be fine."

We all laugh, which makes Danielle cough. Lincoln is to her side in a flash.

There's a free chair at the foot of the bed and I head that way. Once I'm settled, I pull the blankets down a little more.

Ryan has Danielle's skin, an olive-y complexion that will serve him well when he gets old enough to appreciate it. He also has Danielle's long eyelashes.

I can't stop looking at him.

He's a perfect little thing created by a love between two people, a love that was almost broken apart. I think back to when Lincoln almost moved to California and when Danielle almost broke up with him, and I realize—none of that matters. That was all just a stepping stone to get them here. In this moment. With this child.

Already, I know I'd die for this kid. I can see glimmers of my brothers and I hidden in his features, and when he opens his little eyes, he watches me like we've always known each other. It's simply unbelievable and I'm only his uncle. What must Lincoln feel like?

"After you master eating and sitting up, I'll give you a run down on the family," I tell my nephew. "You're a lucky little guy. This family is the best out there, so if you had a choice before you got here, you did good, buddy. But you're going to need some quick tips. Like . . . watch out for Barrett around election time, and whatever you do, don't touch anything on Graham's desk."

Lincoln laughs, reaching for the baby. "Time for him to come back to Daddy."

"Linc is a baby hog," Danielle jokes. "I've only gotten to hold him a few times."

"Because you're asleep and that's not safe," Lincoln notes.

I place Ryan back in his daddy's arms after giving him a little kiss on his soft forehead.

"I'll let you guys get some rest," I say, getting to my feet. "Everyone else has gone home. Mom, Cam, Sienna, Ali, and Mallory," I laugh, "said to call them if you need anything."

"We'll call Graham," Lincoln shrugs.

"Naturally," I laugh. "Congratulations, guys."

"Thank you, Ford." Danielle waves from the bed as I head to the door and let myself out.

The elevator ride is short and the air is still warm and balmy as I find my truck beneath the parking lot lamps. On auto-pilot, I unlock the door, slide my key in the ignition, and pull out onto the road.

My muscles ache from sitting on hospital waiting room chairs all day, but my mind is in overdrive.

Seeing Ryan tonight and watching Lincoln and Danielle has burned something into my soul. Before now, Ellie was a part of my past and someone I wanted to test the waters going forward with. Now, I realize she's my past. And my future. There's no other way around it.

When my sisters' friends trolled the malls on the weekends, Ellie would show up at the trails with a pair of ripped jeans and climb on the back of my four-wheeler. When they were having their hair done, she was taking care of her dad. When they were wearing sequins and makeup and falling over themselves to get my attention at the pool, I find this girl in flip-flops and a messy ponytail ignoring me as she sits on the banks of a muddy lake.

She was the first girl I ever met that didn't give two shits that my last name was Landry. I'm not sure when she even realized that, to be honest. Ellie challenged me, made me question everything I'd ever thought. Even at sixteen, her soul was so much older.

When I complained about having to get a new tux to attend a charity function with my mother, it was Ellie that suggested it would be more helpful to take the money we were spending on our attire and donating that to the charity. While the people in my life were making a show of their help of others, it was Ellie that gave her only winter coat to a little girl at school because she didn't have one and shared her lunches every day with a kid that lived down the road from her and had nothing.

How do you not love that? Especially when she's the most naturally beautiful girl you've ever seen? When just looking at her seems like it fills a hole in your heart that you were born with and can't plug otherwise.

My mind goes back to Ryan and the feeling in the room I just left. The look on Lincoln's face and the love that Danielle has in her eyes when she looks at my brother and her son. I've only had one person look at me like that, and I sure as hell have only felt that way about one woman.

I grab the wheel and whip a U-turn in the middle of the highway.

Ellie

"AH!" MY HEART LEAPS IN my chest the same time I literally jump at a noise from the back. "Damn it," I grimace. "Grow up, Ellie."

I'm such a chicken when it comes to being alone in the dark. Put me in the woods in the middle of the night and I'm fine, but put me in a store on Main Street in Savannah and I'm a big 'ol baby.

It's people that scare me. Crazy serial-killers or demented lunatics that sneak into the bathroom when the curtain is closed or are hovering over you while you sleep. It's also the ridiculously good-looking men with blond hair and the most incredible blue eyes and crooked grins that terrify me. Those that fit the latter description are the most dangerous of them all.

Humming a tune and shaking it off, I pour more paint into a pan and pick up the roller. It spreads evenly on the wall. There's something calming about the fluidity of the motion.

Violet and I were supposed to take today off. She wanted to spend the weekend getting the last few pieces of her apartment put together. I thought a free day sounded perfect, but the quiet afforded me too much time to think.

I've been here for the last ten hours.

The streetlights glow on the other side of the black paper we hung in front of the windows to keep prying eyes out until we're ready to debut the store. The traffic outside has slowed. Only a random car now and then can be heard roaming down the road.

I roll the brush back through the paint and have it nearly touching the wall when a knock raps against the door. Instantly, my heart lodges in my chest.

The roller splashes in the paint, spattering my shoes with mint green drops, as I scramble to find my phone. The knock comes again, a little louder this time.

"Shit!" Grabbing my device, I stand facing the door. I don't know what to do. Should I call 9-1-1? Should I start screaming now? After all, no one knows I'm here. That means two things: One, no one should be looking for me, and two, no one will be until tomorrow sometime, in which case my body will be stone cold by then.

I'm dead. A goner. A missing person's report in the making.

Creeping to the window, I pull back the paper a tiny bit and peek out. And suck in a breath.

Ford is standing under the light in the front, his hands stuck in the pockets of his khakis. A green polo shirt is stretched across his chest. He looks tired, his posture not quite as perfect as it normally is.

His head tilts to the side and he catches me spying. His shoulders lift and then drop, as if he's thinking the same thing—he's not sure why he's here either.

I attempt to keep my face as sober as possible when inside my traitorous body is doing a round-off back tuck.

I want to be irritated with myself for reacting this way. Frustration is what I should feel, not a blip of excitement.

He moseys towards me, slipping one hand out of his pocket. It's planted near mine on the other side of the glass. My fingers bend, as if trying to make contact with his. His do the same.

I pull back.

"Can I come in?" he asks.

Forcing a swallow, I look him in the eye. "Why?"

He shrugs again, but doesn't respond. That gives me nothing to work with.

"I'm busy," I say.

"Painting."

"How did you know?"

A finger is carefully pressed against the glass on the other side of my forehead. "You're wearing more of it than whatever you're painting," he smiles.

Blushing, I look away. Here he is, standing before me looking like he walked out of a dressing room at a men's store and I look like Cinderella, minus the ball gown. Not the impression I wanted to make.

"I can help," he offers. "I'm good with my hands." He tries to hide his smirk, but fails miserably.

I try not to show my ever-growing amusement. "I'm sure you are."

"You don't remember?"

The double pane of glass between us seems to disintegrate, melted by the fire that just kicked up between our bodies. Of course I remember. Every cell of my being remembers his touch. It's impossible to forget how one brush of his finger seemed to switch on an energy inside me.

"Barely," I lie.

"I could remind you."

"You could leave."

"You're right. I could. But I don't want to." He leans towards me until his face is directly across from mine. "And I don't think you really want me to either."

His eyes plead with me, pull at my heartstrings. And no matter how mad I want to be at him, no matter how dangerous this specific man is to my existence, I relent.

"Fine." I'm opening the door before I can be logical about it. I regret it as soon as I do.

He slips in easily, smelling all delicious, with the confidence he carries like no other. It's not vanity or arrogance, nor is it some holier-than-thou persona. It's a charisma, a self-assuredness, a faith in himself that rolls off him with complete and utter ease.

"Thanks for letting me in. I wasn't sure you were going to."

"I wasn't sure I was either," I admit. "I probably shouldn't have, but no one has ever accused me of being a good decision maker."

"Why do you say that?"

I shrug, turning away to try to center myself. My brain feels like a frazzled wire, every emotion crossing with the other and leaving me a giant walking disaster. I plead with myself to keep it together, to stand my ground. I've waited for years to show him I was better off without him. Now's my chance.

"Since you're here, I thought I could tell you that I've talked to Violet and she agrees—we don't need security." I stare at a little dribble of paint rolling down the wall. "We're just wasting your time."

I hear his shoes against the floor, stepping closer. "I don't do anything that wastes my time."

My breath catches as his hand rests on my shoulder. His palm is heavy and warm, and I could easily tilt my head just a few inches to the side and rest it against his forearm. I've done it a hundred times.

"I want you to know," he begins with a gruff to his tone, "that if you honestly don't want me here, I won't come. I respect you too much to do that."

"You'll just walk away. Trust me, I believe that."

It's a direct reference to the past, a jab at him in the most juvenile way. I know he catches it, but he lets it slide.

"I never said that." He circles around until he's standing directly in front of me. "I never said I'd leave you alone. I said I wouldn't do that to you here, not at your business."

I don't know how to take that. I'm not sure I even want to read into it. I just know my cheeks are hot as hell and my stomach is flipping all sorts of ways.

"What do you want, Ellie?"

"What I want is for you to go away so I can look into some voodoo light stick and have you erased from my memory altogether so I can live a life without knowing you exist."

"Tell me how you really feel," he chuckles, lifting his hand from my shoulder. Instantly, I miss it. "I see you're still blunt like your dad."

The look in his eye is genuine, as is the clarity in his voice. They always got along—two country boys with a lot to chitchat about. His concern makes me happy.

"I was over that way today," Ford says. "You think I could swing by and say hi to him sometime?"

I want to say no because that's too personal. My dad is my territory and it feels risky to let Ford bleed into that. Still, I know Dad likes him and seeing Ford would make his day. "He'd probably love that."

"So would I."

I lift the paint roller again and try to concentrate on covering the wall with the mint green Vi and I picked out.

"Need help?" he asks.

Looking over my shoulder, I see him slipping off his jacket. I nearly choke when the hem of his shirt lifts when he tosses his jacket on a nearby box and I see the edge of the ridge going from his hip to his groin.

"Not really," I say, trying to force myself to look away.

He doesn't seem to notice anything other than my stubbornness to let him lend a hand. He flashes me a disapproving look.

I continue stroking the brush up and down the wall.

"Talk to me, Ellie."

"About what?" I ask through parched lips.

"Anything," he says. "I just want to hear your voice."

"What if I say I hate you?"

"No one hates me more than I hate myself."

"I might be close. Besides," I add, "I think you're way too self-centered to hate yourself."

"That's about the third time you've called me self-centered."

"Yeah. So? What's your point?"

His jaw sets firmly in place. "I'll admit I've done some hedonistic things, namely to you, but I'm not some asshole on an ego trip, El."

"Could've fooled me."

Turning away from him, I go back to painting. I'm a half a stroke up the wall when he plucks the roller out of my hand.

"Hey!" I object as he drops it into the pan with a thud. "What do you think you're doing?"

He steps towards me. I take one back.

He's eyeing me like I'm an opponent on the other end of a table, one that he's ready, willing, and able to bend to his will.

Throwing my shoulders back, I look him straight-away. "I asked you a question."

He moves towards me again, but I can't go back any farther without touching the freshly-painted wall.

"I'm sorry."

They're both the simplest and hardest words in the English language and can be the sweetest to hear or the most bitter. Watching them topple out of mouth with that fire in his eyes is a mixed bag.

"I bet you are." There's a swagger to my words, a hint of moxie that I don't try to hide. "You're not ignorant. You're just a typical man."

His chuckle dances over my skin as the blues of his eyes darken. "What do you want me to say? That I fucked up?" He stretches his arms out to both sides. "Is that what you want to hear?"

"No," I bark back. "It's not. I don't want to hear anything from you. I don't even want you here!"

My throat burns as he steps closer, my eyes widening in anticipation of his next move. The look on his face is unreadable. All I know for sure is that a conversation I've been curious about for years now is about to come to a head.

"I was nineteen, Ellie. I didn't know what to do."

"I was eighteen. I didn't know what to do either," I point out.

"You said you were pregnant, and all of a sudden, reality hit me."

"Would it have been that bad, Ford?" I ask, the chip on my shoulder sitting pretty. "Would it have been so terrible to have been linked to me that once you realized you were free, you had to flee the state? Hell, you had to flee my life altogether?"

"That's not what happened—"

"Oh, it is what happened," I snort. "Once we realized I'd jumped gun and it was stress, not pregnancy, that delayed my period, you were out of here."

"Ellie," he begins, "listen to me. That's not what I was thinking."

"Then how do you explain coming to me the week after and just breaking up with me, giving me some bullshit excuse that you had to 'go find yourself' or whatever it was." I laugh angrily. "I knew what you were doing. You were getting away from me."

He charges forward, and as I step back, my shirt sticking to the freshly painted wall. It's a distant observation because his blazing eyes won't let me look anywhere but at him.

He pins me in place, his body just inches from mine. His lips twitch as he considers his next words. "I *was* getting away from you," he admits. "Because I was sure I was fucking you up. I'd been so careless with you, so cavalier. When you told me you thought you were pregnant, I realized I wasn't that much different than my brothers, El. Here I was, the one that always prided himself on being the simple guy, the one that didn't need the silver spoon, acting as entitled as the rest of them."

There's a wave of emotion pooling across his eyes. "Not that it's an excuse, but I kind of broke. I had all this pressure to figure out which college to go to, which major to go after that would put me on a Landry-approved career path, and I just wanted to be me. Only I didn't know what 'me' even meant. I just felt like a fuck-up, to be honest."

"You were never a fuck-up," I tell him. "There's no way you believed that."

"I did," he says quietly. "And all I could think was that I was bringing you with me as I was spiraling down this hole. I wasn't worried about me, Ellie. I was worried about you."

"Really, Ford?"

"Yeah." He reaches up tenderly and brushes a strand of hair off my face. "Then that fight when I told you . . ."

I gulp. "Not my best memory."

"Mine either."

We exchange a sad smile as we both sort through those memories. I can't even look him in the face.

"We don't need to talk about this," I say, trying to go around him, a lump stuck in my throat. He steps in my way. "It doesn't make a difference. We're just wasting our breath."

"Maybe it doesn't make a difference," he admits, "but I want you to know I'm sorry. If I had to do it all over again, I would've figured out how to stay with you. You're the best thing that ever happened to me."

The tough me is gone and in her place is an eighteen-year-old girl that's wanted to hear those words all her adult life. I wish for a witty comeback, something to lighten the feeling between us, but there's nothing.

"Do you love me, Ellie?"

"I don't even know you," I whisper. "How could I love you?"

"Did you used to love me?"

"Yes."

His eyes flutter closed, and he holds them there for a long minute. When they open, there's a fire there I haven't seen before. He reaches for me, but I catch his hand mid-air. Something catches my attention.

In between his thumb and forefinger, there's a tiny star tattooed into his skin. It settles in the bend of his hand. It seems like an odd choice and an even stranger location for a tattoo, especially for guy like him.

"What's this all about?" I ask, running my thumb over it.

When I look at him, I see a gentleness in his face that nearly melts me.

"Do you remember the night we climbed into the top of your neighbor's hay loft?" he asks. "And we sat there for hours, talking and laughing and you trying to show me constellations and getting it all messed up?"

"Yes," I whisper. "That was the first night that we . . . Um . . ." I look down.

"The first night that we were together." He puts his finger beneath my chin and lifts it so I'm looking at him. "This tattoo is my reminder of you."

My chest compresses, my breathing gets shallow, as I try to process what he's saying.

"I got it here, in the bend of my right hand, so I see it, and regardless of what I'm doing—eating, writing, firing a weapon—I see you." His cheeks flush. "Well, not really. But I think of you. I'm reminded of you."

"Ford, I don't know what to say to that," I admit, dropping his hand. Flooded with a warmth like the desert in mid-summer, I can't stop looking at the little star.

He blushes. "It was a late night in San Diego and I may have had too much to drink. The guys dragged me to a tattoo parlor and they were all getting something inked and I walked out with this." He looks at the star, a faint smile crossing his lips. "Picking out a tattoo is a lot harder than you think it will be."

"I couldn't get a tattoo. I'm afraid I'd hate what I chose down the road."

"I didn't think I could either." He drops his hand and looks at me. "I knew if there was one thing I wanted, it had to be something that I'd never regret."

My heartbeat quickens as our eyes lock together.

"I may regret some things, or even a lot of things, that have to do with you. But those regrets are all from the way *I* acted." He takes a step towards me, his chest rising and falling more quickly. "You are the only person in my life that ever just let me be me. I mean, I love my family. You know that. But I always felt so much . . ."

"Pressure."

"Yes," he says, blowing out a breath. "There was, there *is*, pressure to make good choices, do the right thing, toe the line in some ways that I'm not interested in doing."

"Is your mom still doing all those fancy charities?" I ask with a grin.

"Yes," he laughs. "I understand them more now. It's her way of giving back in the way she understands."

"I still think you could just donate all that money you spend on setting it up to the Shelters for Savannah or the Food Pantry."

"You'd be happy to know," he grins, "that Lincoln and Danielle have started a charity in town. I'm not sure of the ins and outs of it, but I know Dani is passionate about under-privileged kids and they do a lot of charity work with those types of things."

"Really?" I ask. "Maybe we could team up and do a back-to-school drive together or something."

"She'd love that. Mom always wants to help and then it becomes this glamour thing. Dani is more like you."

"Are you saying I'm not glamorous?" I tease.

"Your sneakers with paint splattered over them are so, so glamorous, Ellie."

He laughs, a warm, rich, captivating sound that feels like a balm to so many of my wounds. It doesn't fix anything, obviously, but it does soothe me somehow.

"You always did have a way with words," I joke, sighing for dramatic effect.

"You should give me a chance to show you how much better I've gotten with words." He shoots me a smile so sinful I have to look away.

"I bet you have."

"I've gotten better at a lot of things," he whispers.

He searches my eyes as if he's asking for permission and in my amped-up state, I'm not thinking clearly . . . because I smile. It's a tiny fissure in my persona that he takes full advantage of.

My back suctions against the paint behind it as Ford cages me in. One foot on the outside of each of mine, a hand planted on the wall on both sides of my face. My knees wobble the slightest bit as he leans down and feathers his lips over mine.

They're as soft as I remember and my eyes flutter closed as my chin angles towards him, wanting more. We move together effortlessly, like there hasn't been a decade since the last time we did this.

My bottom lip drops open and that's all it takes for him to deepen the kiss. His tongue finds mine, exploring my mouth, the heat of his breath bringing up my temperature hundred-fold.

I can feel his kisses shoot through my bloodstream, regrouping again in between my legs. My hips tilt just as he presses his body closer to mine and I feel his hardness through the fabric of our clothes. My clothing pulls, sticking to the tacky wall behind me.

Moaning into his mouth, my body goes lax. Any sense I had moments ago to keep this in check—to keep it somehow to kisses—is long gone. Instead, my hands are roaming beneath his shirt and splaying over his chiseled abdomen.

As he takes my face in both of his hands, continuing his delicious assault on my lips, I drag my hands all over his body. Across his stomach, along his hips where the muscles are cut to perfection, up his sides and around to his back. Each movement causes those muscles to flex beneath my palms and with each ripple, I lose a little more judgment.

We're going so fast, trying to fit so many years of not having into this moment of having that his fingers are fumbling with the button of my jeans before I realize what's happening. I shimmy my hips, helping them drop to the floor. He grins salaciously.

"Spread your legs." It's a command, an order, given with such authority I shiver.

I'm nearly panting as I widen my stance as much as the jeans pooled at my feet will allow. The wall is warm against my bare skin, my hair feels like it's glued to the space behind me. All of that is forgotten as desire pools everywhere from my vagina to my breasts.

He holds up his right hand, showing me it's paint free. Not that I care at this point. I'd take a trip to the ER as long as I got off first.

I'm nearly trembling with anticipation as I wait for his touch. I gasp when his finger slides into me, my legs almost buckling. He draws his finger through my slit while his bright blue eyes watch my reaction.

"Damn," I hiss, my back arching at the sensation. Lacing my fingers through his hair, I bring his face down to mine. There's nothing sweet about it this time; it's frenzied, capped off by a moan into his mouth as he slips one, then two, fingers inside me.

My body hums to the tune of Ford's insertions. As he intensifies his pace, adding another finger to the mix, I think I'm going to lose it.

I feel how wet I am and know I must be dripping down his hand. The insides of my thighs ache from the build-up of the orgasm that's well on its way.

He kisses me hungrily, ravenously, even, as my hips work against his fingers, absorbing every fraction of friction I can get. Everything moves at a million miles per hour as he uses his free hand, lifts my shirt, and frees my breasts from the lace bra. Paint smears through my hair and along the side of my face in his haste to rid me of my clothes.

"Ford," I breathe, my eyes rolling in the back of my head. He rolls one of my nipples with his fingers while the other hand continues its onslaught of my pussy.

"This is the most beautiful sight I've ever seen," he whispers.

I feel his gaze on me as heavily as I feel any other part of him. It feels just as heavenly.

Tilting my hips even more, craving the final couple of steps to climax, he presses a simple kiss to my lips.

His hand slides from my breast, down my stomach, and splays his hand on the top of my legs. Using his thumb, he presses on my clit. One touch sends me over the edge.

"Fuck," I groan as an eruption begins in my core. Like a flash flood, it crashes through me with no warning. "Ford!"

I buck against him, meeting him thrust for thrust. He presses and pushes on every part of me that he knows will elicit a spark of ecstasy. He works me over like he wrote the book on how to make me come. In a way, maybe he did.

He brings me down as expertly as he took me up. Slowly, he allows me to drop from the clouds and land, shakily, on my own two feet.

When I open my eyes, he's grinning ear-to-ear.

"That was . . ." I don't know what to say, so I giggle.

"That was awesome."

"You got nothing out of that."

"Oh, sweetheart. I got more out of that than you did."

"But . . ." He's making no move to do anything else, no indication that there's more where that came from.

As if he reads my mind, he nods. "That's all that's happening tonight."

I look at him curiously as I pull my jeans back over my hips. They stick to the paint, making it harder than normal to get in place. "Whatever you say," I say, fastening the button. "It felt amazing."

I stall mid-zip as his grin turns wicked. He holds his hand up in the air. My juices are all over it, his fingers covered in my come.

His eyes on mine, he brings them to his mouth. My jaw hangs open as he licks his fingers. "It tastes better than it felt."

My cheeks turn red as I scramble to regain my composure. He has every upper hand in this situation and now that I'm not all worked up, I see I'm at the disadvantage. And a complete mess.

My hair is matted to one side of my head, the ends of my ponytail acting like little brushes and rubbing the green material all over my shoulders.

Before I can figure out what to say, he heads towards his coat.

"Where are you going?" I ask, trying to work my hair into some semblance.

"I need to get home and get to bed," he says nonchalantly. "I have a meeting on the golf course first thing in the morning. That'll be two days golfing and I don't particularly love it in the first place."

"Oh."

Whether I expected him to stick around or offer to take me for coffee, or a shower, I don't know. But I didn't expect this—whatever it is.

He's faces me with a smug look on his face, his jacket slung over his shoulder. "Did that prove I'm not selfish?"

Before I can answer, he's out the door.

Ford

RUNNING THE TOWEL OVER MY head, I toss it in the sink. The charcoal grey linen drops into the bowl as Trigger's yawn echoes through the marbled room. The yellow lab lies in the corner, curled up on a burgundy rug that I paid way too much for but knew she'd love.

I lean against the counter and look at myself in the mirror. My hair is sticking every which way from the shower, my eyes wide awake despite having been up far too long.

It's nearly two in the morning and I'm not closer to sleep now than I was hours ago. I've tried working myself out until muscle failure, pouring over security plans for Landry Security, shooting the shit with Sienna over tacos that she brought over under the guise of being bored. I know she was searching for gossip. I gave her nothing.

There's this crazy feeling in the pit of my stomach like something big has happened. Like I scored tickets to watch my favorite band perform in a sold-out concert or I beat my record five-mile time.

My cock comes back to life as soon as I close my eyes and see her face. Her head tipped back, the sexy-as-fuck sounds emitting from her throat as she gave me full access to her sinful body.

"I have to figure this girl out," I tell Trigger. "Want to give me some tips?"

She opens one eye and closes it again.

"Come on. Just one. Give me one thing that will win her over."

This time, only her mouth opens to yawn.

"You're a terrible best friend."

Rubbing her behind her ears, I flip off the light and pad down the hallway. Pictures of my family, of friends from the military, and some photos I took around the world hang on the walls.

My house is unlike my brothers'. Whereas theirs are modern and sleek, some of them elegant and sophisticated, mine is comfortable. Sure, I have marble counters and state-of-the-art sound systems and things like that, I also have a pool table in the living room. A hot tub on the back deck. A basement with a full exercise room and sauna.

Venturing into my bedroom, I flop on the chocolate-colored blanket. Closing my eyes, I wonder what it would feel like to have Ellie here.

I imagine feeling her next to me, hearing her sing in the shower, smelling her coffee in the morning before I wake up. I wonder if she's as messy as she used to be and if she still likes to eat breakfast in bed.

Trigger waltzes in and curls up in the corner. Before she can get too comfy, I give her a warning.

"Better get used to the idea of having another woman around here," I tell her, slipping under the covers. "Come hell or high water, I'm going to make her mine again. Just you wait and see."

Ellie

I HAVEN'T SEEN ONE-THIRTY IN the morning in a long time.

Stretched out on the couch, a fleece blanket pulled on top of me, I flip through the endless stream of channels on the television.

"Over a thousand channels and not a thing to watch," I groan.

I wonder vaguely if that's true or if I'm so preoccupied that I can't get engrossed in anything except the one infomercial about the copper pots. I really kind of want those.

A man comes on the screen with light-colored hair and wide shoulders, and that's all it takes to zap me wide awake again. It's not Ford, obviously, but it's close enough to cause my mind to jump back into overdrive.

My body is still charged, singing his praises every time I brush my legs together or clench my belly. That delicious pull from a good, hard orgasm still sits in my gut.

I'd forgotten what that felt like. I can't remember the last guy to make completely lose control like that, to completely wipe away every thought but the feelings exploding inside you. That's how I felt tonight.

I close my eyes and instantly see his face. Not the Ford now, but the Ford then. He was so cute with his cheeky grin and athlete's body. I adored him on the verge of infatuation. That's why it hurt so much. That's why it was so devastating.

Losing him almost made me lose me. Only by a stroke of luck did I land in Florida and only with a few lucky breaks was I able to make it through school. If for no other reason than I was determined to make something of myself to spite him. I did that. And so much more.

In a roundabout way, Ford may be to thank for making me the woman I am. Clearly it wasn't intentional. But the successes in my life are spurred by the need to never be a burden to someone and never have to rely on someone . . . and that's because of him.

Maybe having him walk away was more hurtful because I was young and didn't understand life. Or, maybe it was just due to him being my first love. Either way, it goes to show that there will always be something special about Ford that complicates things to a degree that's almost lethal.

That's why I can't do it again.

Ellie

"I DIDN'T EXPECT TO SEE you here."

Mallory's voice rings out behind me, her naturally chipper tone like a burst of sunshine through the yoga studio. I look up to see her toned body clad in purple yoga pants and a lime green top.

"You look like an eggplant," I laugh. "A gorgeous one, but an eggplant anyway."

"It was all I had clean," she admits. "I hate laundry."

"I don't know of anyone that likes laundry."

Finishing my stretch, I pull my legs to me and wait for her to join me on the mat.

Mallory has classes every day of the week, but mornings are the least busy and my favorite. I love the quiet. Today, in particular, I need the zen. I also wanted to show Mallory I'm not angry with her.

She plops down beside me and smiles. "I'm glad you came. I was wondering if I should come by Halcyon or if you'd just toss me out on my eggplant rear."

I can't help but laugh. "I considered quitting you," I wink. "But I'm stressed and yoga helps and this is my favorite studio. So I figured I'd better not quit you yet."

"Thank God for small favors," she sighs. "Please know I didn't mean to make you mad with the whole Ford thing. Sometimes I just think I have a brilliant plan and act on it and then realize later I might've kind of crossed boundaries."

"You think?"

She blows out a deep breath, her cheeks pinking. "I thought maybe I could bring the two of you together again. I love a good love story and felt like that information was dropped in my lap for a reason."

"I know you meant well." I grab my toes and lean towards my knees, hoping this gives me a minute to figure out what else to say.

"I'm probably prying, but how did things go? I know his side of it, but what's yours?"

I sit back up and look at her. My first reaction is to ask what he said about me, but I talk myself out of it. I want to come to terms with my reaction without having his and hers thrown into the mix any more than they already are.

"I have really mixed emotions about him," I admit.

"Want to talk about it?"

"Not really. I'm not sure where to even start. Besides," I say, getting to my feet, "I could probably talk through it for hours and be as confused as I already am."

She laughs, standing as well. "Can I cross one more boundary and say something else?"

"You're going to do it either way, aren't you?"

"Probably," she grins. "Look, I know it's been awhile since you've really spent a lot of time with Ford. It's been years, Graham says."

"Almost ten."

"Right. So, I wanted you to know that while I don't know what Ford was like growing up, I do know him now. He's a giant pain-in-my-butt, eats all the pie, and routinely gets Graham so worked up that I think he's going to have a heart attack and die."

Despite the words out of her mouth, Mallory has a smile stretched from ear to ear.

"He's also ridiculously intelligent, funny as hell, and the kindest Landry in the bunch." Mallory's voice softens. "No one has a bigger heart than Ford. No one looks at people and immediately sees the good, not the bad, like him. He's pretty special, Ellie. I wouldn't have sent him your way if he wasn't."

My shoulders slump. "I spent so many years being mad at him. Venomously angry at first, then more bitter, I guess, as time went on. It's weird now to see him face-to-face after having felt that way for such a long time."

"I bet it does, and I didn't think about that."

I drag in a deep breath and blow it out, hoping to push away some of the confusion in my brain. "When I hated him, at least I knew how to deal with that. It was almost safe, in a way. But now . . ."

"Now what?"

"Now I'm not sure how I feel."

It's the most honest thing I can think of to say. After mulling it over for hours, having his smile flit through my mind at random times, hoping I run into him at the gas station—I don't want to know *if* I want to know how I feel.

"Liking him is too easy," I concede. "It's that boyish grin that does me in."

"Not that I'm looking because I'm not, but it might be his body that does me in if I were you," she winks.

I can't help but laugh, knowing just how right she is. But physical attraction isn't my problem. I'm a red-blooded female, after all. The problem is something deeper, something more difficult to see.

"Let me ask you something, Mal."

"Sure. Anything."

"Is he really the good person you say he is? What I mean by that is does he date a lot? Does he go through women like crazy? You know, is he nice to people?"

Holding my breath as she considers my question, I wonder if she'll be completely truthful. Will she try to sell me on the guy she likes or will she dig deep and find the one time he was a jerk, like leaving a girl high and dry after he realizes he doesn't want to be with her.

Like what he did to me.

Her features soften. "He hasn't seriously dated anyone since I've known him. Sure, he's been with girls but none that he's brought around any of us. So that should answer that part of your question."

"What about the other?" I ask, my chest tightening with anticipation.

"He's the nicest guy I've ever met."

The simplicity in her statement speaks louder than anything. It's like those few words say everything she can say. There's nothing else to add.

My shoulders sag at the sincerity in her tone. "That's good to hear," I whisper.

"I know getting involved with someone, anyone, is hard. You really put your heart out there and hope they treat it kindly. When I gave in to Graham, I remember hoping he wouldn't treat me like a contract closure if he decided it didn't work between us. I worried about that."

"That's the thing . . . Ford did treat me like that before. He didn't want to be with me anymore and it was just like, 'bye,'" I sigh. "I've had guys do that before, obviously. We all have. But he's not just another guy. He's Ford. He was my first love, my first everything, to be honest. There's so much more tied up in things with him. A part of me feels stupid for even considering getting involved with him right now when Halcyon is getting off the ground, I just moved back home. Why invite the possible drama?"

"Life is complicated, Ellie. Look around at the people you know. Are any of their lives easy?"

"Yours seems pretty cush right now," I tease.

"I spent an hour this morning arguing with Graham about a mug that was left in the sink last night," she says, rolling her eyes. "I wouldn't trade Graham for anyone in the world, but let me tell you, it's not easy dating someone like him."

"He's pretty intense, right?"

"And high maintenance," she laughs. "The man has to have every-thing done a certain way. His clothes have to be facing a specific way in the closet. Can you believe that?"

"You're serious?"

"Yup, but I'm breaking him. Slowly."

I think about her words as she jogs off to welcome a few customers.

Ford certainly is complicated, but being with him is also so easy. It always has been. But maybe that means it's so easy because there's nothing too deep about it. Maybe it's a sign that our lives will cross from time to time, but there's nothing to put roots in.

Mallory's hand lands on my shoulder, making me jump. "It's about time to start class. But I wanted to give you one last piece of advice I've learned since I met Graham."

"Shoot."

"If you can walk away from Ford, do it. That means he's not the one for you."

My heart pulls at the thought of not seeing him again. It already hurts to think of going days, months, years again without having him in my orbit.

"In every other relationship I've ever had," Mallory adds, "I've always felt like I could leave and survive if I wanted to. I know if I tried to leave Graham, he'd come after me. And I'd want him to. I'd need him to."

With that, she heads to the front to greet her customers, and I'm left sitting on the mat to think.

Ford

THE LATE AFTERNOON SUN BEATS down, heating the interior of Graham's SUV. I crank on the air conditioner and get a snarl from my brother.

"What is it with you and the AC?"

"It's ninety degrees in here," I say, pulling the collar away from my neck. "I'm sweating like a motherfucker."

"Remind me to make you drive separately next time," he laughs.

"I'd be happy to, especially since you failed to inform me you have a meeting after ours that I'm going to wait out."

He looks at me over his shoulder. "I didn't know about that until we got in the car. I've waited to talk to this guy for two weeks. You're going to have to deal."

A sign catches my eye and I squint through the sunlight. "Hey, Halcyon is like two streets over."

"So?"

"Drop me off there."

Graham huffs. "Do you think I'm your dad? Like, 'Hey, Graham. Take me here and then come back to pick me up'?"

"Would it kill you?" I deadpan.

On a dime, the SUV takes a right and heads north.

"Ah, thanks, G," I grin.

"You can be such a child."

"If it makes you feel any better," I laugh as we take another right and pull up in front of Ellie's store, "you've made this child very happy."

"Get out of my car before I'm late," he says, smiling. "I'll text you when I'm on my way to get you."

"Yes, Father."

"Asshole," he mutters as I climb out and slam the door.

I jog the few paces to the front door, my heartbeat picking up. I tell myself it's because of the burst of exertion, but I know better.

There's been no exchange between us since I left her standing, covered in paint. It's killed me not to call her or send her a text. Hell, it's been nearly impossible not to just drive to her house and scoop her up and kiss the ever-loving fuck out of her.

I knew once I broke the barrier, things would change. Seeing her respond to me in such an intimate way, watching her put her guard down and let me in, only solidifies how I feel.

She's mine.

Not in some mock-caveman way. It's not like that at all. She's mine because as much as she belongs with me, I belong with her. The catch is I've said a lot of stupid things, made a lot of promises, and set up a lot of things that I didn't follow through on. She won't trust my word. She shouldn't. It's up to me to show her who I am and how I feel.

That I love her.

The cool air of Halcyon hits me in the face as I step inside. Violet and Ellie are on the floor, sandwiches and chips in front of them.

"Hey, ladies," I say, nodding quickly at Violet and then setting my sights on Ellie. A pair of cut-off denim shorts showcases her toned legs and a plain black tank top is stretched across her ample breasts. With her messy ponytail, she's a sight I could watch for days.

"Hey, Ford," Violet chirps.

"Hi." Ellie smiles at me, absentmindedly combing a hand through her hair. Green smears are laced through the dark strands. I pretend not to notice.

"I hope you don't mind me stopping by," I say. "I was riding with Graham and he had a meeting. I thought I'd see if you ladies needed any help instead of waiting in the car for God knows how long."

"We were just wrapping up lunch," Violet says, mischief in her eyes. "I do hear you're a good painter though."

"Violet!" Ellie hisses, making us all laugh.

"That's what she says, huh?" I tease.

"She did," Violet continues, dodging a thrown water bottle from her friend. "She said—"

"Don't you dare!" Ellie springs to her feet, a smile on her face. "Between the two of you, you embarrass me to no end."

I pin my eyes to hers. "Baby, there is absolutely nothing to be embarrassed about."

Her cheeks ratchet up a darker shade of pink. "Can we change the subject?"

"Yes," Violet offers. "Let's talk about that little smear of green paint on Ford's forearm that conspicuously matches the green in your hair."

Ellie charges back, threatening Violet, as I chuckle. Pulling my phone from my pocket, I see Sienna's name on the screen.

I motion to them I need to take the call and head to the back. "Hello?"

"Hey, Ford! Are you busy?"

"It depends on what you want."

"Well, I need a ride."

"Why?"

She sighs dramatically into the line. "I rode with Camilla to get manicures and she went first. She was finished when I was just starting, so she said she was going to run a few errands and come back to get me. I can't get her to even respond to my texts now, and I'm tired of sitting here. I'm only a few blocks from Landry Security, so I thought maybe you'd take pity on your baby sister and come get me."

"You could walk," I offer.

"It's a hundred degrees out there!"

Ellie's voice drifts to the back and I get an idea. "Can I call you right back?"

"You aren't going to leave me sitting here too, are you?"

"Get an attitude and I just might leave you to an Uber."

"Call me back," she growls and hangs up.

Moseying to the front, it's Violet that catches my eye first. I toss her a wink.

"Who was that?" Violet asks carefully, trying to make sure that's what I intended her to do.

"My sister Sienna. She's stranded at a nail place and needs a ride."

A look of understand flickers through Violet's eyes. "Weren't you dropped off here?"

"Yup. I told her she'd have to take a cab or something."

Violet looks at Ellie. "Why don't you take Ford to get her?"

Ellie's jaw drops as she looks at Violet and then me. "Um, well, I . . ."

"You totally don't have to," I say. "Really. She can call someone else. It's fine."

"But you were just saying you needed to run out and grab some thumb tacks and stuff, right?" Violet prods. "Let me finish what we were doing and you run Ford to grab his sister."

"But I . . ." she gulps. "Are you sure?"

"Yes," Violet says, nudging her towards me.

"If you don't want to, Ellie, it's fine," I grin.

She searches my face and I can almost see the cogs turning. Finally, she throws back her shoulders and smiles. "Let me grab my keys."

Ellie

WHAT THE HELL AM I doing?

It takes two attempts to get the keys in the ignition. Ford is too close, looking entirely too sinful, and smelling way too freaking good to think clearly.

In my little car, he completely dominates the space. It's like my brain refuses to work with him in the passenger's seat next to me. Where he could reach out and touch me. And move his fingers to my—

"Ellie?"

"Ah!" I say, jumping back in my seat. My hands clasp over my heart as it stalls in my chest. "You scared me!"

"Saying your name?" he laughs. "What on Earth is wrong with you?"

"Nothing," I mutter, pulling my sunglasses over my eyes in hopes he doesn't see me blush. "Where is Sienna?"

He gives me the address, and I pull out onto the street. We drive for a few miles with no sound besides the radio quietly playing a hip-hop station Violet had on this morning.

"Do you listen to this?" he asks, turning the sound up. "This is horrible."

"It was all Violet," I laugh. "I usually listen to country."

"I knew I loved you."

Pressing a swallow, I try to let those words go in one ear and out the other. I'm sure it was just a slip of the tongue, a casual use of words people say each and every day.

I knew I loved you.

I gulp again.

A song by a popular artist comes on the radio and he taps his foot against the floorboard in rhythm. The insistent tip-tap begins to drive me up the wall.

"Okay," I say, flipping off the radio. "Let's talk."

"Okay. Let's talk," he repeats.

"What are you? A canary?"

"A canary?" he laughs. "You mean a parrot."

"No, a canary. Canaries talk."

"Do they? I don't think so."

"Look it up," I laugh. "We had a canary when I was little and it talked."

He gives me the cutest, silliest look. "I'm sure it did."

I smack him on the shoulder. That's all it takes for the air to shift. He must feel it too because he cranks up the air conditioner.

"I've been hot all fucking day," he grumbles.

I want to comment that he looks fucking hot every time I see him. I could make a note about how hard his shoulder just was when I hit him and how I'd like to roam my hands down his biceps and feel him flex his body while he's up against mine. Or on mine. Or under mine. Or inside mine.

"Hey!" he laughs, grabbing the top of the steering wheel. "Pay attention or I'll drive."

The car evens back out as I feel every ounce of blood rush to my face. "Sorry."

"You feeling okay today?" he grins. "You're flushed."

"I'm fine."

"Yes, you are," he whistles. "I keep thinking about last night."

"I wanted to talk to you about that, actually," I gulp.

Glancing at him over my shoulder, there's a look of surprise on his face.

"I don't know what came over me," I start.

"I know what came over me. All over me, actually . . ."

"Damn it, Ford," I blush. "Stop."

"Fine. I'm sorry. Continue."

He's not sorry. Not a bit. The smirk set deep in his cheeks tells the truth.

Sighing, I take a left towards the salon.

"Look, El. I'm not sure what you're thinking, but I'm not sorry about what happened," he says. "If you want me to say it was a mistake or apologize for something—"

"No," I say hurriedly. "I, um, I don't want you to apologize. I just didn't expect that to happen, and I'm not sure what kind of signal it puts out."

I can tell he's grinning as he shifts in the seat so he's facing me. "What kind of signal it puts out?"

"Yeah."

"Sexy as hell? Does that work?"

I don't look at him. If I do and see his eyes on me like I think they are, I might pull over and ravage him on the side of the road.

"If you're insinuating that I think it meant anything more than you wanting something I could give you in that moment, I don't," he says, all teasing gone from his tone. "I'll be honest and say I hope it means that you're opening up to the idea of maybe spending some time with me."

"Seems like a slippery slope."

"I'll have you know I'm passing a huge innuendo with that one," he laughs.

"You have a one-track mind today," I grin.

"That's your fault."

I sense movement to my right. Out of the corner of my eye, I see his arm reaching forward just before his palm lands on the bare skin of my thigh.

Goosebumps ripple from the spot, like a stone thrown on a lake. With every wave, my body comes alive.

Much to both my relief and regret, he doesn't move his hand.

"To clarify, my mind is always two-track with you," he almost whispers. "That's how I know you're special."

As if the universe is finally giving me a break, I pull to the curb of a salon nestled in the back of a strip mall. A gorgeous blonde girl is standing in the front with an oversized pink bag and purple tips to her hair.

"Is that Sienna?" I ask.

He removes his hand from my leg, the skin instantly feeling cold. I turn the air conditioner down.

He rolls down his window and waves at his sister. Her face lights up and she half-runs to the car.

"Thank you," she says as she climbs in the back. "I'm going to kill Cam."

"Where'd she go?" Ford asks.

Sienna just rolls her eyes in response. "Thanks for coming to get me, Ellie," she says. "It's nice to officially meet you. Cam has said you're a pretzel in the yoga studio."

"Things I'd like to know," Ford murmurs before Sienna shoots him a look.

Ignoring him, I pull back onto the road. "I've only practiced for a couple of years now. I'm not nearly as good as your sister."

"I think she's getting lots of practice in contortion these days," Sienna laughs, watching Ford for a reaction. He glares at her.

I have no idea what I'm missing, but I laugh too. "Sounds like she's getting a workout."

"Trust me when I say if you saw the apparatus, you'd be wishing—"

Ford silences her with one pointed look.

"Sorry," Sienna grins, slipping back into the seat. "Oh! Take a right here!"

I do as instructed, and in a few minutes, we are sitting outside a cute little white house with black shutters.

"Who lives here?" Ford asks.

"A friend of mine," she says, leaning up and kissing him on the cheek. "No worries."

"Should I accompany you to the door?"

This time it's her that silences him with a look.

"Fine. Behave yourself," he mutters. "And if you don't hear from Cam, call me."

"She's fine. No, she's more than fine," Sienna laughs, ignoring the look from her brother. "Thanks again for coming to get me, Ellie. I really appreciate it."

"It was nice meeting you," I reply.

"Same here."

With a final bright smile, she's up the stairs of the little house. I pull away before Ford can try to catch a glimpse of the person inside. This frustrates him, but he doesn't mention it.

"Did you hear that?" he groans, stretching his legs out in the small space in front of him.

"No. What are you talking about?"

"My stomach just rumbled."

"Poor thing." I swerve through traffic and hit my next turn-off.

"Definitely poor thing. You should feed me."

Scoffing, I glance over my shoulder. "That's no way to ask a girl on a date."

"I wasn't asking you on a date."

"You weren't?"

"Nope," he says, the last consonant exaggerated. "You'd say no."

"Probably," I grin.

"So I was not asking you on a date," he goes over again, "but I was suggesting we share a non-date meal with each other."

"So you were breaking the date ice with a drive-thru meal?"

"Exactly," he chuckles. "Let's get a hamburger."

Before I can respond, he's digging in his pocket and pulling out his phone. "Fucking Graham."

"What?"

He sticks out his bottom lip. "He's on his way to get me."

My giggle drifts through the car, a lightness in my soul that I want to grab on to and hold forever. "You sound like a child."

"That's what Graham said."

"We both couldn't be wrong."

I turn left, heading back to Halcyon and away from the fast-food chains dotting the right side of the road.

"I guess we're going to have to go on that date after all," he says easily, like it's the default answer.

"Or not."

"Come on, Ellie," he says in a faux-whine. "I've already had my fingers—"

"Stop!"

"Fine, fine," he sighs. "Just go to dinner with me tonight. Let me have a moment to swoon you."

"Swoon me?" My face is lit up with a smile so wide it makes my cheeks ache. "You want to swoon me?"

"I want to do more than that, but I'll settle for a good swoon first."

Pulling my car in behind a jet-black SUV, I flick off the ignition. "I can't."

"Don't give me that."

"I can't," I tell him. "I have plans tonight."

"Come on!" A dark-headed version of Ford shouts from the window of the SUV.

"Fucker." Ford climbs out the passenger's side door. He sticks his head back in and makes one final attempt at winning me over. "I'll take you anywhere you want. Fancy dinner? Picnic? Milkshakes and French fries? You name it and I'll make it happen."

"I really can't, Ford."

His face falls. "Okay. I'll try harder."

"Ford—"

"See ya later, beautiful."

He jogs to the car in front of us, climbs in, and they take off down the road, leaving me swooning behind.

Ellie

THE EVENING AIR IS THICK and warm. Beads of sweat form along my forehead as soon as I exit the car. Scents of freshly hewn wood, oil, and the stench of cement permeate the air as I walk to the construction site.

"Hey, Ellie!" Bernie, the site superintendent, greets me with a wide smile. "I was wondering if you were coming tonight."

"I had a few things creep up at Halcyon. Sorry I'm late."

"Don't apologize! We're glad you came." He walks by my side as we head into the little trailer they use for an office. "How's the shop going? You about ready to open?"

"We're getting there. It's so much work."

"If anyone can do it, it's you."

"Thanks," I grin. "Where do you need me tonight?"

"We're actually clearing a little area on the north side of what is going to be the house pad."

"Oh, Bernie. Don't use words like north to give me directions. You know better than that."

He laughs heartily. "I'm sorry. Head to the pad and walk around it. You'll see some people dragging out the final trees and big stones, things like that."

"Great. I'll head that way."

I check-in on the clipboard, find my hardhat, and head back out onto the site. Out of all the charities I love, this is one of the closest to my heart.

When I was a little girl, our house burned down. I must've been five or six at the time. I remember watching orange and blue flames screaming out of our roof, windows, and where the front door used to be. I didn't worry about my clothes or baby dolls or teddy bears. I remember being terrified about where we would live.

Shelters for Savannah is one of the reasons why my family wasn't homeless. Through their generosity, we had a warm, safe place to regroup and because of their extraordinary kindness, we were able to rebuild. That house, constructed with so much love, sweat, and tears, is the home my father still lives in to this day.

Rounding the corner, I see the team of volunteers clearing an area just like Bernie said.

"Hey, everyone!" I say, pulling my gloves from my pocket. "Where do I start?"

They all say hello as Wendy comes forward and asks me to fill a wheelbarrow with debris and haul it to the waste bin.

I get to work, picking up rocks, trash, and debris and loading them into the cart. My boots sink a little in the soil. My heart, on the other hand, is lighter than air.

I haven't felt this happy in such a long time. Although a part of me wishes I had gone to dinner with Ford, a bigger part of me feels so much joy being here. Giving back. Repaying the favor we were shown.

"You never fail to amaze me," Wendy says.

"And why is that?"

"We don't see a lot of girls your age out here getting dirty."

"Ah, I guess it's in my genes," I shrug. "I was never much of a girly-girl."

"That's good for us, I guess."

With a spring in my step, I take the full wheelbarrow and begin pushing it across the ground. The weight of it causes it to sink into the earth and it makes it super hard to get to the trash. Volunteers whiz by me like a beehive, everyone doing their part for the greater good.

I pull up to the garbage and begin transferring my haul. Twisting to grab a metal can that fell off the side, my hand pauses in the air.

A tall, lanky figure is on the other side of the site. He's shoveling a pile of gravel into a trench.

Forgetting all about the can, I stand and watch him. He's dressed in a pair of ripped jeans and has a purple t-shirt on with ARROWS emblazoned on the front. A white hat is pulled low on his head.

His body moves in long, graceful strokes. Even from afar, I can see his muscles under the sheen of sweat soaking through the back of his shirt.

It's sexy as hell.

And it's Ford.

I laugh in disbelief. He's here. Here. At a Shelters site on a random day for a random family in a random neighborhood. Why?

"Hey, Wendy," I call out as she pulls a tree beside me. "Is he here often?"

"Who, honey?"

"Him." I point to Ford. "Is he here a lot? I haven't seen him before."

Her head cocks to the side as a smile takes over her full lips. "He's never been to this one particularly, to my knowledge. I worked with him a couple of times on the south side of town over the last year or so." She quirks a brow. "You know who that is, don't you? He's a Landry."

"I know," I whisper, watching him work.

"You don't see that much—a man like that out here with the rest of us. Gives us some hope for humanity, huh?"

"It sure does."

Wendy goes about her task and leaves me standing with my wheelbarrow.

A shovelful of rocks falls off the end of Ford's tool, and as if he feels my eyes on him, his head slowly rises to mine. It takes no time at all for our gazes to lock. Like a band is pulling us together, we both walk towards one another.

"What are you doing here?" I ask as we meet in the middle.

"Same thing as you, I guess." He takes his gloves off. One hand comes to the side of my face and he brushes it gently. "Every time I find you in the wild, you have something on your face. The first time I saw you, you had mud everywhere too. Remember that?"

"Yes. I almost fell into the lake that day."

"If that shirt would've been wet when I found you . . ." He wiggles his brows. "We are both probably better off you just always have dirt on your face."

"Maybe it's always there so you have to touch me."

"I don't need a reason to touch you, sweetheart."

We exchange a soft grin, like there's a secret between us.

"If you would've told me you were coming here, I would've brought us a picnic," he chuckles. "We could've done this and then had dinner. I'm easy, you know."

"That's what I hear," I joke. "Do you do this often?"

"Yeah," he confesses with a slight shrug. "Sometimes. A girl I knew once upon a time went on a rant about how you should get your hands dirty and all this nonsense."

"Did she?"

"She did. She was a smart one." His eyes darken. "And so fucking beautiful . . . even with dirt on her face and paint still stuck in her hair."

"There is not," I giggle.

"Oh, there is," he laughs. "But it brings back such great memories I think you should just leave it there permanently."

I kick a rock, watching it roll across the soil. Forcing a swallow, I try to untangle the thoughts twisting together in my mind before I do something stupid.

Unfortunately, it's one of those moments when my libido works faster than logic and I hear the words from my lips before my brain knows what's happening.

"Did you hear that?" I ask.

"What?"

"That was my stomach rumbling."

A cheek-to-cheek smile spreads across his handsome face. "I did hear that, actually. You should let me fix it after we're done here."

With a flutter in my chest, I return his smile. "I'd like that."

Ford

MY FOOT IS HEAVY ON the accelerator, in part because I'm worried I fucked up.

I should have never let her out of my sight.

In my twenty-eight years of life, I've never once feared being stood up. Not even with Brittany Belview, the hottest girl in the tenth grade. But tonight? I'm kind of terrified.

My truck rolls to a stop in front of her house. It's a small brick one-story with neatly trimmed hedges along the front. The steps leading to the porch need painted and I find myself calculating if I have time this weekend to accomplish that task.

"Slow down," I mutter as I head to the front door.

Glancing down at my clothes before ringing the bell, I smooth out an imaginary wrinkle from my shirt. I had no idea whether to dress up or down because we really didn't hash that out. In lieu of any direction, I threw on a pair of khakis and a blue button-down. Figuring it didn't look like I expected too much, yet made an effort, I left the house with a bit of confidence I can't quite find just now as I press the doorbell.

The door swings open and I let out a sigh of relief. She's dressed in a pair of leggings and a red top that showcases every curve on her body. Her hair is still wet from the shower, her face free of any makeup.

I must be staring because her face flushes. "I know I look like a mess, but—"

"I was just standing here thinking you've never looked more beautiful."

She looks at the floor. "Thank you, Ford."

"You need to thank your mama." I step over the threshold and take in her abode.

The walls are white, the floors a honey-colored hardwood. There are pictures everywhere and little accent pieces in blues and golds. It reminds me a lot of my own house, but with an Ellie flair.

"I like your place," I comment as she shuts the door behind me.

"I looked around the city forever to find a place that I felt like I could call home. I thought my realtor was going to quit. Luckily this came on the market and I fell in love."

"It took me forever to find mine too. I had this list of things I wanted and my realtor said I was too picky," I chuckle.

"What did you want in a home?"

We sit on a sofa covered in pillows beneath a window. She tucks her legs up beneath her like she did when we were kids. It makes me smile.

"I wanted to be out of city limits. That was the first thing," I tell her.

"That doesn't surprise me. You've always been a country boy."

"I couldn't stand living with neighbors this close. I need my privacy. I also wanted a big space for a yard, not just trees and shrubs. I want a place to run and let Trigger out to play."

"Who is Trigger?"

"My baby," I tease. "She's my yellow lab and she's insanely jealous of you."

Her eyes grow wide. "Of me?"

"She knows her place as the love of my life is being threatened."

She laughs, shaking her head. "Well-played. For the record, I don't particularly love being in town either. But this place is close to Dad and close to Halcyon and close to Violet. So it makes sense."

"It's not close to me."

"I don't know where you live," she says sweetly.

"We'll have to fix that soon."

We share a quiet pause, something moving between us that neither of us wants to break. I reach for her hand and she lets me take it. Our fingers laced together, her delicate palm nestled in mine, I set them on my thigh.

"Was coming back to Savannah an easy choice for you?" she asks.

"At the end of the day, yes," I say. "My family is here and I like living close to them and working with them on a daily basis. I can appreciate that now. There's something really organic and fulfilling about that."

"It's amazing how well you all get along. I mean, out of six of you, no one hates anyone. That's impressive."

Nodding, I think through all my siblings and realize she's right. "None of us feels any bad way about anyone else, I don't think. Whatever one of us does, we know the others have their back. Actually," I say, giving her hand a squeeze, "Barrett called me today. His party has been talking about him running for the Presidency in a few years."

"That's amazing," she grins.

"It is. It feels like the last election just ended, but I guess things work fast in politics."

"That's what they say," she shrugs.

"But to your point earlier, he was asking if he were to run, would I join his security team."

Something about that catches her off guard. "Really? What would that entail?"

"I don't know," I admit. "I guess that's something we'll have to wait and see if it comes to fruition."

There's a slightly awkward silence that's capped off by her slipping her hand away from mine.

"What about you?" I ask. "What's the future hold for you?"

"I don't know either," she contends. "I want to get Halcyon off the ground. Maybe go for my Master's degree at some point after I pay off this round of student loans."

I start to say something, but close my mouth.

"I feel like I'm coming into my life right now, you know?" she asks. "Things are starting to work out for me. I'm back home. I can help Dad out. I can give back to this community that I love so much."

"I understand. I feel that way too. I feel like this is the precipice to the next part of my life. I've done the nomadic, roam-the-world part. Now I'm ready to settle down, have some kids, do that whole thing."

"I'm not ready for that."

It's more the tone than the words that catches my attention. She looks me in the eye, her resolve undeniable.

Although it's not what I want to hear, not by a long shot, I try to remain as passive about her declaration as possible. "I was driving by where the old drive-in theater used to be. Do you remember that?"

"You took me there to see Jaws on the Fourth of July. Remember that?" she laughs. "We took a kiddie pool and filled it up with buckets from the bathroom."

"I'd have done anything to see you in that bikini," I wink. "Man, I was desperate."

"You were. But it was kinda hot."

"Just kinda hot? Damn. You're a tough sell."

"It's like real estate," she says, her voice lowering just a touch. "It's all about the comps."

"What are you comparing me to?"

She eyes me with an impish grin. "Maybe I'm comparing you . . . to you."

My pants all of a sudden feel too tight as her gaze heats my blood and it pools in my cock.

"So I'm hotter now than I was at seventeen? I'll take that," I tell her.

"You are definitely hotter now than you were then," she says, looking me straight in the eye.

I grasp her hand again. Instead of putting it back on my leg, I rest it on my lap.

Her chin lifts ever-so-slightly and I know she feels how much I'm dying for her right now. Without breaking our gaze, she presses her hand against me. The pressure she applies is just enough of a taunt that my teeth grind together as I attempt to keep myself from throwing her backwards and fucking the daylights out of her.

"I say we have two choices right about now," I say as she begins to press slow, torturous circles against my throbbing length.

"What's that?"

"We can get off this couch right now and go to dinner."

"Or?"

"Or we can get off on this couch right now and you can be dinner."

"OPTION NUMBER TWO, PLEASE."

I can't believe I just said that.

Before I can open my mouth to try to take it back, I'm on my back on the floor.

"Ah!" I shriek, my giggle a little wobbly from the sudden movement. "Ford!"

He wedges himself between my legs, planting his hands on either side of my face. He looks down at me with a wicked smile.

All thoughts of not being in this position right now are gone. Even if I wanted to tell him I didn't mean it, I couldn't. My libido has officially taken over and as I look into his eyes and feel his thickness bulging from his pants, I'm good where I am.

I make a point of lifting each leg and wrapping it firmly around his waist, locking my heels together at the dip of his back. The purposeful movement is as much for me as it is for him. It lets us both know I'm all-in. At least for now. At least for this.

"If this goes an inch farther, it's on. I'm warning you," he grins.

"You have a window of opportunity here," I whisper, winding my hands in his hair. It's silky and soft, and I gently tug a handful of it so his face lifts to me. "Take it. Or leave it."

"Yes, ma'am," he grins.

His head dips slowly until his lips are hovering over mine. I wait one, two, three seconds until I can't take it anymore. Lifting my chin, I brush my mouth against his and I know what he means by, "It's on."

An urgency is just below the surface. His struggle, as real as mine, to keep this under control is a losing endeavor. His tongue licks a long swipe against my mouth, and as I moan, his volleys against mine.

His breath is hot, his skin smooth as I drag my hands down the side of his face and cup his cheeks in my palms. The curve of his jaw is masculine, almost sharp, as it rests against my fingertips.

As he kisses me senseless, I roam his body—down his neck, across his shoulders, down his sinewy, muscled sides. Tugging on his shirt, I bring it up far enough to get my hands on his back. Traversing his body, it's like rediscovering a road you once traveled all the time, only to find all the dips a little deeper, the bends a little sharper. The body a whole lot sexier.

"Ford," I moan against his lips as he rocks his hips forward. His cock presses against me, solid as a piece of steel. My entire body hums, begging for him to touch me. Caress me. Make love to me. I'm so keyed up I can't think. I can't hear. I can't do anything but feel for the first time in forever.

He breaks the kiss, but goes back in and kisses me once more. Then another time. Then a fourth. By the fifth kiss, I'm giggling. When he pulls back, his eyes are shining. "I could kiss you all night."

"I hope you do," I say, fumbling at the buttons of his pants. "But can we do that without these?"

He does a push-up and on the up-swing, pops up to his feet. Standing over me, he looks even taller, wider, than he really is. "Up." He reaches for my hand and pulls me to my feet.

Lifting the hem of my shirt, he drags it over my head. I'm left standing in front of him in a nude-colored lace bra and a pair of leggings. My thighs press together in a failed attempt to stop the ache pulsing so hard, begging for attention, that it's almost all I can concentrate on.

"Damn," he whistles. He takes a step back and looks me up and down, his gaze like fire as it skims my body. "You are beyond gorgeous."

"Your turn," I say, motioning to his shirt. "Off with it."

He sheds the fabric in a second and discards it to the side next to mine. His body is like looking at a magazine cover for men's health. His shoulders are broad, tapering down to a narrow waist. His abs are cut into perfect squares with long, lean lines running down the sides. My fingers itch to touch him, drag my nails down his tanned skin and feel the smoothness of his powerful body.

Right before I do, I see a small tattoo vertical down his right side. It's a rifle with a combat helmet on top. Winding around it are three little red flowers. When I look at him, he swallows.

"I had three buddies killed overseas. That's for them."

"What about that one?" I point towards a line of script going from his front to his back around his left ribs. "Who you are and whose you are" is etched in elegant script in his skin.

"It's something my grandma used to say. I got it as a reminder to remember who I am in the scheme of things and where I belong. I thought it was stupid back then, but now, I get it."

"Where do you belong now?" I husk.

He closes the distance between us, his eyes burning a hole in me. "Right fucking here."

As my breathing picks up, his follows suit. As his fists begin to clench, my hands start to move as well. He closes the final few centimeters with barely a move and his thumbs dig into my hips.

It's like a button has been pressed.

He slides the fabric down my legs, his palms flat against me as he goes down. Chills creep up in the wake as I watch him drop to his knees. He lifts one leg, pulls the leggings off, and then moves to the other. As he stands, his fingertips trail up my body as if he's afraid to break contact.

I grab the front belt loops of his pants and yank him towards me. He smiles. The latch is unfastened and the zipper lowered in a few quick seconds. He steps out of his pants and green boxer briefs as I unfasten my bra and discard it to the side.

Only now do I see him in all his glory—chiseled, carved, and cut to absolute precision. His cock is long, the head of it swollen, as it waits at attention.

My pussy pulses, wetness dampening my thighs. I'm tempted to reach down and relieve some of the pressure myself, but I'm afraid to move. A sheen of sweat dots Ford's body as he narrows his eyes.

"Come here," he orders.

His arms extend to the sides and I step into his personal space. He wraps me up, locking his hands at the small of my back, and kisses me again. I let my arms dangle off his shoulders and embrace the feeling of being encompassed by Ford.

His hands glide over the top of my butt and cup the underside of each cheek. I'm lifted up, and instinctively, I wind my legs around his waist. I grab his cock in my fist and pump it a few times. Ford's eyes roll back in his head as he rewards me with a growl.

"Does that feel good?" I ask, knowing damn good and well it does.

"Not as good as this is going to feel." He drops to his knees, making me yelp at the sudden change in position. I hang on to his neck as he leans forward, dropping me carefully onto my back.

As I settle back onto the floor, I'm met with a look from him that makes me almost combust.

The side of his lip curls into a mischievous grin, the blues of his eyes looking deeper, darker as he hovers over me.

I think he's going to kiss me, but he doesn't. Instead, his lips find the side of my face. He trails a set of kisses from my cheek, across my jaw, and to my ear. Then he goes down my neck, drawing his tongue down my skin and then blowing on the wetness left behind.

I shiver, lifting my hips towards him.

A low chuckle rumbles from his chest as he continues his kisses and licks over my breasts.

His assault is heavenly. He treats my body like it's a temple to be worshipped. Unrushed. Leisurely showing me how much he's enjoying this.

Propping back up so he's looking down at me, he smiles. "God, you're beautiful."

"You're going to make me blush," I giggle.

"I want to make you blush. And smile. And giggle like that. It's the best sound I've ever fucking heard. Well, maybe it is. There's one I'd like to compare it to."

He maneuvers himself so that his length sits at my opening. I can feel the head of his cock teasing me, promising to split me in two.

"Please," I beg, letting my knees fall to the side.

"Please what?"

"Please fuck me."

He looks pleasantly startled. "I wasn't expecting such a dirty mouth on such a pretty girl," he jokes. "But I'd love to fuck you." He moves his hips so his cock dips just a little farther into me. "How hard do you want it?"

"Hard enough that I can't think of anything but you in the morning."

"Baby," he grins, "if I have my way, we'll still be doing it in the morning."

My response doesn't come fast enough. Any thoughts I had are pushed away by the sensation of him sliding inside me. It's a slow, sensual thrust, an inch of his rock-hard cock at a time gliding through my wetness.

His eyes are locked on mine, but I can't keep them open. If I do, I think they'll pop out from the surge of pressure vibrating through every piece of me.

Tilting my hips upward to meet his, he finally hits the back. Instead of pulling back and restarting the descent, he pauses. My body is full to the brim, stretched to a point that it's almost, but not quite, uncomfortable.

I exhale a breath and open my eyes. He's still watching me.

"Does that feel okay? You're so tight, sweetheart," he says quietly.

"It feels incredible," I tell him. I cup his face in my hands and lose myself in his eyes. "Move. Please."

He pulls back in the same, slow way he entered me before rocking his hips forward and filling me once more. With every push, then pull, I'm built higher and higher.

He moves from kissing me to caressing my breasts to kissing me again. My ankles lock behind his waist once more. He lifts my ass so that my shoulder blades are all that is touching the floor. His fingers dig into my hips, searing the flesh in the best possible way, as he guides my body on and off of his cock.

I feel the burn in my core, the flame taking on a life of its own. It spreads through my thighs, down my legs, through my stomach and up, up, up to my face.

"Ford," I cry out, meeting him thrust for thrust, "I'm going to come.

I can't take this much longer. Ah!"

He slams into me harder, the head of his dick pounding the back of my vagina. It's relentless. Unyielding. And absolutely wonderful.

"Ford!" I almost scream as streaks of color swim over my vision. The flames inside me burn like a raging wildfire, and before I can say another word, an orgasm tears through me without warning.

My legs stiffen as I'm assaulted with the hardest, most spectacular climax of my life. My teeth clench, my body shakes, as Ford's thumb massages my clit in smooth, small circles.

He continues sliding in and out until, as I'm coming back to Earth, he pulls out. His come sprays across my body, the warm liquid dotting my breasts and stomach.

I'm too tired to care, but not too tired to watch.

He's so undeniably sexy with his head thrown back, mid-moan, his Adam's apple popped in his throat. He grunts, my name laced in the sounds of his desire.

Finally, his hands drop to the side and his face pulls forward, grinning. "You okay?"

"I don't know," I say, pretending to consider the question. "You may have to do that one more time just to be sure."

"I'd be happy to help you figure that out," he laughs. "But I did realize I wasn't wearing a condom," he says, like he's feeling me out to see if I'm angry or cool with it. "I have one in my wallet, but I . . . I honestly forgot about it."

I let that sink in as I watch him search my face. "I'm clean. I mean, I just had my yearly and they test for everything."

"Me too," he grins. "Well, not my yearly, but I'm clean."

"And I'm on the pill so we shouldn't find ourselves in another *situation*."

He gives me a strange look, one that I can't quite read. Instead of trying to figure it out, I yawn.

"Although I'm starving, I think I need a nap," I say, yawning again. Glancing at the clock over the mantle, I realize why. "It's getting late. It's almost ten."

"Ten is late? You're a wuss," he laughs, standing and beginning to gather our discarded clothes.

"Are you a night owl?"

"I usually head to bed around one or so. I work a lot at night. Work out a lot after work. I have a system," he laughs.

"Am I interrupting your system?"

He stops in the middle of picking up a shirt and looks at me. "You're the best interruption I've ever had, Ellie."

There's no denying how I feel in this moment, no way to pretend the look he's giving me doesn't make me want to hit pause on life and stay right here for the rest of time.

"You want to order take-out?" I offer. "Otherwise, I'm going to have to get another shower, dry my hair, put on makeup—"

"You don't have to do any of that to go out with me," he says with a smile. "But I won't say no to hanging out with you here and eating food from a box. I'd prefer it, actually." He hangs his head to the floor. "I'm boring, I know."

"Can I tell you a secret?" I ask, getting to my feet. "I'd rather stay home too."

"Really?"

"Really." I head down the hall, fully aware that he's watching my ass. "I'm going to clean up. You figure out what's for dinner."

His chuckle follows me in the bathroom.

Ford

THE CEILING FAN WHIRLS AROUND, causing Ellie to shiver every now and then as we lie together in her bed. I use it as an excuse to bring her even closer to me. She doesn't resist, just smiles in her sleep and repositions her face on my chest.

After a nap, a pizza delivery, a shower, followed by round two, we both fell asleep. It's now nearing eight in the morning. I don't know what time she usually gets up, but I know there's no way I'm going to disturb her.

My clothes are on a chair in the corner of the room, my phone tucked safely in one of the pockets of my pants. In less than an hour, that phone is going to ring. It's going to be Graham and he's going to be pissed.

There is a meeting scheduled at Landry Holdings at eight-thirty. It's a meeting I'm going to miss because I'm not about to shorten this moment for anything in the world by untangling our bodies just to get my phone.

Glancing down at her, I take in her pouty lips that are pressed together like they want kissed. Her lashes are splayed against her cheeks, her arm stretched lazily over my stomach. It's a beautiful sight. It's an even better feeling.

I might have suspected that I couldn't fully connect with another woman because my heart was still with her. It was one of the only explanations why I found a fatal flaw in every date I had, in every girl that I even vaguely considered dating. They just weren't right. Something was slightly amiss and I couldn't quite put my finger on it.

My finger—hell, my whole hand—is on top of it now. It's absolutely clear that I have two choices: live alone for the rest of my life or fight like hell for this. For her. For us.

There might be two choices, but there's only one answer.

Ellie begins to stir, rolling away from me and stretching.

"Shh," I whisper, trying to bring her in beside me again.

Her beautiful eyes pop open. "Are you going to let me sleep all day?" she laughs sleepily.

"I'd let you sleep all week if that meant I got to hold you."

"What time is it?"

"Almost eight or so."

She furrows her brows as if she's just waking up and putting all the pieces together. Before she can comment, my phone rings through the silence.

"Shit," I groan. Reality has officially broken through. "I really need to get that."

After she wiggles to the side, I unfold my body and pad across the floor. Her gaze is hot against my back, searing my skin as I grab my phone and bring it to my ear.

"Hello?"

"Where the hell are you?" Graham asks.

"Occupied."

"Damn it, Ford. Just because Lincoln has shaped up a bit, doesn't mean you have to fill the vacancy."

"Easy there, captain," I laugh. "Hoda will be there. She has the files, and I went over everything with her yesterday. She knows where I stand. You don't really need me."

I listen to Graham's tirade, slipping on my pants and shrugging on my shirt. It's hard to pay attention to what my brother is saying as Ellie sits up in bed, her breasts perky, her nipples in stiff peaks.

She climbs out of bed, her ass so perfectly round I want to palm it. I'm only reminded of the call when I hear Graham mutter a string of profanities.

"Relax, Graham. I heard everything you said."

"You did fucking not."

"Okay. You're right. I didn't. But I get the gist of it."

He sighs. "Moments like this, I loathe being the only responsible one."

"I'll make it up to you."

"I'll add it to your tab," he says. "Oh, before I go—Barrett will be in town in a couple of days. Mom wants everyone at the Farm for dinner. She said something about Linc wanting to get together anyway so it's perfect timing. I'll text you when."

"I'll be there. Talk to you later."

Placing my phone back in my pocket, I stretch my arms over my head and catch Ellie watching me.

"What?" I ask.

"I love listening to you talk to your brothers."

"Why is that?"

She shrugs. "You feel so . . . safe with them, I guess. Like it seems like you can say whatever you want and you know if you called him back right now, no matter how mad he is at you, he'd help you."

"True," I state. "He would. Any of them would. Well, maybe not Lincoln right now, but he has an excuse."

She disappears in a closet and returns in a purple and white robe. I hate her body being covered and away from my sight. It feels like a barrier, a way to keep me out.

"Want to meet up for lunch?" I offer, feeling her out.

"I have a meeting, actually."

"Dinner? Or we could go fishing."

"I haven't been fishing in forever," she admits. "Probably not since I left for school."

"Let's do it then."

"Maybe some other time."

"I'm sorry. Did I miss something here?"

She crosses her arms over her chest. "What do you mean?"

I mimic her posture. "I thought we were passed this whole thing."

"I can have dinner and an orgasm and not lose my mind, Ford."

"Seeing me again is losing your mind?" I ask in disbelief. "You're going to have to explain that one, El."

There's no attempt to explain, no words thrown my way to demonstrate why she's now pushing back a little. She just stands there and watches me in that adorable little robe I want to rip off her damn body.

"Fine," I sigh, stuffing my wallet in my pocket.

"Fine what?"

"I'll just keep thinking of ways to win you over."

Her arms drop to her sides. "Stop trying. Just let things be."

"And risk losing you? Risk letting you think I don't care? Sorry, babe. Not happening."

"Listen, I love being with you . . ."

"And I love being with you. So what's the issue?"

"The issue is just because we had sex doesn't mean things have somehow changed between us."

"Babe. Everything has changed."

The air changes, everything now heavier than it was moments ago. Her eyes are filled with an uncertainty that I want to kiss away.

"I'm not going to lie and pretend I don't feel something different with you than I've felt with anyone else."

"Good to fucking know."

She shakes her head. "That's part of the problem, Ford. I don't know how much of this is just some kind of hold-over emotion from a carefree time in our lives and how much of it is real."

"You don't think this is real?"

"I don't know," she breathes. "I hope it is. But before I go jumping in this with you—whatever that even means—I need to know this isn't something we're doing on a whim."

"Even if it is, *and it's not*, what would be wrong with that, El? We're two adults that want to spend time together."

"Spending time together is fine. I quite enjoy *spending time* with you," she adds cheekily. "But none of that changes where I want us to go. Not right now."

"Ellie, I want to—"

"Your knight awaits!" A voice, a very *male* voice, booms from the entryway.

My gaze snaps from Ellie to the doorway, back to a wide-eyed Ellie. "Who in the hell is that?" I ask.

"Where are you?" he shouts again, his voice much closer. "Ellie?" The last syllable wraps around the doorway as he steps into view. He takes me in and stops dead in his tracks. "And who are you?"

"I was going to ask you the same thing," I warn.

"Hey, Heath!" Ellie's voice is too loud, too chipper, to be believable. "How are you?"

"Um, I'm okay," he draws out, still looking at me. "Confused. But good. Maybe getting better, depending . . ."

"Want to make some introductions?" I ask, my brows raised.

"Heath, this is Ford Landry. Ford, this is Heath Breckenmeir, my friend that obviously doesn't realize the key he has is for emergencies only." She glares his way.

"He has a key?"

"For emergencies," they say in unison.

I take in my opponent. He's thin, too thin to be able to put up much of a fight. He's wearing wire-rimmed glasses and his black hair is more perfectly styled than any man I've ever seen. Then he smiles. Wide.

A phone rings in another room and Ellie's hand smacks her forehead. "Could this timing be any worse?"

"I'm kind of appreciating it right about now," I note.

"I'm definitely appreciating it," Heath snickers. "Go get the phone, Ellie."

"Why don't you answer it?" Her voice is almost a plea, which makes his snicker turn into an all-out laugh.

"Oh, no, sweetheart," Heath grins. "This is your problem. I'll stay right here with Ford."

I cringe at the term of endearment, my fists balling at my side. "Go on, *sweetheart*," I say pointedly to her.

She looks on the verge of panic, but as the ringing starts again, she throws her hands up, mumbles something under her breath, and storms out. Once she's out of sight, Heath moseys my way.

"I'm just here to go with her to a few wholesalers today," he tells me. "So while that alpha-male posturing you're doing right now is so fucking hot, you can ease up a little."

I don't respond.

"Or not. For the record, I'm really, really gay."

"Good to know."

"Heath!" Ellie's voice shouts from the kitchen. "Will you come here for a second?"

He tosses me a wink before joining her in the front. I meander to the doorway and listen to their conversation.

"What did you tell him?" she hisses.

"I told him I'm gay," he admits. "There's no chance he swings both ways, is there? Hey!" he yelps as I hear a smack that makes me grin.

"Would it have killed you to pretend we have something going on?"

"And why would I do that?"

"To buy me some time."

"Because you need to get your head together after he just fucked the shit out of you?"

"Heath. Really?"

"Yes, really. Now, circling back to your question, I couldn't pretend anything. I couldn't take my eyes off that hunk of man meat," he says.

I bite my tongue so I don't laugh out loud.

"Second," he continues, "I'm not about to get on his bad side. Did you see his biceps? Wait. You've seen his biceps and his triceps and his . . . Come to think of it, I hate you."

"Get in line, buddy."

"You just got dirty with GI-fucking-Joe. I'm proud of you, Ellie. Maybe you're not too old to learn new tricks after all."

A laugh comes roaring out of my mouth before I can stop it. I grab the last of my belongings from the table and stick them in my pockets before joining Ellie and Heath in kitchen.

"I need to head to the office," I tell them both. Looking at Ellie, I grin. "I'll call you later and we can pick up the conversation we left off."

"Sure."

Wrapping my arm around her narrow waist and pulling her towards me over the start of her faux objection, I kiss her loudly and with as much force as I think is legal square on the lips.

"Thanks for last night," I wink.

"Ford!"

"Oh, I can't even . . ." Heath nearly squeals.

When I release her, she stands breathless, a little wobbly on her feet, as I head to the door. "I'll call you this afternoon, Ellie."

"Hey!" Heath calls after me. "You forgot mine."

Ellie

"I'M A LITTLE PERTURBED," HEATH says, his eyes still on the door. He straightens his yellow polo shirt.

"I can't wait to hear this," I sigh.

"I feel . . . cheated."

I look at him blankly.

"Like you've been holding out on me," he adds.

With a roll of my eyes, I head to the coffee pot. As expected, Heath follows on my heels.

"Friends don't not tell friends about hot guys, Ellie. You know this."

"You're right. They don't," I say, looking at him. "But we aren't friends anymore."

He grins. "Does this mean I can make a play at your lover?"

"How hard would it have been for you to pretend to be going on a date with me?" I ask, ignoring his jab at a reaction.

"Hard," he says, making a face. "Besides, I feel like if I had done that, Mr. Landry would've either pummeled my handsome face, and let's face it, I would not look good with a crooked nose. Or he would've kept you from the cock."

I look at the ceiling. "Where is Violet when you need her?"

Heath plops on a barstool at the island and stretches his long, skinny legs out. I don't look at him.

"Don't ignore me," he demands.

"I hate you," I laugh.

"No, you don't," he says, laughing too. "Now, let's talk about what matters."

"Okay. I need to figure out the best things to put in the window displays. We're looking to attract a customer that—"

"No. No, no, no," he says. "Let's talk about whatever I walked into today."

"You didn't walk into anything."

"There were feels everywhere. I may be gay, but I'm not blind, honey."

I rest my head against his shoulder and breathe in his overly expensive cologne. "Why do you always smell so good?"

"Because I have exquisite taste. Landry Love falls in that category, so spill it, sister."

"He was my first love. My first . . . everything."

"Like, everything-everything?"

"It was in a hayloft," I remember. "I was scared to death. He was so easy with me, so sweet. It wasn't some planned thing. We were just sitting there, looking at the stars and . . ."

Heath sighs happily. "And I'm guessing you had a mini-replay of that today?"

"Yeah," I giggle. "Kind of. I mean, it was so much better, obviously, but you get the idea."

"I do and I have so many questions."

"None of which I'm about to answer, Breckenmeir."

"Answer me this," he says, shrugging his shoulder so I have to sit up. He looks at me out of the corner of his eye. "Are you together?"

"No."

"Why not?"

I look at my nails and wonder when I had a manicure last.

"I'm waiting," he needles me.

"I could easily lose myself in him."

"Sounds like a great plan."

Trying to put my feelings into words is a lot harder than I expect. I know exactly what I'm thinking, but how do I make that understandable to someone else?

"It's obvious he's smitten with you," he notes. "And it's just as apparent you're in love with him."

"In love?" I laugh. "You saw us together for five seconds."

"I knew it in one."

"Well, I knew I loved him the minute I saw him," I say softly. "I just need to know that this time, if there is a 'this time,' it's for real. That it's not just some phase in his life that he can walk away from if he feels a whim."

Heath twirls around on his behind so that he's facing me. He studies my features.

"I need to know," I gulp, "that the universe hasn't paired us up to waste some time between life events again. I don't want to be his stepping stone, Heath."

"You want to be his landing pad."

I shrug, not sure if that's what I want or not. "I don't know. I know this time around is . . . more." I stand, brushing off the seat of my pants. "I'm not a kid. I have a business I've worked my ass off for. I have plans, dreams . . ."

"Dreams of him?" Heath asks simply.

It's a question I don't answer.

Ford

THE BACK PORCH WELCOMES ME like an old friend. A whiskey barrel sits by the sidewalk. There are no flowers planted inside like there used to be when Mrs. Pagan was alive. There's a green rug with WELCOME written across it and I wonder if it's the same one that welcomed me the last time I was here.

I make my way across the concrete and to the screen door a few feet away. Sounds of a gunfight can be heard inside the little kitchen on the other side.

The steps creak with my weight, the door squeaking as I knock on the wooden frame. My eyes adjust to the light. I see Bill Pagan sitting at the round table Ellie made in shop class her junior year. It's shoved to the wall between the refrigerator and cabinets, just like it was the last time I was here.

"Ford Landry," he says with a nod. "Come on in."

The kitchen looks like I'm walking back in time. Everything is exactly where it was years ago—a time capsule, almost.

If I closed my eyes, I could see Ellie's mom, Gloria, standing at the stove. I could smell her pot roast cooking in the oven and see her home-made pie crusts rolled out on the counter to my right.

I sit at the chair next to the refrigerator. "How are you, Mr. Pagan?"

He gruffs, waving a hand through the air. "Don't start with the 'Mr. Pagan' bullshit."

"Sorry," I grin. "How are you, Bill?"

He doesn't answer for a moment, just stares at the television in front of him. Finally, he looks at me and answers me with a question of his own. "How are you?"

"I'm good," I reply. "Ellie says you're doing well."

"Yeah, well, I don't tell her everything."

My brows pull together as I try to make sense of what he's saying. Do I press for more information? Is he being facetious? I don't know. He's a hard man to read, and I've been gone a long time.

"You been traveling the world?" he asks.

"I've seen some of it," I admit.

"Is it as bad as they make it out to be on the news these days?"

"Parts of it. Parts of it not." I stretch my legs out in front of me. "I'm glad to be home though."

He nods, taking me in. "Ellie was pretty upset when you left."

My heart sinks in my chest. I figured this conversation may happen, but I guess it's going to happen sooner than later. "I apologize for that, sir. Trust me when I say it's eaten at me all these years."

"I bet it has."

"I wish I would've handled things differently."

"You were young and dumb. But I suspect you aren't either one these days."

"I'm sure as hell not young," I laugh. "I hope I'm not dumb."

He tips his head my way. "You're sitting here. That tells me you aren't too stupid." He goes back to his television show for a while. "You know, when you first came around a long time ago, I wasn't sold on you. You drove up in that fancy truck of yours, dressed up and talking all smooth. I didn't figure your intentions were very good."

"I remember that," I chuckle. "You made things hard for a while before you really gave me a chance."

"I only gave you a chance because of Gloria," he admits. "She always was a sucker for a good-looking man. That's how she got me, after all."

We enjoy a good laugh. He grabs the remote and turns down the volume.

"I miss her," he says softly. "Every morning I wake up and listen for her piddling around."

My chest tightens as I watch the pain haunting his eyes. I can relate, in my own way, because that's how I feel about Ellie. I can't imagine how I'd feel if I was with her for decades and then lost her.

He looks at me with a sobriety that catches me off guard. "She was a good judge of character. And she liked you, Ford."

"I liked her too, Mr. Pagan."

He lets my address slip, his mind focused on something else. In a movement so unlike him that it makes me flinch, he reaches across the table and lays his hand on top of mine.

"You're going to be around awhile this time?" he asks.

"That's the plan," I breathe, unsure as to what he's getting at. "Why are you asking me that?"

He pulls his hand away, a resolution in his eyes. "You leaving the first time is probably the only reason I'm still around."

"What are you talking about?"

"In a really short time," he says, the words clearly burning, "you left Ellie. Then her mother got sick and left us both. I'm all she has now."

He looks away, gathering his courage and pride. I lean back, giving him space in every sense of the word. I try to put two and two together, but can't. My head is spinning.

"The doctors say the cancer is back," he says, clearing his throat. "I haven't told Ellie and I'm not going to."

"But Bill—"

He shakes his head adamantly. "She's happy. She's got the store now and things going her way," he sighs. "I'm tired. I don't want to go through all that nonsense again. And I don't want her thinking she should've pushed me to do it or feeling guilty about it in any way. I don't want her over here, wasting her time, doting on me like I know she would."

"Isn't that her choice?"

"No," he barks. "It's mine." He gives me a look, one that makes me back down. "I asked the doctor if the medicine would work and he said probably not. It's stage four and I'm old and that's that."

"I'm really sorry," I say, feeling like a complete idiot. I should have something better to say, but I wasn't expecting this. Not by a long shot. "Can I do anything to help you?"

"I just . . ." He clears his throat again. "I need to know Ellie will be okay. That's all that matters, and it's the one thing I can't guarantee."

He forces a swallow, trying to drown the emotion that's thick in his gruff voice. We don't look at one another because I'm not sure which of us would break first.

I know what he's asking me and I can't imagine the balls it takes to ask this of anyone, much less of me. The guy that walked out on her once.

"I sit here day after day with no one to talk to," he says quietly. "I've let everything go. My friends stopped coming by. Hell, I don't even go after my mail anymore. They bring it to the porch like I'm some kind of invalid." Tears dot the old bad-ass's eyes and it causes mine to water. "I just sit here and wonder what will happen to her when I'm gone. Because she's . . ." He chokes back a sob.

It's me now that's reaching across the table and placing my hand over his. It shakes beneath mine, the skin loose and cool against my own.

"She's hard-headed as hell," he laughs nervously. "She's stubborn just like me. When she's difficult, I just focus on that heart of hers and the eyes that remind me so much of Gloria."

"She's a lot like her mama," I say, withdrawing my hand. "But it's the parts of you in her that make her who she is."

He grins, wiping his hand down his face. "I know she's irritated with you and I know I've just dumped a load of shit on your lap. That's probably not right of me to jump into this with you just walking in the door."

"I'm honored you'd think enough of me to have this conversation."

"You're the only one I'd have it with."

"That means the world to me, sir," I nearly whisper.

"I was hoping you'd come back. Even after all these years, I still had my hopes pinned on you."

"I had mine pinned on her," I grin.

He searches my eyes, as if he's trying to find the thread of dishonesty. Finally, he takes a long drink from a plastic cup.

"Mr. Pagan—Bill," I correct myself, "I know it might seem out of left field . . ." I look him dead in the eyes. "You have my word that Ellie will always have someone watching out for her."

"You mean that?"

"I wouldn't have given you my word if I didn't."

The relief that leaves his body is evident. His shoulders drop and I think for a moment he might slide out of his chair.

"You have no idea what that means to me, Ford." He takes another drink, this time the cup shaking just a bit. "You love her, don't ya?"

"With every ounce of my being. As a matter of fact," I say, squirming a little in my chair, "I was wondering if I can manage to convince her at some point to marry me. How you feel about that?"

His eyes light up. "Are you thinking that way?"

"I've thought that way since the first time I saw her. I should've done it years ago, but 'young and dumb,' as you say. Would that be okay with you? I mean, I have to get a plan together or else she'll say no for the hell of it," I laugh.

With pride as wide as the Grand Canyon, he laughs. "That sounds about right." He extends his hand and I take it in mine. "If it comes to that, you have my blessing. And I hope to God it does."

"Me too."

"Can I ask you for your word on one more thing?"

"Absolutely."

"Please don't tell her about my sickness."

"Yes, sir," I say warily.

We shake hands, but exchange something far deeper than a simple handshake at his kitchen table.

Bill clears his throat. "Been fishing lately?"

I settle back in my seat and find a story to distract him from his life for just a little while.

Ellie

"ELLIE! THERE'S A DELIVERY GUY here to see you!"

Violet's words ring through Halcyon, startling me as I daze off in space. It's not something I do regularly; most times I'm completely focused on the task at hand. Most times, I guess, I'm not coming off of a few days with Ford.

The last few days have been incredible and not just for the sex, although that's been the reason I've been late to work every day since our first official date night. He's been sweet, considerate—everything I could want him to be.

If it were anyone else, it would be trying too hard. But it's Ford. With his disarming smile and authenticity surrounding him like a shield, there's no way to take it any other way than he wants me to be happy.

The words that come out of my mouth and the things I do don't match up. I tell him I can't see him the next day because I know I shouldn't. But when he sends a text for lunch, my fingers just type out three little letters. When he shows up at the store when I'm ready to walk out, I get in his car. I know I'm getting in far too deep too fast and it'll probably bite me in the ass, but for right now, I'm wearing waders and hoping for the best.

Turning the corner, I start laughing. "Is that for me?"

"Are you Ellie Pagan?"

"I am."

"Then these are for you."

Giggling, I take the items from him. There are two fishing poles—one long and one short—and a tackle box that's heavy. "Thank you."

He laughs too. "Honey, if you're into fishing and it doesn't work out with whoever sent these, you know where I work."

"I'll remember that," I say, nodding as he waves and exits the building.

"He sent you fishing stuff?" Violet asks. "That's . . . unique."

My cheeks ache from smiling. "That's Ford," I say simply. "He's thorough."

"I can tell," she snorts. "You've been smiling like that for a while now. And for the record, it's been fun to watch."

"Thanks, Vi."

"You're welcome. Now put your survival gear in the back and help me move this shelving unit."

"Be right back." I stroll to the back and put the gifts against the wall. But, before I go help Violet, I whip out my phone. He answers on the second ring. "Hey, you."

"Hey, pretty girl," he says, his voice kissed with the same easy joy I feel in my gut. "How are you doing today?"

"I just got a delivery."

"You did, huh?"

"I did. It looks like someone wants to take me for some fun in the great outdoors."

"I like the way you phrased that," he laughs.

"I like it too. Maybe we can make that happen."

A flurry of papers being moved trickles through the phone and I hear another man's voice.

"If you need to go, that's fine," I offer.

"Yeah, I do. My father is here to go over some family stuff," he sighs. "Can I call you in a little bit?"

"Sure. Have fun!"

"Not until it's in the great outdoors," he teases. "Talk to you soon."

"Bye."

With a final glance at the gifts in the corner, I skip out of the room to help Violet.

Ford

THE FARM IS LIT UP like it only is when everyone is home. It's really not about the lights, it's like there's a glow, an excitement, when all of us are in the same place at once.

I park my truck next to Barrett's SUV. Before I can climb out, I get a text.

> *Ellie: Have fun with your family tonight. I will just cuddle with my new fishing lures.*

> *Me: You can come if you want. I'll come get you right now. Just say the word.*

> *Ellie: I'm good. Thanks. ;) Me and the lures will watch some trash television.*

> *Me: Text me if you change your mind.*

> *Ellie: I will. But I won't.*

> *Me: I'd rather be in the outdoors with you.*

> *Ellie: Me too. The lures are smelly. Now go do your family stuff.*

> *Me: Grr . . . Bye.*

Ellie: Bye. <3

As I get out of the truck, I see Troy standing next Barrett's SUV in a navy blue suit. My buddy from the military, now Barrett's personal security guy, grins when he sees me.

"Long time no see!" He pulls me in for a quick hug. "How are you, Ford?"

"I'm good, man. How are you? How's my brother treating you?"

"Things are good," he says. "We're all getting adjusted to the new routine of the Governor's mansion." His laugh permeates the warm evening air. "Can you believe I'm working in the Governor's mansion?"

I shrug. "I don't know why the hell not?"

"I owe you, Ford," he says, all laughter gone from his voice. "Without you and your family, I don't know what would've happened to me."

"I told you things work out."

"Yeah, but not like this. You took my life and turned it on a dime. I just . . . Every day I wake up and put on a suit and think, 'What the fuck?'" he laughs. "It's unreal."

I head to the steps. "Just be thankful Graham didn't find you before Barrett or this conversation would be much, much different."

Troy laughs, his voice trailing behind me as I step inside the Farm. It almost feels like Christmas walking in and hearing everyone's voices. We used to do this a lot. Now it's harder to do with everyone striking out on their own, living in different places, having their own commitments.

"Hey, Ford!" My mother wipes her hands on a towel and greets me with a kiss on both cheeks. "How are you, handsome?"

"Good. Man, it's loud in here," I laugh, holding an arm out for Huxley. He wraps his arms around my side. "How are you, Hux?"

"I'm good," he grins up at me. "Did you see Lincoln's baby?"

Tugging his Arrows hat over his eyes, I laugh. "I did. He's cute, huh?"

"Yeah." Huxley takes off across the room, plopping in a giant beanbag my mom bought him and picks up an electronic of some sort.

Surveying the room as I head to the kitchen, I see everyone but Camilla.

"Hey!" Barrett greets me. "Shit, Ford. I think you get bigger every time I see you."

"That's what she said," Lincoln cracks.

"And some things never change," Alison laughs, joining us. She gives me a quick hug. "How are you?"

"Good. How about you? Getting the feel of Atlanta?"

Her eye shine as she blows out an exaggerated breath. "It's a lot to take in. And now with him considering . . ." She looks at Barrett and makes a face. "I shouldn't have said anything."

"No, it's okay," he says, pulling her to his side with a smile. "Talks are getting more serious about the Presidential thing."

"Are you going to do it?"

He looks at Alison. "We've been talking about it. It's definitely not a question you can just answer, you know? Speaking of which, I'd like to talk to you about it later, if you don't mind?"

"Sure."

"Hey, son." Dad's hand rests on my shoulder. "Good to see you."

"Hi, Dad." I turn to see him cradling Ryan in his other arm. He's cuddled against my father in a bright blue blanket looking as peaceful as can be. It's a sight I'm not used to—my brusque father, the head of our family's empire, holding a baby.

"What?" he asks.

"It's just a little . . ."

"Weird seeing you with a baby," Barrett finishes for me. "Lincoln's baby at that." He chuckles. "It's still hard to imagine our baby brother with a baby of his own."

"My junk works just fine," Lincoln imparts, joining our little circle. "The two of you better get on it and prove your manhood."

"I think I'll leave this conversation," Alison blushes, peeling herself away from Barrett.

"Why? You don't want to have my baby?" Barrett teases her. "That's not what you said—"

"Barrett! Please," she sighs, her eyes wide, imploring him to hush. Her reaction makes us all laugh.

"Behave," our father warns his eldest.

Lincoln reaches for Ryan.

"He's perfectly fine, Linc," Dad says.

"Yeah, but I want to hold him."

Dad makes a face, but lets Ryan go. "One of you is going to have more kids just so I can hold one of them."

They continue to banter back and forth, joking and teasing, but I excuse myself. Waving at Sienna and Danielle in the kitchen, I head to the back porch.

A light breeze twirls the ferns hanging around the porch, the swing creaks on its chain as it moves easily back and forth. Besides the chaos of the house at my back, it's absolutely serene.

This is why this is my favorite place on the planet. A place where I can tune out the world, ignore the anarchy of whatever is going on in life, and just think.

My heart is heavy as I sit in the swing and try to separate all I'm feeling. Hearing my family talk about having babies, seeing my father hold Ryan, feeling all the love in the house is an amazing feeling. It's like all the pieces are fitting together just like they should. All of them except mine.

Just a few weeks ago, I was content with being a bachelor. A booty call here and there was enough to keep me satisfied. Maybe I felt the fissure in my life, the crack that was unfulfilled, but I never knew how deep it ran until I saw Ellie again.

When we're together, I'm hopeful things will work out between us. Even if she tries to push me away, it just feels so organic, so *right*, that I'm sure it will end the way it should.

But what if it doesn't? What if she means it when she tells me she wants things to slow down?

It's funny—all I can see as my life now are moments with her. What becomes of that vision if she chooses not to take part?

"You okay?" Graham steps onto the porch and leans against the rail. He looks out over the lawn.

"Yeah."

"Good." He turns to face me. "I need to talk to you about something."

"Well, I want to talk to you both about something." Barrett comes around the corner and stands next to Graham.

"Go ahead," Graham sighs. "Come marching in here and take over. This isn't the fucking Governor's mansion, you know. I'm in control here."

"You wish," Barrett laughs. "I was mentioning earlier to you, Ford, about maybe running for the Presidency."

Graham takes a step back. "So this is a real consideration?"

Barrett shrugs. "Maybe. I'm not sure if I want to go that far or not, to be honest."

"What's Alison say?" I ask.

"She says she'll support whatever I want to do," he smiles. "But I don't know. It's asking so much of everyone . . . including you guys."

"How does it affect us?" I ask.

"Well, you'll be subjected to scrutiny everywhere you turn, for one. For two, I'd want you to be a part of whatever we do. Especially after Nolan's betrayal, I trust no one."

Graham scowls. "I get that. But you know Washington is the land of the least trustworthy people in the universe, right?"

"I do," Barrett laughs. "I'm just asking you guys to think about it and let me know what you think."

"Okay." I look at Graham. "Your turn."

"I got a call this afternoon that I needed to go down to the impound and pick up my car."

"What?" Barrett asks, his brows raised to the sky. "What happened?"

"I obviously confirm my car is where it's supposed to be and Mallory's is too. So I make a call downtown and it's Camilla's car."

Barrett and I exchange a look.

"Our little sister has been running around Davis Avenue. Or her car has, anyway."

"What the fuck is she doing down there?" I ask. "There's nothing but trouble on Davis."

"Is she home?" Barrett asks. "She's not here tonight."

"She's not here because she doesn't want to see me," Graham says. "She told Mom she was sick, but it's all to avoid me."

I scoot over in the swing to make room for Barrett. "Did she offer any reasonable explanation as to why she, or her car, was out there?"

"She essentially told me she's a grown woman and I should mind my own business," Graham smirks. "I pointed out that grown women don't typically need to ask their brother for an allowance."

"Bet that went over well," Lincoln laughs, joining us outside. "Swink, Swink, Swink. She's a good girl gone bad. I kind of like it."

"I always thought it would be Sienna," I note.

"You thought what would be me?" Sienna climbs the stairs from the side of the house. "And don't even say you thought I'd be the first to have a kid because that shit isn't even funny." We all laugh as she punches Lincoln in the arm.

"I was saying I thought you'd be the bad egg of the family." I give her a smile. "But look at you, all Miss Goodie Two Shoes."

"Want your ass kicked, Ford?"

"You think you can do it?"

"No, but I know someone that can," she singsongs. "And her name rhymes with belly."

Barrett's jaw drops. "Ellie? What have I missed?" He looks at Lincoln. "You've managed to not tell me this? You tell me all kinds of stupid stuff and you miss this?"

"Well, I'm a little preoccupied these days," he scoffs. "I have a baby, you know."

"Let's focus on the subject at hand," I plead, looking at Graham. "Give us the plan because we all know you have one."

"The address the car was found is a bar . . ."

Sienna sighs loudly to get our attention. "You guys, just leave her alone."

"That's hard to do," Lincoln winces. "Considering y'all have decided to be little secret keepers."

"Yeah. Just tell us what's going on and we'll drop it," Graham offers.

"I can't," she pouts. "I'm sworn to twin secrecy."

My brothers and I all look at each other, slow grins slipping across our faces.

"I hate that look," Sienna says, her eyes going wide. "She's fine, you guys. I know you're worried but it's fine. I promise."

Barrett and I stand, Graham turning towards the house and Lincoln nodding. We all head to the back door.

"Where are you guys going?" Sienna calls after us.

We ignore her. Filing into the house, the girls and Dad look at us like we're crazy.

"What's going on?" Dad asks.

"We have something to do," Barrett says. "Don't worry. Troy will drive us." He gives Alison a quick kiss and waves to Huxley. "I'll be back in a bit, okay?"

"That's fine," she grins, Ryan nestled up against her.

"That's a good look on you," Barrett winks before moving towards the front door.

Lincoln clears his throat. "I better stay with Dani."

"No," Dani laughs. "You better go with your brothers."

"But—"

"Ford," she pleads. "Make him go."

"Let's go, lover boy," I say, getting him in a headlock. "Say goodbye, Linc."

He fights with me until we're both on the ground. Arms and legs are flying as we maneuver to get the best position.

"Boys, don't you break anything," Mom warns. "I thought we were past this and got the good crystal back out!"

"I quit!" Lincoln shouts as I twist his arm behind him. "I quit. Fuck, Ford!" he laughs.

I roll over onto my back, out of breath. We lay next to each other laughing.

"You're responsible for those two," Dad tells Graham. "Get them back in one piece."

G extends a hand to Linc and I and pulls us up.

"I thought we were going to do yoga tonight?" Mallory pouts, wrapping her arms around Graham.

"When I get home," Graham promises.

"But . . ."

"Hey, Mal?" I call, following Lincoln to the door. "This is what you get for your Ellie bullshit."

"Ford!" she whines.

"I agree with Mallory," Sienna chimes, a little panic in her tone. "Daddy! Make them stay here."

"They're grown men," Dad notes. "What do you want me to do?"

I look at Mallory and wink, which only irritates her more. "Come on, G! Night out with the boys!"

Ford

"SIENNA IS BLOWING ME UP," Lincoln laughs from the front seat of the SUV. "Should I reply or ignore her?"

"Ignore her," we all say in unison.

"If she wants to be an accomplice in this, she can take a little of the heat," Graham points out. "I've spent so much fucking time on Swink and her bullshit when all Sienna has to do is tell me what she's doing."

"It's obviously a guy," Lincoln points out.

"It's obviously a guy she knows we'll flip a lid about," I say, catching Troy's eye in the rearview.

"Am I going to need bail money?" he asks.

We chuckle as he takes the final right-hand turn towards the bar where Camilla's car was towed from.

"I ask you one thing: don't let Barrett get hemmed up," Troy says, looking at me. "If shit is going to hit the fan, at least have the decency to let me get the Governor out of there first."

He pulls the car in front of an old brick building with a series of letters partially lit across the top in a faded red lighting. It looks like the dump you'd figure would be on Davis Street. As we all climb out of the SUV, we take in the sight before us.

"What in the ever-loving hell is Camilla doing here?" Lincoln turns to Graham. "You sure you got the right place?"

G flashes him a look, chastising him for second-guessing his facts. Lincoln shrugs and enters. We all follow behind him.

The Gold Room, as we come to learn the fine establishment is called, isn't aptly named. There's nothing gold or expensive or even "room-y" about it.

A long bar extends down the center of the wall to the right, pillars hold up the ceiling up along the middle of the building. Tables with cheap plastic chairs dot most of the free space, save a little area in the back. That's reserved for a couple of pool tables and what looks to be a makeshift dance floor that appears to have the same eighties-style paneling as the walls.

"You think Cam has turned to stripping?" Lincoln jokes, nodding at a semi-hidden stripper pole situated behind a partition.

I shove him in the back, causing him to propel forward a few feet.

"I was only kidding," he laughs. "I'm sure Graham is gracious enough to give her enough money to keep her from that."

We slowly make our way to the bar. There are only a couple of patrons in the place. They're spread out, some at tables, a couple at the far end of the counter.

"Let's have a drink, shall we, boys?" Barrett takes the lead and sits at a bar stool at the end. We file in to his left and wait for the bald-headed bartender to come our way. He sees us, that much is for sure. He also purposefully makes us wait.

"There goes his tip," Lincoln mutters, earning another bump on the shoulder from me.

Troy stands discreetly by the front door, not missing a beat.

"What can I get you?"

I turn to see Nate, if his name tag reads correctly, looking between the four of us. His eyes are assessing, trying to figure out what we're doing here.

"Four shots of tequila," Lincoln relays. "You have any Patrón?"

Nate gives Lincoln a look as if to say, "Really?" Muttering something under his breath, he turns to the cabinet behind him. After a few seconds of rummaging, he pulls out a bottle and blows a layer of dust off it. "Yup."

"We'll have that and give the asshole to my right a double," Lincoln says.

"Fuck you," I laugh. But before I can change the order, Nate is down the bar.

"Tequila, Lincoln? Really?" Barrett asks. "Do you know the last time I've shot tequila?"

"Not my fault you're a proper politician these days," Lincoln winks. "Besides, don't you want to see Ford and Graham get all fucked up?"

"I will not be getting fucked up." Graham shoots Lincoln a look. "Now focus, boys. Let's do some . . . what do you call it, Ford?"

"Recon. We're on a recon mission."

The shot glasses are placed in front of each of us, Barrett's spilling over a little. Troy looks concerned when Lincoln asks that the bottle be left in front of him.

We raise our drinks and shoot them at the same time. It's not so bad going down, but I forgot the fire once you open your mouth.

"Ugh," I say, licking my lips. "I hate that shit."

"Purifies your blood," Lincoln laughs. He points at Graham. "Want another one?

"When in Rome . . ." He holds out his glass and Lincoln fills it back up.

"Fuck it." Barrett offers his up for a refill too. "Give some to Ford. Don't leave him out."

"I'd never leave him out," he grins. "He's the one I'd like to get bombed."

"Good luck," I snort.

The clear liquid fills the glass again. I cringe as my brothers wait for me to lift it to my lips. It goes down a little better than the first, but still tastes awful. The glass clinks against the bar top as I feel the fire again.

"All right. Now to business," Barrett says. He looks around the room and I follow suit.

There's an exit sign behind us that's dimly lit. Over by the nook holding the stripper pole, there's a nondescript door.

"Wonder where that leads?" I say, moving my eyes that way. "Door to the left. By the pink chandelier."

"How do we even know if she was here specifically?" Barrett asks. "Maybe she got dropped off here and went elsewhere."

"Yeah. Because if you were getting picked up by someone, this is the place you'd choose," I say sarcastically. "The only reason you'd be here is to be *here*."

Lincoln pours everyone another shot and we take this one without thought. He looks proud.

"Hey, Nate!" Lincoln calls.

The bartender makes his way to us, looking irritated. "What's up?"

"We're looking for someone," Lincoln says.

"Aren't we all?"

"Hey! That's a good one," Lincoln laughs. "But we really are. She's short, blonde, green eyes. A pain in the fucking ass."

"A set of big ol' titties?" Nate leans against the bar so he's eye to eye with Lincoln. He's challenging him, there's no doubt about it, and becomes very clear he knows who we are. And who Camilla is.

Lincoln grins, but I can see his jaw pulsing. Instead of replying right away, he pours us all another drink. I down mine. I see Graham pushing his away out of the corner of my eye.

Nate shoves away. "I see a lot of whores in this place. Hard to tell them apart after a while."

"Why ya gotta be a dick, Nate?" Lincoln asks, shaking his head.

"Why ya gotta come in here causing trouble, Landry?"

Just like that, all cards are on the table. Not that we had cover, but if we had anything going for us at all, it's now blown into the abyss.

"We aren't here to cause trouble," Graham cuts in. "We're just looking for our sister."

"She ain't here," Nate says, spreading his arms to his sides. "Do you see her?"

Barrett leans forward, giving Nate his best campaign-esque smile. "We don't want trouble. We're just concerned."

"Why?" Nate snorts. "Because you think maybe your little sister has fallen to the dark side?"

"We didn't say that," Graham says calmly.

"Maybe," Nate says, keeping a few feet back, "your little sister just likes a little real cock laid to her."

"Easy . . ." I warn.

Nate laughs. "I'd venture to say there's nothing easy about it."

"You motherfucker," I say, lunging across the bar. Troy is at my side, Lincoln on the other, before I know it.

"It's time to go," Troy says, jerking me backwards. I shake off his grip and give him a look letting him know I'm fine.

Nate grins. "Do you boys need anything else?"

Lincoln slams a couple of bills down and sits his glass on top of it. Without taking my eyes off him, I pour another shot and down it. Slamming my glass against the bar, I wipe my mouth with the back of my hand. "If you fuck with her, you fuck with all of us. Do you hear me?"

"I hear you," he winks. "Now listen to your minder there and get the hell out of here before word gets out the Governor is sitting in the Gold Room. I don't think you want that, do you?"

Nate flashes Barrett a look, letting him know with a few well-placed calls, he can turn this visit into a PR nightmare.

"Let's go," Barrett says.

I wait for them all to file ahead of me before I turn back around. Nate is looking at me.

"You know, not everything you see is what you get." He raises his brows. "Your sister is a big girl, Landry. She can take care of herself."

My hands plant on the bar and I look him dead in the eye. "She can. And if she can't, she has me. I'm not the Governor and I don't give a fuck what is written about me in the papers." I turn to go, but wheel back around. "If you allow her in here, I want you to know that I personally hold you responsible for her safety and well-being. You got that?"

Something changes in Nate' eyes. I see it happen. He nods subtly before I turn and walk out to a much-relieved look on Troy's face.

"Let's get the hell out of here," Barrett says, climbing into the back-seat.

With a last look at the Gold Room, I pile into the SUV and we speed off towards the Farm.

Ford

HODA TAKES A FEW FINAL notes before closing the notepad. "I think I have it, Mr. Landry. I'll send the estimate over now." She stands, smoothing out her dress, grinning.

"What?"

"You've seemed really happy the last few days. That's all."

"Really?" I smile at her in a tell-tale sign that she's right. It's amusing to me that she's noticed.

"I like seeing you like this. I don't know what's causing it, but I hope it continues."

"I didn't know you were so invested in my happiness, Hoda."

She laughs and heads towards the door. "If you're happy, you make my life easier."

"Is that some kind of veiled way of saying you don't want me stressed and acting like Graham?" I joke.

"You said it. Not me." She heads back to her office, closing the door softly behind her.

Glancing at my phone, I look for a missed call. A missed text. Anything from Ellie, but find nothing.

I turn back to my computer in hopes of getting something done when Hoda pokes her head back in again. "Mr. Landry? I'm sorry to bother you again so quickly, but Camilla is here to see you."

"Oh," I say surprised. "Send her in."

The lid of my laptop closes with a quick snap. Swink doesn't just drop by to see me in the middle of the day. As a matter of fact, she's pretty scarce to all of us these days. Her arrival has me curious. And worried.

"Hey, Ford," she says, her tone terse. She breezes in, her posture perfect from years of instruction from our mother. Her blonde hair, the most like mine out of all of our siblings, is tied at the nape of her neck.

"This is a surprise." I watch as she sits across from me, smoothing out her emerald green dress. It's a throwback to the old Camilla—the one before she decided to be a renegade.

She lets loose a heavy breath. "I came to talk to you because you're logical."

Leaning back in my chair, I take her in. Her forehead is marred with a line of wrinkles, her blue eyes shining with a seriousness she doesn't wear often.

"Because I'm logical? This should be a fun conversation if you're coming to me appealing to my logic." I lean towards her and grin. "You know what that tells me?"

"What's that, Ford?"

"It tells me you think you can persuade me to go along with whatever bullshit you're selling more easily than to Barrett or Graham or Linc."

Her jaw sets. "Apparently I was wrong. You're just as irrational as the rest of them."

"We aren't irrational, Swink."

"Oh, so going to The Gold Room was rational?"

She nearly glares at me, which makes it hard not to laugh. She's this little thing in a glitzy-label dress trying to battle with me. It's hard to take her seriously.

"Do you have any idea what The Gold Room is known for?" I ask, smirking. "Tell me, Oh Brilliant One, how smart it was for you to be hanging out at a place that's best known for its happy endings."

"You don't know what you're talking about!"

I laugh. "You're right. Because I've only been there precisely once in my life. Would you like to tell me more about it, Cam?"

"Where I go shouldn't matter to you. I'm a grown woman."

"You're my little sister," I warn. "You'll be my little sister when you're fifty. Got it?"

"You're just as bad as the rest of them!"

"What do you want me to say? Just go get mixed up with the wrong people? Just go hang out on Davis and good luck to you?"

"How about a little faith that I know what I'm doing?" she volleys back.

"I'd love to do that. Really. But it's hard when you're so fucking secretive and then G gets a call—"

She springs to her feet. "Don't get me started on Graham!"

The rise in her voice sparks something inside me. The edge of brattiness catches me wrong. Whether she thinks she's right or wrong is one thing, but to pretend that all of us, Graham specifically, are out of line is another.

Fuck. That.

"Don't get you started on Graham?" I ask coolly. "Okay. That's fine. But I'm going to ask you to consider who works their fucking ass off to make sure that you can go to the mall and buy those fancy labels you like so much."

She flinches, falling slowly back into her seat.

"You say what you want about Barrett and Lincoln and I. But Graham?" My elbows resting on the edge of my desk, I look her in the eye. "You must be out of your damn mind if you think for a second that anything he does or says isn't in your best interest. Use your head."

"How does anyone know what's in my best interest besides me?"

My chuckle has little to do with amusement and more to do with my struggle to contain the frustration I feel. "Oh, I don't know. Because we're your family. Because we don't see the world through rose-colored glasses. Because we don't stand to gain from any interactions you have except to see you happy and healthy."

"I am both," she says, getting her nerve back. "I've never been happier, as a matter of fact. I wish you all would stop seeing me as some little girl that's clueless and trust me to make my own decisions! It's like you think

I'm not following along Landry protocol so someone has to intervene. I don't need an intervention."

"If you want to be treated like a big girl, Cam," I say, looking her square in the eye, "we're all happy to do that. Be sure you're ready for it."

My words hit their target. She falls back slightly in her chair, the fight leaving her eyes. While it gives me some relief that she hasn't completely lost her mind, it does cause a little bubble of regret to begin to form.

I sigh. "I know what it feels like."

"What?" she mumbles.

"I know what it feels like to look around our family and feel . . ." I struggle to find the word, " . . . different than the rest of them."

This gets her attention. Furrowing a brow, she adjusts in her chair. "What could you possibly know about not fitting in around here? You're Ford. The hero. The one of us that's never done anything wrong but be a feather in our parents' cap?"

Laughing, I shake my head. "Oh, Cam."

"What?" she asks, joining my laughter. "It's true. Even when Barrett was the Mayor, I know Mom and Dad worried about some of his . . . extra-curricular activities?"

"Nice way of putting it," I wink.

"And Graham is definitely Dad's favorite, but even he worries sometimes that G will make the wrong decision or is working too much. And Lincoln . . ."

Our laughter starts up again, that one not needing an explanation.

"But you?" she shrugs. "You're Ford, the military boy. The pride of the Landry family. The one that took after Grandpa Landry and went the honorable route. The one that—by listening to our parents rave to their friends—can do nothing wrong."

I don't know how to respond to that. I've never thought about it like that, didn't think it *was* like that. It certainly doesn't feel like it. It never has.

"Did you know I went into the military *in part* because I didn't know what else to do?" I ask her.

She responds with a confused look.

"I graduated from high school and had no idea what I wanted to do. I had Dad shoving me towards business. I swear he had this vision of Graham and I working together, his office right in the middle," I laugh. "Then I had this baseball scholarship sitting there from Texas . . . and I didn't know what to do."

"Good problems to have."

"I felt so . . . *different*," I say, giving her word back to her. "I couldn't see myself wearing a business suit every day, crunching numbers and scheduling meetings like Graham. Kill. Me. Now."

"But that's what you do now, right?"

"Sort of, but I'm also in a very different time of my life now, Cam. I would've hated this ten years ago." Shoving back from my desk, I stand, letting the chair roll back and bump the window. "The point is that I didn't want to follow along with what everyone wanted me to do. I couldn't imagine playing baseball every day. What's the point in that?"

She grins. "Lincoln found one."

"Linc found a couple thousand with nice racks," I laugh. "And good for him. That's what made him happy. It wouldn't have me." Sunshine beats in and warms my skin as I watch the cars below struggle to get to their destinations. "This family is so goal-oriented," I say, more to myself than to Cam. "It's all about the next check-off point, the next level, the next dollar. I had a really hard time with that for a while."

I turn to see my little sister looking at me. She looks so young sitting there and I calculate how old she is. Then I consider how I felt at her age.

I was just starting to figure out who I was then. I'd seen enough, done enough, been exposed to enough to know what I wanted. What I liked. What I hated. If someone would've told me at her age I was wrong for feeling a certain way, I'd have been pissed. Just like she is.

I ran away from my problems and fears. At least she's fighting for hers.

"Talk to me," I say. "What's going on?"

Her eyes flip to the floor as she wrings her hands in her lap. "I met a guy."

"I know."

"How do you know?" She looks up at me again. "Did Sienna say something?"

"Sienna has your back to the grave."

"Then how do you know?"

"This isn't my first rodeo, Cam. It was obvious to everyone weeks ago."

She fights the smile stretching across her face, and it's then I know—she's much deeper in with this guy than any of us thought.

"Who is he?" I ask.

"It doesn't matter."

"Oh, it matters." I quirk a brow. "What's his name?"

"Look—"

"Why are you doing this?" I sigh. "Just tell me his name so I can figure out who the hell he is—and by that I mean who he is to the rest of the world and not just Camilla Jane Landry."

Her courage is back. She narrows her eyes. "You know why I won't tell you?"

"I'd love to know."

"Because you won't give him a chance."

Putting my hands in my pockets, I sigh. "Is he that bad, Cam?"

"No. He's fantastic."

"But we'll just hate him right off the bat because he's so fantastic?" I groan. "I can't deal with this."

Falling back in my chair, I open my laptop. The screensaver waits for the password. I start to type it in when she speaks.

"What if I told you," she says, gulping, "that he's kind to me? Sweeter than anyone I've ever met? What if I said that he'd do anything to protect me, that he's loyal . . . like you? What if he was a businessman and started a company from the ground up to take care of his family?"

I consider this. "I'd ask to meet him to see for myself."

"What if I'm not ready for that?"

"Cam . . ." I bow my head. "I can't guarantee you that I'm not going to search around and see what I can find out."

"Ford—"

"But," I say, giving her a look, "I will promise you that when the time comes that we meet, I will give him the benefit of the doubt."

This puts a twinkle in her eye. "You will? Honestly?"

My shoulders slump as I admit defeat. My natural inclination is to go all crazy-brother on her right now, but I know better. I know how she feels. She needs someone on her side, someone that knows what it's like to want to color outside the lines a little bit. Someone to tell her it's all right to break protocol.

"As long as he treats you well—"

"He does!"

"And he doesn't get you involved in anything dangerous or illegal—"

"He wouldn't do that, Ford."

"Then I'll meet him with an open mind. Soon," I say, giving her a warning look. "I'll meet him soon."

"Soon . . . ish," she responds. Waltzing around my desk, she places a kiss on my cheek. "I knew you were the logical one."

"That may be true," I tell her. "But remember one more thing, Cam."

"What's that?"

"I'll also be the first one to kill him."

She giggles as if she thinks I'm playing and almost skips towards the door. "Thanks for talking to me, Ford."

"Any time," I sigh.

"One more thing," she says, her hand on the knob. "You said you left in part because you didn't know what else to do. What was the other reason?"

My shoulders fall. "Story for another day, Cam."

"Fair enough. See ya later, Ford."

I know for the first time what Graham must feel like. Thank God I'm not him.

Ellie

I GLANCE AT HIS TEXT again.

Ford: I'll pick you up at seven. Don't wear anything nice.

It's three minutes until seven, he isn't here, and I'm dying to see him.

My fingers begin to fly across the keyboard, demanding information, when I hear a knock at the door. Just knowing it's him makes my heart flutter.

It's so funny how having someone in your life that's supposed to be there changes everything. Mornings are a little easier because I might get to see him. Laundry isn't as mundane when you're mentally putting together outfits so you look on top of your game when you see him—a man that always looks great no matter what. Each minute can be changed by a single thought of him and something he said or a way he looked at you.

I haven't seen him since yesterday morning. He had a family commitment last night that I was invited to, but didn't feel comfortable attending. Today was a hellish day for both of us at work. It feels like too long since I saw him and that's nerve-wracking.

"Hey," I say before the door is even pulled open.

He doesn't greet me with words, just a deep, soft kiss that is almost as if he needs the contact or he may suffocate.

Pulling away, I giggle. "Nice to see you too."

"I been trying to get over here for the last forty minutes," he groans. "There was an issue with the event Landry Security is doing tomorrow night and the organizer from their end is incorrigible."

"That sucks."

"It does. But now I'm here and everything is better," he admits.

"Not everything," I sigh. "I was just texting you."

"What for?"

"Well, I was antsy, really," I laugh. "But your instructions to dress down have thrown me a little. I dress down already, so dressing more down . . ." I make a face.

"You could keep dressing down, and I think I'd like it even more."

There's a hint of innuendo in his tone, a little shimmer in his eye, and I take a step back. Pulling the neckline of my shirt down to expose a sliver of cleavage, I say, "Oh, dress down like this?"

I'm over his shoulder before I know what's happening, my shrieks of laughter filling the house. One hand squeezes my butt, holding me firmly against him.

"What are you doing?" I laugh, pointing to the bedroom door. In a matter of seconds, I'm on my back and he's on top of me.

"Exactly what you just asked for," he grins.

"I don't recall asking for anything." I run a fingernail down the side of his face.

His eyes heat, his Adam's apple bobbing so sexily that I almost gasp. His fingers work the button of my jeans and they're slipped down and discarded, along with my shoes and socks.

The air is cool as it touches my skin, but my temperature rises as I watch Ford undress. He maintains eye contact the entire time, ridding himself quickly of his attire.

As he climbs back on top of me, I drape my arms over his neck. I press a kiss to his lips. "Just looking at you is like foreplay," I admit. "Damn it, Ford."

He grins, allowing me to roll him over and sit my pussy over his cock. I can feel the heat radiating off me, my wetness making our bodies slip as I gently rock my hips back and forth.

"I can't wait," he says, lifting his hips. He palms his length. As he positions himself against my opening, I lick my lips.

"I want you inside me. I want you so deep that you—oooh!"

In one deft movement, he slides in me. My body feels amazingly full, like every sensory organ is being overwhelmed in the most delicious way.

"Like that?" he growls.

"Yes."

Moaning, my head falls back and the ends of my hair swish against Ford's thighs. He digs his hands into my hips and I rock back and forth, craving as much contact as I can make.

"Damn," I hiss, rolling my hips slowly. "This is heaven."

He lifts his hips, sinking even deeper into my body. I feel my wetness when I reach behind me and palm his balls.

"Fuck," he murmurs, throwing his head back into the pillows.

I massage them, watching the look of pure delight dance across his face. "Feel good?"

"So fucking good."

As I release him, he flips me to my back. My foot goes flying, knocking over the menagerie of things on my bedside table. The sound of little candies pouring onto the bed rattles through the room.

I giggle, trying to move so the hard pieces don't get under me. It's futile. Every adjustment I make allows more to roll beneath me.

"Shit," I laugh. "That's kind of a mood killer."

"That's all it takes to ruin your mood? Guess I'll have to work at getting you back where I want you."

I lie still, watching him methodically pick up one piece of candy in each color. "Be still," he warns as he places a red one in the hollow of my throat. "Don't move or it'll fall."

He shoots me a devious grin as he places another candy between my breasts.

"What are you doing?" I ask, trying to stay still.

"Shh . . ."

A purple candy sits just beneath my chest and a yellow one is placed in my belly button. With a smirk to die for, he watches my reaction as he sets an orange one at the apex of my thighs.

My breathing gets more ragged as he positions himself between my legs. His hair is mussed up, his eyes downright sinful.

"What now?" I whisper.

He shuffles to the side, placing a green one on the peak of my closed lips. Maintaining eye contact the entire time, he lowers himself push-up style and swipes the candy from my lips. I grasp his biceps, feeling the muscles flex under my touch.

As my jaw slacks in response, he takes advantage and enters my mouth with his tongue. He kisses me with a fervor I reciprocate.

When he pulls back, I pout.

"Trust me," he winks. Lowering himself again, he forms an O over the candy at the base of my throat and sucks it into his mouth.

I hiss, sucking in a deep breath. My nipples harden, peaking, begging for attention. "This better not take too long."

"You're going to have to be patient," he warns, swallowing the candy.

He moves down my body, appreciating every curve and bow of my figure with squeezes and kisses as he goes. I feel his cock hard against my leg as he repositions himself. My pussy clenches in response.

He draws my nipple into his mouth, rolling the hardened bead around his tongue. I knot my hands in his hair and pull, letting out a drawn-out moan.

"You're killing me," I tell him, dying.

His tongue drags hot and wet across my chest, catching the candy on the way to my other nipple. Using the candy as a prop, he rolls it over the tip of my breast. I writhe against his body, beginning to lose my mind.

He moves lower down my body, swiping the next candy and then sucking the piece from my belly button. His mouth is hot, his tongue heavy as he drags it across me.

I suck in a quick breath, my skin on fire. Goosebumps spatter the surface, my hips rising, begging for action.

Looking up at me as he gets settled between my legs again, he grins. "Need something, El?"

"Yeah. You. Inside me."

"I'll be happy to do that. In just a second . . ."

I growl, falling back into the pillows.

Nudging my thighs apart with his elbows, he presses a kiss to the inside of each of my legs. I feel small bits of pressure parting me and I look down to see him pressing candies along my slit.

"What are you doing?" I ask, my jaw hanging open.

Ford splays his hand at the bottom of my belly and uses his thumb to apply pressure to my clit. "Hold still," he smirks.

"Hurry up, Ford," I groan. "You're being mean."

"I'm about to be very," he says, leaning forward, "very," he hovers his mouth over my opening, and as I begin to moan, he whispers, "nice."

His breath trickles over my opening, warm and heady. Just as I begin to object, he runs his tongue up me, capturing the candies with his tongue.

"Oh my God," I say, as he grins devilishly at me. Before I can process anything, he buries his face between my legs.

"Ah," I say on an exhale, trembling. My knees literally quake, my eyes squeezing shut as he makes another leisurely pass to my clit.

"Hurry up. Ah!" I voice as he dips a finger inside me.

"Hurry up?" he laughs. "Baby, I'm just getting started."

Ellie

He takes me in head-to-toe as I fix my hair. I ran a brush through it after our detour to the bedroom, but it's still wild.

"You look perfect," he beams. "Go get in the truck."

We lock up, toss my fishing poles in the back, and take off down the road a couple of hours later than we anticipated.

The windows are partially down. My hair begins to blow like crazy around the cab of the truck despite the elastic securing it. I'm trying to smash it down when he reaches behind my seat and retrieves a Tennessee Arrows baseball hat.

"Thanks," I say, taking it and pulling it snug over my head.

Ford takes my hand, locks our fingers together, and rests them on the middle console. He holds it tight, brushing his thumb against the side of my palm. They fit perfectly together, his hand nearly encompassing mine.

"I had an interesting conversation with Camilla the other day," he says, rolling up the windows so we can hear.

"Oh, yeah?"

"She was telling me that whoever she's gotten involved with makes her happy. Her eyes lit up, you know?" He glances at me out of the corner of his eye. "I've never seen Cam like that. I keep thinking about it."

"Is this the guy that you were looking for? At The Gold Room?"

"Yeah," he chuckles. "The Gold Room. I mean, if that name doesn't tell you everything you need to know."

I laugh, giving his hand a squeeze. "How'd the conversation go? I mean, did she come clean with you about who he is?"

"No and she won't."

I let him mull over whatever he's thinking. After a few long seconds, he takes a deep breath. "In the military, I learned how important it is to surround yourself with people that you trust. You are only as strong as the weakest person in your unit. The same theory applies in life too."

"I can see that."

"I hope she does too before she gets in too far." He gives my hand a final squeeze and then releases it. Grabbing the wheel with both hands, he steers the truck off the road onto an old path.

My heart leaps in my chest. "I forgot where this was!" I exclaim, not believing what I'm seeing. "It's so overgrown now. I drove out here the other day and couldn't find it. Oh, Ford!"

The grass is freshly cut on both sides, but the path still shows signs of neglect. It's washed out and bumpy and the truck shakes as we creep down the trail.

I unfasten my seatbelt and lean forward to take in the place I met Ford one summer afternoon a long time ago.

The trees are green, the grass lush and tall. Flowers bloom in the opening as we approach the sparkling water.

Everything is bigger, more mature, than I recall. The tree I used to prop myself up against seems to have tripled in size over the years. I head towards the water while Ford locks up the truck.

"It's as peaceful as I remember," I breathe when he joins me. The air is fresh and clean, with notes of evergreen that resonate somewhere deep inside my soul. "I used to come out here and sit over there, by that giant oak tree, and just watch the water ripple for hours."

"You were sitting right over there the first time I saw you," he smiles, pointing towards an old dock that is half-falling into the water. "I remember riding up on my four-wheeler and seeing you. I couldn't understand why you were here all by yourself."

I lean against his side, feeling his heartbeat against my cheek. "I'm sure I remember that day more because I met you than why I was here, but I do remember." My arms slide around his waist and lock on the other side. "I had a horrible time of school that day."

My eyes close as it all plays out in front of me like it just happened. Ford must sense the heaviness of my heart and runs his hand down my back.

"I never really had a lot of friends in school," I say. "I mean, I had lots of friends but never those close friends that feel like your people, you know? Never a tribe or a squad or whatever those dumb names are girls call them. It was fine most of the time, but sometimes it bit me in the ass."

He squeezes my behind, making me smile.

"The day you found me was a tough one. There was this little boy in our school in a wheelchair. Something was physically wrong with him, but mentally he was pretty much on par with the rest of us. He just couldn't speak clearly for whatever reason. You had to be patient with him but it would come."

I grin as I remember his lopsided smile. "His name was Scott and he was really sweet. We had the same lunch. The day I met you, I had taken my lunch over and sat with him and his helper, this lady assigned to him by the school. Sitting there making him laugh was far better than listening to the girls gossip and compare the best lipsticks."

I mentally walk the hallway from the cafeteria to the bathroom and go into the stall. The sound of their footsteps squeaking against the linoleum rings through my ears.

"I overheard them making fun of me for sitting with Scott, making these disgusting jokes about him drooling and flailing around," I remember. "I just hid in the stall and listened. I couldn't find the courage to go out and confront them because I couldn't believe I was actually hearing it."

"People are evil," Ford says. "It never ceases to amaze me how mean they can be. They don't need a reason; they'll find one. Anything to make themselves feel better."

"It was the first time I'd experienced that. Girls had been mean to me before but whatever. I could let that roll, for the most part. But to say those things about Scott? It really bothered me. It still bothers me."

"So you were sitting out here that day thinking about that, huh?"

"I was. My dad used to bring me here to fish on the days he'd let me skip school and hang out with him. I'd never seen another soul out here before. It was my quiet refuge until you came over that hill raising hell on your four-wheeler," I laugh. "What were you doing out here that day, anyway?"

"I don't really know," he admits. "I was always off by myself. No one in my family or the guys we went to school with liked to ride dirt bikes or ATVs or go fishing or whatever. They were more into chess and newspaper-worthy events," he grins. "That day, I was riding around on one of the adjoining properties and ran into Mr. Kauffman. He owns this one. He told me I could ride around out here, so I took him up on it. Then I found you."

Standing on my tiptoes, I meet his lips with mine. It's a soft gesture, one that isn't driven by lust or lost time but, instead, maybe a love that you only find once.

"I remember you turning around," he chuckles. "You gave me this look like you thought I was going to kill you or something and all I wanted to do was kiss the girl with mud down the side of her face."

"I think you did kiss that girl," I wink.

"I did. And then I was hooked." He takes my hand and leads me to a burgundy and white quilt beneath a tree. A picnic basket is sitting on one corner.

"You made me pinky swear that I wasn't a serial killer," he laughs. "Do you remember that?"

"It seemed legit at the time," I say, embarrassed that he remembers.

My heart is full, memories flooding back like they only can when you're at the location they took place.

"This is the best date spot ever," I whisper. "Thank you for bringing me here."

We sit on a blanket stretched out under a tree. Ford lifts the lid to a picnic basket. I laugh as he pulls out two glass bottles of root beer, a bag of chips, and two peanut butter and jelly sandwiches.

"It's not gourmet," he laughs, his cheeks flushing. "But I got stuck in the office until late and I wasn't about to stop and buy burgers." He hands me a sandwich wrapped in plastic wrap. "I'll happily buy you whatever you'd like when we leave, but—"

My hand rests on his forearm, stopping him mid-sentence. "This is perfect."

He takes me in carefully. "It's not. I don't think I could ever come up with the perfect way to show you how much I think about you."

I twist his wrist and press my thumb against the little star in the bend of his thumb and pointer finger. "You did."

Tossing my sandwich beside me, I crawl across the blanket and curl up in his lap. He locks his hands around my waist and nuzzles his face in the crook of my neck.

"So, I was talking to Barrett last night," Ford says. "I think he really might run in the next election cycle."

"Really?"

"Maybe. He and Graham and I had a long discussion about it. He has reservations, naturally, and is afraid he's being thrown into a lion's den."

"That's what D.C. politics is, isn't it? A giant lion's den."

"Yeah, that's what I said," he chuckles. "But politics is Barrett's thing. He's been testing some ideas out, tossing around platforms that he could run on. One of them," he says carefully, strumming his fingers against my arm, "is the idea of bringing back the family dynamic in this country."

"Like sit-down dinners and things?"

"Yes. Kind of. I understand it like he wants to make the country think more about doing things as a community, helping one another. Being involved in their neighborhoods. That kind of thing."

"That's sensible," I agree. "I like it. I think it would resonate well with a lot of people."

He takes a deep, calculated breath. "A part of the reason he was asking Graham and I for our thoughts is because, to pull this off, he'd need his family to have his back."

"Of course you'd support him, right? I'm not following you."

Turning in his arms, I see the hesitation in his eyes, the lines forming around his mouth. Forcing a swallow, I wait for some kind of bomb to drop because I know it's coming. It's written all over his face.

"The thing is," he pauses, "he'd want to incorporate us into his campaign. Really walk the talk, so to speak."

He gauges my reaction, his features falling as I sit up. My stomach flip-flops, my mind scrambling to get to the point and to get there fast.

"So you'd be going to D.C.?" I ask flat-out.

"If he won. He proposed me being on the security panel of his campaign. I could do a lot of that from a home base—Savannah or Atlanta, for now. But once the actual campaign would start . . ." He blows out a breath. "God knows what it would entail, to be honest."

"Wow."

"I know this is a lot to take in, but I wanted you to know it was being discussed."

I nod, forcing back a lump that's forming rapidly in my throat. "Thanks for telling me."

"I'm not sure he's even going to do it, Ellie. And if he does, I have no idea what my role will be."

Sitting criss-cross applesauce on the blanket facing him, I consider what that life would be like. Or if there would even be one for me included in that plan.

There's no interest on my part in spending weeks and weeks alone while he travels the country with his brother. I have no desire to relocate anywhere, much less to the shark tank of Washington.

I see the resolution in his eyes. I know the loyalty he has to his family. And, sadly, I know where I rank.

"You're overthinking this," Ford says. "Don't. Don't start playing out a million scenarios, Ellie."

With a half-laugh, I shrug. "How can I not? At least this time, I have a little warning."

"What's that supposed to mean?"

"It means I can prepare for you to move on this time and not be blindsided like before."

His sigh is sarcastic, frustration laced all through his tone.

"Look," I say, "I get you want to support your brother. You'd be a dick if you didn't. But that's a huge commitment you're making—"

"I *might* make."

"You might make," I correct.

Before I can say anything else, his gaze catches mine. The brightness of the blues is gone, and in their place, is a reluctance I've feared seeing in them since they day he walked into Halcyon. It's a shadow of the look I saw when he broke the news he was enlisting. It's enough to make my stomach curl.

I have a hard time pulling a lungful of air in as I look away.

"Let's not get ahead of ourselves," Ford says. "Nothing has been decided."

Maybe not for him. But there has for me.

It takes all the courage I have to turn my head to face him again. I paint a smile on my face and even manage a laugh. "Let's eat these sandwiches before they get soggy."

He wants to press the issue, but smartly decides to let it go. We go about unwrapping our picnic in silence.

"Listen to what happened at work today . . ."

Ford begins a story about how a contract almost fell through, but he managed to save it in the end. I stop listening after the first couple of sentences and just nod and smile every now and then.

His cologne fills the air and weaves with the pine scent from the trees around us. My gaze drifts to the dock to my right and I think back to the little girl I was so many summers ago, the little girl that was broken by a boy that moved along to something better.

I'm not her anymore.

Ellie

"DAD?" THE SCREEN DOOR SQUEAKS as I enter the house. The television is on, his chair pulled out, but he's nowhere in sight. "Dad?"

My stomach pulls as I head through the house. The hair on the back of my neck is standing on end, the result of the odd vibe in the home I grew up in.

The dining room looks normal, everything in place. I turn into the living room and call out again, "Daddy?"

My mom's Christmas cactus sits beneath the window undisturbed. The throw pillows that I don't think have been moved since I moved them last are perched where I left them. The remote control is on the armrest of the recliner. Dad is gone.

"Dad!" I'm digging in my pocket for my phone when I let out a shriek. "Ah!"

I fall into the wall, a picture of me as a little girl shaking against the paneling with the force. "You scared the crap out of me!"

Dad stands in the bathroom doorway, looking shaken. A yellow washcloth is held over his forearm, a small scrape marring his cheek.

"What's wrong?" I gasp, getting to my feet and rushing towards him. My heart is pounding, veering out of control.

"Oh, nothing," he grumbles. "I fell out in the garden. Didn't see the rake and went sailing into the zucchini."

"Are you okay?" My purse hits the floor with a thud. Much to his dismay, I peel back the cloth and take a look. The wound isn't deep, but looks nasty anyway. "Did you put stuff on this?"

"Yes," he sighs like I'm ridiculous. "It's a scrape, Ellie."

"Is your face okay?" I reach to touch it and he pulls away.

"I'm fine." With a shake of his head, he marches by me. Grabbing my purse, I sling it over my shoulder and follow him.

"You don't need all that zucchini anyway," I huff as we enter the kitchen. "Just let it rot to the ground."

He sits in his chair in the kitchen, slumping in defeat. He refuses to look at me, so I know I have to tread lightly. He clams up if he doesn't want to talk. If that's the case, I could sit here for ten hours and get not a word from the stubborn man.

So, I change tactics. "How's the garden? Besides the damn zucchini," I ask, sliding into the chair by the fridge.

"Tomatoes are coming out of my ears. Want some?"

"Sure."

He doesn't take his eyes off the television. "I put a bag on the porch hoping you'd come by. Better use 'em up quick."

Picking up a lighter on the table, I fiddle with it. I've had an edgy, distracted twitch all day.

After Ford dropped me off yesterday and I told him I had a headache and he should probably just go home, I've been a ball of nervous energy. There's an overwhelming feeling that I'm on the cusp of a major fall and I can't stop it. That no matter how hard I claw away at the rocks on the face of the cliff, it won't make a difference. I'll free fall anyway.

"Finished painting Halcyon today," I tell my father. "It looks really good. Want to take a ride and see it?"

"Not today, pumpkin."

Tossing the lighter on the table, I lean back in my chair. "How did you know Mama was the one?"

He seems intrigued I'm asking this by his raised brow and tight lips, but doesn't call me out on it. He doesn't ask if this has anything to do with Ford, and I don't volunteer it.

"Your mother was the only one."

"That's sweet, Daddy."

"Maybe, but she was the only choice I could make."

"You mean to tell me no one else wanted you?" I tease. "I thought I heard something about you being as handsome as they come, and Mama saying you looked like a hunkier Sam Elliott?"

He grins like he always does when he thinks about his younger years. "Well, I did have my pick of 'em. Ladies were lined up from here to Atlanta to get a look at your Pop. One night I had three dates with three different women."

"You were a man whore," I gasp. "Daddy!"

"I was indeed," he grins proudly, "but that was before your mama came to town." He looks back at his Western. "There used to be a place you could go and watch a show for a dollar and a half. I was there one Friday night and there she was, sitting on the tailgate of Buddy Loren's truck. Prettiest thing I ever saw."

"Did she just leap off the truck and run to you like they do in the movies?"

He snorts. "It took me six weeks to get her to go on a date with me."

"That man whore reputation probably sunk you," I point out.

"Probably. But I got her to agree eventually." He looks at me again. "I knew she was the one a few weeks after our first date. I was down by the coast, looking over the water and the sun was setting. The sky was this purple color and I remember standing there thinking how beautiful it was and I wished she was there to watch it with me."

I wait for more, but he just looks at me. "That's it?"

"That's it," he shrugs. "That's the moment I knew that I wanted to share all the things in my life with only her. That's really what being The One means, ain't it?"

"Oh, Daddy," I sigh.

"I reckon you're asking me this for a reason."

"Maybe."

I pick up the lighter again and start fiddling with it. "His brother is going to run for office again."

"I saw that on the television. They were talking about him being eyed for the Presidency."

"Yeah."

"Why does that have you bothered?"

"I'm pretty sure it would affect Ford too. Like, he'd have to go off with Barrett and do those things. Maybe even move to Washington if he won."

Dad just looks at me.

"Well?" I ask. "Don't you see?"

"See what?"

I look at the ceiling. "I'll be honest with you, Daddy. I love him."

"I know you do."

"But . . ." I look at his handsome, wrinkled face. "But I don't know if I'm willing to put everything on the line for someone that just takes off when they feel like it."

"He hasn't gone anywhere."

"Not yet," I scoff. "But isn't the past the best indicator of the future? Isn't that what you used to drive into my head growing up?"

"You know what I loved most about your mama?"

"Absolutely. Her pot roast. Everyone knows that."

He cracks a smile, but stays focused. "What I loved the most was that she let me . . . evolve. Try new things. Remember the time I had that ponytail?"

"Those pictures will never be shown to your some-day grandkids," I say, making a face. "That was horrible!"

"It wasn't the best," he laughs. "But your mother didn't say a word. She let me pick mushrooms when I really should've been mowing the lawn and she didn't say a peep when I wanted to switch careers from the railroad to truck driving. Then I got hurt and that was over before it started," he notes. "But the fact of the matter is, she let me grow."

"So what you're saying is, I should just let Ford do what he wants because I'm the girl?"

"Hell, no," he laughs. "The rest of my speech goes a little something like this: she let me evolve, yes, but I always listened to her. I always heard her feelings out and we compromised. I didn't always get what I wanted, but I got the chance to be heard. Marriage is a delicate balance, Ellie Dawn."

"Whoa," I say, holding my hands out. "Let's not start talking about the m-word."

He flicks the mute button on the television and pushes the remote a little off to the side. "Do you have an inkling that you want to see someone else?"

I don't. Not a bit. But the look on his face, the severity of his features, keeps me from replying.

"There's nothing guaranteed in this life, pumpkin. I've lived a long one, seen a lot of stuff. There's not a thing you can say for sure you'll have in the morning. Not even another breath. That can be paralyzing when you think about it."

"That's true," I say softly. "It's a weakness of mine, actually. I get to thinking about what tomorrow will be like and I just get scared. I'm afraid to make the wrong choices. I'm afraid of being hurt." I look at the table, cuts from knives and dinners and burns from pots and pans over the years scuffing the surface. "I fear regret."

"You can't do that. You can't let fear of the unknown make you stop living." He begins to blink rapidly as a wet sheen sweeps across his eyes. "Don't turn into me, Ellie."

"That wouldn't be a terrible thing," I say over the lump in my throat.

"If you do one thing for me in your whole life, I want you to do everything. All the things you're scared of, all the things I wish I did."

"Like date four men at once?" I tease.

He chuckles. "No, like not getting stuck at a nine-to-five. Take vacations. Get sunshine . . . and get your mail." His voice cracks and I fight tears but they come anyway. I have no idea what's sparked this from him, this sort of life manifesto or whatever it is, but it's killing me to see him in this way.

I reach to pull him into a hug but he bats my hand away. "What I'm saying is for you to figure out what puts a smile on your face and give that a try. Try new things. Let Ford try them too. If it's a mistake, then you'll know and you don't have to wonder. Besides, life is entirely too short to live with so much caution you're frozen."

Considering his words, the truth literally hurts. It stings my chest, makes tears well up in my eyes. "I think Ford does that, Daddy. He puts a smile on my face."

"I was hoping you'd say that," he whispers. He moves the cloth from his arm and I see that it's stopped bleeding.

"Let's go to dinner," I offer. "Let's do something outside of this house."

"Thank you, pumpkin, but I'll stay here."

"But you just said . . ."

"Go on," he grins. "Have a good dinner and tell that boy I said hi."

"You're more than welcome to come," I insist. "We can go get a barbecue sandwich at Porter's."

"I'm tired. My back is starting to hurt a little bit so I'm going to go to bed."

I stand and kiss him on the head. "I'll come check on you tomorrow."

"I'll be fine," he sighs.

"Behave and I might even bring you a sandwich tomorrow," I wink before heading to the door. Before I push it open, I hear him say my name.

"Ellie?"

"Yeah, Daddy?"

"I love you."

"I love you too."

Ellie

I COULD PROBABLY PRY MYSELF off this couch and do something productive. I'm sure I could, actually. I don't feel too bad physically, besides a little iffy in my stomach from anxiety.

It's mental exhaustion that has me down for the count. If not, lying on this couch for the past three hours should've revived me.

Closing my eyes feels good for about five seconds, just long enough to quiet everything in my brain. All that does is allow everything to kind of reboot and start from scratch, and I have to work my way back through it from the beginning.

Besides Ford, I now have my dad to worry about. He promised this morning when I called to check on him that he was okay. There's something in his tone that worries me.

My stomach twists and churns. I lay a hand on top of my belly button and listen to it actually gurgle. It's gross.

Deciding to try to force myself to take a nap, my eyelids don't touch before a knock sounds on the door.

"You've got to be kidding me," I mutter, throwing off the fleece blanket and getting to my feet. Stumbling to the entryway, I call out, "Who is it?"

"It's Ford."

It doesn't go unnoticed that my nerves quell just a little as I unlatch the lock. He hears it and opens it himself.

Stepping inside, he does a quick once-over.

"What's wrong?" I ask, tugging my t-shirt down.

"Just checking on you. You haven't called me back from this morning."

"Sorry. I didn't mean to worry you," I say as he bends and kisses my cheek. "I got busy and I haven't felt good today. I came home early and couched it."

"You should've called," he says, taking my hand in his. "I would've brought you some soup or something and couched it with you."

"I'll be fine. Just tired, I think."

He leads me to the living room and sits. Before I can take a spot next to him, he pulls me on his lap. I don't argue. Instead, I curl up against his chest and listen to his heartbeat, steady and strong.

My body relaxes, my shoulders softening, and I sink deeper into him. He wraps his arms around me and holds me tight.

"I was going to make you get all dressed up and take you dinner," he whispers. "I wanted to show you off."

I grin against his shirt. "Not tonight."

"I'm okay with sitting with you like this all night. No complaints from me."

We sit quietly, the only sound coming from a talk show on the television.

"I talked to Danielle today," he says. "She loved the idea of partnering up with Halcyon on a back-to-school fundraiser in the fall."

"Really?"

"Really." He kisses the top of my head. "I told her all about you and she can't wait to meet you."

Fisting his shirt in my hands, I squeeze my eyes closed. "Do you really think that's a good idea, Ford?"

"What? You meeting Danielle? Yeah. You'll get along great."

I pull away and scoot off his lap. "I'm sure she's fabulous. And thank you for mentioning Halcyon to her. That means a lot to me."

He pulls his brows together and takes me in. "What are you getting at?"

"I just . . . I think we've been going a little too fast."

I flinch when he laughs. It's not what I'm expecting. Not at all.

"Fast? Are you kidding me right now?" he asks. "Hell, I've been doing everything I can to slow this down."

"I didn't realize you didn't want—"

His index finger lies against my lips, silencing me. "If I had my way, you'd be moved in with me already, beautiful."

I beg my heart to behave and not start swooning. I can't. Not this time. This time, I have to be an adult and think.

"Ellie? What's wrong?"

"I, um, I just think we need to take a step back."

"Why in the hell would we do that?"

"We're just barreling along here, being complete hedonists, and not thinking about the ramifications later," I say, the words spilling out quicker than I can keep up. "We are on such different pages in our lives and there's no sense in keeping this up when we can see if we'd just look that we can't—"

His mouth is pressed against mine, his hand palming the back of my head. The words are scooped up with his tongue as I sigh the rest of them in his mouth.

Not having a choice to kiss him or not is a relief. I'd have said no, but maybe I wouldn't have meant it.

This is where I'm happy. This is where I want to be, wrapped up in his arms, breathing him in. It just doesn't mean it's the best place for me.

He breaks the kisses, tapping one on my nose, before pulling away. "Let's try this again. This time, without a hundred-word ramble," he grins.

I clear my throat, my lips still stinging from his delicious assault. "Okay. What I was trying to say is that I think we need to not press this thing between us any farther than it already is. Not right now."

"And . . . why would we do that?"

"We want different things, for one," I sigh, standing up. Making my way to the mantle, I figure it's far enough away from him to think. "You want . . . I don't even know what you want," I admit. "That's a problem."

"I want you. How hard is that to wrap your head around?"

"You say that, but then you tell me you want to get married, have kids, get a dog . . ."

"I have a dog and she's epic. If I tried to replace her, it would hurt her feelings."

"You know what I mean," I say, rolling my eyes. "You want this cookie-cutter life, and I just don't know that I want that."

"Why not?" He scoots to the edge of the sofa, resting his elbows on his knees. "You love me. I love you. Maybe we haven't said those things yet, but it's as fact as the day is long."

A soft smile tickles my lips and I sit on the edge of the fireplace stoop to stop the shakiness in my legs. "You say that, and then you say you're going to go trekking all over the country. That's not really conducive to a family lifestyle, Ford."

"I said I might do that," he groans. "Might, as in maybe. Possibly. Not definitely."

"I can tell you I definitely don't want to live that way. I want to live here, with my father, my business, my roots. I don't want a long-distance relationship. I have no interest. Zero." I pick up a magazine and roll it in my hands. "But I know you have to go with your brother."

"I don't have to do jack shit."

"But you will. Because that's who you are. Because that's the man I adore."

He leans back against the cushions and puts his hands on his face. "Why do I feel like you've just shoved a mile away from me?"

When I don't answer, he finally looks at me. There's fear etched on his face. I see it, too, when he forces a swallow.

"Ellie, baby, don't do this."

"I'm not doing anything," I promise. "I just . . . I'm between a rock and a hard place here."

"Why do you think that? I don't get it."

"If I give in to you and just go with the flow, follow my heart . . ."

"You don't trust me." It's more of a question than a statement, a phrase uttered with disbelief. "You don't, do you?"

"It's not that I don't trust you. It's just . . . what happens if in a year from now, I'm sitting here alone with a baby and you're off God knows where doing God knows what? Then what, Ford? Do you think that's the life I want?"

His jaw hangs open as he exhales, narrowing his eyes like he can't believe what he's hearing. I just sit on the stone fireplace and watch him.

"You know it's not. After all, isn't that one of the reasons you claim to have left me the first time? You wanted the freedom to do things and felt like it wasn't fair to make me wait on you or follow you around?"

He runs a hand through his hair, tugging briefly before letting go. "For fuck's sake, Ellie. What do I have to do?"

"I'm not asking you to do anything. I'm just saying that until we figure out where our paths are going, maybe we shouldn't be getting too involved."

He springs off the couch, his body vibrating with irritation. "We shouldn't be getting too involved? You really just fucking said that?"

"You know what I mean."

"You know what? I don't. I don't get a word of this bullshit."

"Think about it," I say, standing up so I don't feel so vulnerable. "Taking a step back gives us some breathing room."

He's across the room and inches from me before I can take any precautions otherwise. His chest rises and falls so hard, I think it's going to slam into mine.

"What if I don't want breathing room?" he asks.

"I do."

He nods, a look of skepticism on his face. "Tell you what—you can have some breathing room if that's what you want."

Even though it's what I said I wanted, my heart crashes anyway. He's still standing in front of me, and I could call this off with one little word, yet I already miss him. I already ache for him. I already crave him and feel the void he's instantly carved in my life.

Tears fill my eyes, but I blink them back. This is what I wanted. I have to remind myself.

That's easier said than done when I see the emotions he's wearing on his shirtsleeve.

"This doesn't change anything," he warns me. "This doesn't change how I feel or what I want."

I can't blink fast enough. A solitary tear trickles down my cheek.

"I love you," he whispers, his eyes shining with emotion. "I love the hell out of you."

My words barely come out over the lump in my throat. "I love you too."

"Then don't you see how stupid this is?"

"It feels stupid," I admit. "But I just want to be careful."

A kiss comes quick and soft, his hands cupping the sides of my face. "I'll call Violet and have her bring you some soup," he says.

"You don't have to do that."

"I told you this doesn't change anything for me."

He holds my gaze for a long moment, and then, with a hefty sigh, he drops his hands. He may as well have dropped my heart as he walks out the front door.

24

Ford

"ARE YOU HUNGRY?"

I step to the side to allow Sienna to make her way in. She holds up two greasy paper bags. "I brought dinner."

"It's amazing you don't weigh seven hundred pounds with all the fast food you eat," I laugh.

"So you don't want it? I even got you a double-double with bacon and extra pickles."

"How can I resist that?"

She grins. "Kitchen or living room?"

"Living room," I say, heading that direction. "I'm not Graham."

"You can say that again," she scoffs. "I accidentally set a glass of water on his coffee table once. He got me a set of coasters for Christmas."

She heads in front of me, dressed in a pair of jeans and a black shirt with some kind of sparkles on the shoulders. On her feet are a pair of heels that make me wonder how in the hell she's even walking in them.

I plop down on the couch and watch her place one bag in front of me.

"One time he insisted I stay at his place when I was home on leave. It was around the holidays, I think," I say, opening the container. The scent of deep fried goodness hits me in the nose. "I took a shower, right? And hung the towel on the side of the shower to dry, thinking I'd re-use it later. I mean, I was clean when I used it."

"I do the same thing," she says with a mouthful of French fries.

Shaking my head, I laugh. "Sometimes it's amazing you are our mother's child."

"What?" she giggles, shoving in another fry.

"Anyway, when I went in to shower that night, the towel was gone and a piece of paper was taped to the door that the towels go in the hamper."

"You're kidding me."

"Nope."

The burger oozes condiments as I lift it to my mouth. "This is so good," I say, searching the bag for a napkin. Before I can wipe my mouth, I take another bite.

"And I was afraid you wouldn't be hungry," she laughs. "You don't normally eat so late, do you?"

"No," I say through a mouthful of burger. I swallow and take a drink before continuing. "I don't want to call it a fight, but Ellie and I had . . ."

"A tiff?"

"What the hell is that?"

"I don't know. That's what Mom calls it," she laughs. "So what happened?"

"The S-word," I groan.

"Syphillis?"

I burst out laughing. "No! Space. She wants space."

"Oh," she says, choking on her drink. "That sucks but it's better than a venereal disease." She gets herself under control. "So what are you going to do? How do you play this?"

"Short from kidnapping her?"

"Kinda illegal, bud. But I know people, and Cam definitely knows people . . ."

"What the fuck?"

"A joke," she says, her eyes going wide like she's been caught in the cookie jar. "It was a joke."

"It better be a joke."

"Can we focus on the problem at hand?" she sighs. "What are you doing with Ellie?"

I give her a final glare to warn her about her idea of a joke. "I'm giving her space. That's what she wants, that's what she'll get." Tossing my sister a napkin, I lean back on the sofa. "I'm going to make her miss me."

"You sounds like a country music song."

"Well, I have the truck and the dog and the woman that's running off. I guess it kind of works," I laugh. "Fuck, that's pathetic. Never tell this to Lincoln."

"Blackmail," she laughs, taking another bite. "But I think it's smart to just give her some room."

"You know what? I'm kinda pissed."

"Really?"

"Yeah," I say, propping my feet up on the coffee table. "She's holding shit against me from years ago. That's not fair."

Sienna wipes her hands off and seems to gather her thoughts. When she looks at me, it's not a look from my little sister. It's a look from a grown woman, someone that's been through things, and that takes me by surprise.

"You know what's not fair, Ford? You dismissing her feelings."

"I'm not doing that."

"You don't mean to, but you are. You have every right to be angry. But she also has every right to be scared if that's what she is. You can't force her through that. What you can do, though, is to let her work it out with you standing by her side."

"Why are you talking to me like this? You're my baby sister."

She laughs, patting me on the leg. "You realize I date. And I do other things that make me—"

"Shut up, Sienna," I laugh. "Seriously. This is not the conversation I want to have with you. You want to talk about that shit, go hit up Lincoln. I'm out."

"I hear Barrett's the kinky one," she giggles.

"Grapes?"

"Yes," she says, shaking her head. "I'm disgusted that I know that about my brother."

"I'm disgusted you even know what sex is."

Sienna laughs as she sips from her soda. We sit quietly for a long while, the only sound coming from Trigger's occasional claws hitting the kitchen floor as she walks back and forth from her food dish to her bed.

I didn't realize how lonely this house could be until recently. Sometimes now I sit here and wonder what it would be like to hear another person in another room, feel someone else's presence. Know Ellie was in the kitchen or bedroom, waiting on me.

"So . . ." Sienna begins, breaking my trance.

"So . . ."

She looks at me with hesitation in her eyes. I can almost see the words sitting on the tip of her tongue, begging to come out. I wait for her to give in. She doesn't.

"What's up, Sienna?"

Sighing, she leans back on the sofa. "A part of me wants to go back to LA and a part of me doesn't."

"So don't go until you're ready."

"But I just feel the need to . . . move. To go. To do. To experience," she sighs again. "I feel like I was a nomad in a past life. A gypsy."

"I think they make their living by fortune telling," I note, taking a drink. "You got a crystal ball somewhere?"

"Very funny." She crosses her arms over her chest and shoots me a look. It's the one that I can't just blow off.

"Okay, I'll play. Why do you want to move or however you say it?"

"I don't know," she whines. "I feel like there's so much out there that I don't know and I'll never see."

"You're in your early twenties. You have time," I laugh.

She rises up. "I'm being serious. I feel like I'm the little sister of all the Landry boys. Like I'm the afterthought, the one no one expects anything of because you assholes have already conquered the world."

"Lincoln had conquests, Sienna. It's not the same thing."

"Hardy, har, har."

"Fine. You want to blaze your own path. You did go to fashion school, remember? You have an apartment in Los Angeles . . . I think? You've been in Savannah more or less for a few months now so I could be wrong about that."

"My roommate there can handle the rent. She has a bigger allowance than I do," she frowns. "Besides, her sister is staying with her now so it's not like they miss me."

"So what do you want to do? Travel? See the world? Get a job with that expensive degree you have?" I say, remember Graham's outrage at how much a fashion design degree costs.

She laughs, thinking the same thing. "Graham about died."

"If he had his way, we'd all be misers, pinching pennies and refilling ketchup bottles out of to-go packets," I say, knocking the takeout bag in front of me.

"Do people really do that?"

I shrug. "I saw it on television once on one of those shows where people do crazy things to save a buck. Maybe you could try that out. I don't think gypsies have a lot of money. Could work."

"I'm being serious, Ford."

"Fine," I sigh. "What are you wanting to do? Answer that."

She blushes and looks at the floor. Picking at the hem of her shirt, the sequins catch the light and bounce it around the room.

When she finally looks at me, I see the sincerity in her eyes. She twists in the seat and squares her shoulders with mine.

"I want to move to Illinois."

"What in the hell is in Illinois?"

"I knew a girl in LA from there. She just moved back home and we've been texting a lot. She does some freelance design work for some of our friends in California, and it's kind of growing really fast. She invited me to be a part of it."

"So you want to move there? And not go back to LA?"

Her smile is contagious. "We'd run the business from Illinois. I'd join as co-CEO and we'd do the work from Illinois, going back to LA if we need to. She's making a fortune, Ford, and Graham's finally freed me up some cash to do with what I want." She sets her jaw. "This is what I want to do."

"Did you not want to design socks like six weeks ago?"

Exasperated, she throws her hands in the air. "That was then. This is now."

"Sorry," I flinch, scooting back a little. "So, Illinois and designing what?"

"Clothes. Computer skins. Hats. Maybe socks," she says, rolling her eyes. "I want to do this."

"I can tell."

"But I need to know if you think it's stupid."

Of course I think it's stupid. Designing computer skins with a fashion degree that's fees could feed a small island for a year is asinine. I know Graham is going to have a major meltdown and Dad isn't going to be thrilled either.

Before I can say that, I see the glimmer of hope in her eye. It's similar to the one Camilla flashed me when she came to me to appeal to my rational side.

"Why did you come to me with this?" I ask.

"Because you're rational."

"Damn it," I laugh. "Do I need to be more of a dick or something so you and Cam will stop asking me for approval for dumb shit?"

"Oooh," she says, leaning forward. "What did Cam say?"

"I'm not talking to you about it because you won't tell me certain things I want to know."

Her bottom lip pouts out. "I can't."

"Tell me this," I ask. "Who will flip out more? Graham? Barrett? Lincoln? Or me?"

"Maybe . . ." she considers this. "Barrett. I think. I don't know. Maybe G? You aren't going to be thrilled either."

My head goes into my hands, my stomach churning. "If this is what having a daughter is like, may God bless me with sons."

"Hey," she says, punching my arm. "You know you love your sisters!"

"I do," I say, picking up my burger. "But I love you more when you go to Graham with your crap."

She laughs as we go back to our dinner, and I realize that even though Sienna drives me crazy, it feels good to have someone else here tonight.

Ellie

"YOU COULD BE WITH FORD," I taunt myself like the crazy person I'm beginning to think I am. Pouring myself a cup of hot tea with honey, I hope it somehow helps me get to sleep.

It won't.

There won't be sleep when my heart hurts so much.

When my body misses his touch.

As my fingers itch to touch him, to feel him grin against the side of my neck in the middle of the night, sleep will be out of reach. Just like he is.

The bowl of half-eaten soup sits next to the sink. Half of it is probably full of tears as I took the soup that Ford asked Violet to bring me and cried on her shoulder.

Carrying my teacup, I make my way into the living room and set it on the coffee table. The pillows bounce as I drop onto the cushions and pick up the remote. There's nothing on but the infomercials I've already watched twice. I almost purchased the copper pots.

"That's how pathetic you are," I tell myself.

Proving that point, I jump when my phone glows beside me. In one quick move, I swipe it up. When I see Violet's name, I almost throw it across the room.

"Hey," I say into the line.

"Are you okay?"

"Yeah. Why?"

"I saw you're still up."

"How did you see I'm still up? It's like two in the morning."

"I was out," she says snarkily. "I happened to see your lights on. Thought I'd check on you."

Tossing the remote on the other side of the couch, I get comfortable. "I just can't sleep."

"Want me to come back by?"

"No," I sigh. "Go home or wherever you're going."

"Ford called me a couple of hours ago," she admits. "He wanted to see how you were feeling."

"He could've called me."

"I believe you said you wanted space." She singsongs it, like she's rubbing it in my face. "You could've called him, you know."

I hate when she's right and there's nothing I can do about it. After a long, drawn-out sigh, I get the nerve to stop the façade and just be frank. I'm too tired to pretend anything else at this point.

"What am I doing?" I ask her. "I'm damned if I do and damned if I don't."

"I have no idea. You're going to have to tell me, friend."

"I'm just so, so tired."

"Fine. Let me walk you through this," she groans. "Boil it down for me. What is it that you are really afraid of? What is the image you see when you have these panic sessions."

Choking back a memory, I clear my throat. "I'm afraid of getting in so deep with him that I'm at his mercy."

"Elaborate."

"Damn it, Vi," I gruff. Getting up from the sofa, I begin pacing the living room. "I can't just switch my feelings on and off with Ford. I love him, Vi. Like, *I love him.*"

"That's good."

"Not if he decides he doesn't love me back," I point out. "What if he gets a wild hare up his ass and wants to go campaigning with Barrett?

I can't do that. We have the store. Besides, I don't *want* to do that. But then what? What happens to me?"

"Whatever you want to happen to you."

"I've worked so hard to get to where I am. To be strong and smart and capable. When I'm around him, I feel myself relying on him. Needing him. I don't want to do that because . . ."

"Because it gives him power," she says, finishing my sentence. "He told me you don't trust him."

Even though she can't see me, I shrug.

"El, you're smart to want to protect yourself. But you can't go through life waiting on the next shoe to drop."

"It just always seems like there's one just waiting to fall."

"There is. It's life. It's what happens," she laughs. "But you'll be okay. You'll survive. Look at all you've survived already."

She's right. I know that. I pride myself on being a survivor and not a victim. But that doesn't make it easier to change the way I see the world.

"I'm not telling you what to do," she says, "but I think you need to inventory your life. Decide what you want in it and what you don't. And be prepared to live with those choices."

Her words hit me like a dose of cold water. I glance at the clock and see it's way too late to call Ford now.

"I'll give him a call in the morning," I tell her. "We'll see if we can work it out."

"Good girl. You're meeting Heath and I in the morning at eight, right? We're supposed to figure out how to style the mannequins."

"I'll be there. And, Vi?"

"Yeah?"

"Thanks for being such a good friend to me."

"You're welcome."

I hang up the phone and head to my room. This time, when I lay my head down, I'm lulled to sleep by Ford's laugh.

Ellie

"YOU LOOK LIKE CRAP." HEATH makes a face as he breezes by me and falls dramatically in the recliner. "And I thought I was having a bad hair day."

"That key was for emergencies," I tell him. "That's the second time you've just barged in. I'm going to take it away."

"Would you rather have dragged your sorry butt off the couch? I could've knocked," he points out.

"He's been this way all day," Violet sighs, picking up my legs and sitting on the end of the sofa. She drops my feet on her lap. "How ya feeling?"

"Meh. I feel like I've been lit on fire and stomped on." Rolling over to my side, I look at Heath. "The yellow polo shirt looks good on you."

"Thanks," he grins. "I thought I looked pretty banging in it."

"Has Ford called today?" Violet asks.

I give her a look.

"He called me," she offers. "He was worried when I told you didn't meet us this morning. I'm supposed to check in with him later. He said he had a meeting with his brothers later today."

"Can you imagine that board meeting?" Heath asks. "It's like a game of How Many Hotties Can We Fit in One Room?"

We all laugh. For the first time in the last two days, I don't feel like

I'm at death's door. My stomach isn't gurgling and my head doesn't feel as stuffed with cotton.

I sniffle to be sure.

"You have the flu or what?" Violet asks. "I was in the bakery this morning and they were saying lots of people have come down with a nasty bug."

"I guess. My dad has it too. I called him a few minutes ago and he said he's been in bed since yesterday. Just feeling wiped out."

Heath adjusts in his seat. "Is that how you feel? Wiped out?"

"Does it look like I've gotten off this couch in a couple of days?" I laugh. "I just want to sleep. But on the bright side, I think I've lost five pounds."

His eyes snap to Violet's. Something, not vomit this time, rumbles in my stomach. "What?"

Violet grins at Heath. "Is it possible . . . ?"

Heath laughs. "Oh, you know it's possible, and if it's not, she doesn't deserve him!"

"What in the hell are you two talking about?" I say, scooting up on the pillow so I'm sitting.

Heath bends forward, his eyes shining. "Has it ever crossed your mind that you're pregnant?"

The vomit is back now in full force. "No," I say loudly. "I'm not pregnant."

My mouth goes dry as the acid in my stomach that was quelled just a few seconds ago is now churning like a volcano ready to erupt. I can't be pregnant. I mean, I can. I could be. Technically. But I can't. Not really. That would just . . .

"Hey," Violet says, her hand resting on my shins. "One thought at a time."

"I have the flu, guys," I insist. "It's what my dad has. I probably caught it from him or the girls in the bakery this week. I mean, I . . ."

Breathing takes effort as what feels like the entire room caves in on me. There's a franticness that I can't control, a slew of reminders of feeling this way once before hitting me in waves.

"I'm going to be sick." I leap up, holding my stomach, and race to the bathroom. As I spill the last few drinks of water into the toilet, I add in a few salty tears.

Violet takes my hair and pulls it to the side, her other hand rubbing small circles on my back. After I'm sure I'm done heaving, I look at her and laugh. It's a sad, terrified sound, more like a crazy person than her best friend.

The wall is cool as I lean on it. Violet sits beside me on the bathroom floor. She doesn't offer me advice or direction or tell me to get up and deal with whatever it is. We just sit there looking at the light blue wall.

"I have the flu," I mutter. My mouth tastes like bile and it almost makes me get sick again. My face feels swollen, puffy, and I really wish that was my biggest concern. Laughing, I look at Vi. "Funny how things put other things in perspective. Now I just wish I was worried Ford might stop by and I'd look like shit."

I look down at my stomach. It looks the same. But is it still the same? Or is it quietly harboring a secret I didn't know?

Forcing a swallow, I look at Violet. She's watching me patiently, the side of her lip starting to curve upward.

"I'm afraid to really consider this is a possibility," I admit.

The room might be spinning. I find a toothbrush sticking out of the holder on the sink and focus on that to keep from falling over.

A series of emotions tumbles through me, and I don't know which to grab on to.

"Breathe, Ellie," Violet whispers.

"It's harder than you think." I blow out a shaky breath and refill my lungs. "I'm not ready for this. I mean, if that's what it is."

"It might just be the flu."

"Maybe. I hope so." Timidly, I rest my hand on my stomach. All I can feel is the gurgle from the acid that threatens to expel, but I close my eyes anyway.

Déjà vu strikes me hard in the feels. I was terrified then. I knew in my soul that I was too young to do it properly, to do it the way my mom did it. I was terrified then. But I may be more scared now.

Would I be ready for this now? Would I be ready to take on all the changes a baby would require? I've been telling Ford I'm not in a place to do those things and I don't feel like I am.

I want to follow through the promises I made to my mother—to see things and do things and live a life that's more than she did. If I have a child, I . . .

"I'm gonna be sick." I heave again into the toilet, the tile floor biting into my knees. Violet kneels beside me and it occurs to me that in the moment I might find out I'm going to be a mother, I need mothering. Certainly this is evidence of failure on my part.

Taking the washcloth offered me, I wipe my mouth and rock back on my heels. "I need to know. I probably have some virus and this is all for nothing. But I need to know."

Violet nods. "Heath ran to the pharmacy on the corner."

"You're kidding me."

"We knew you'd want to know. And maybe we wanted to know too."

"Of course this is about you," I laugh. My tone is shaky and hearing that only makes me more anxious. "I don't know if I can do this, Vi. What would this mean for Halcyon? What would it—"

"One thing at a time. Besides, this isn't the end of the world if it's true."

"Your business partner is going to be a lot less partner-y."

"Good. I'll do what I want," she winks. When I start to object, she laughs. "Ellie, babies are a blessing. Maybe it's not how you planned it. Maybe it's going to make some things harder, I'll give you that. But I've never heard a mother say she wishes she didn't have her child."

My shoulders slump. "I had so many plans. I really feel like my life was just taking off. And now this?"

I close my eyes and try to find the happy place that Mallory teaches us to find at yoga. My center. My zen. Before I find it, Heath appears at the doorway.

"How are we doing?" he asks.

"Fork it over." I extend a hand, palm up.

He flashes Violet a look.

"I know you have it so just give it to me," I order.

With a sneaky grin, he lays a slender box in my hand. It feels like it weighs a ton. The weight of my future lies in this piece of cardboard.

As I ponder whether I really want to do this or not, my phone rings in the living room. Heath goes to get it. When he returns, it's in his hand. "It's Ford."

"It's like he has ESP or something," I groan. "Will you answer it? Tell him not to come by here. Make up some reason because I don't want to see him."

"He's going to want to check on you," Violet chimes in.

"Tell him . . . tell him I have some errands to run today and am leaving in a minute. Tell him I'll call him later."

Heath beams, swiping open my phone and walking away. His tone, almost cooing in the line, makes me roll my eyes.

"You're trusting Heath to talk to Ford?" Violet laughs.

"Only because I'm absolutely sure Ford's not gay." I struggle to stand, my knees wobbly. "That's what got us here, after all."

She laughs. I don't.

I look in the mirror. My face is worse than I even imagined. Broken blood vessels in my cheeks from straining, puffy eyes, drained skin.

Violet's face pops up next to mine. "Want me to stay or go?"

"Go. In the hallway. I'll tell you when I know something."

She squeezes my shoulder and disappears, closing the door snugly behind her.

The box feels like a bomb in my hand, ready to go off at any minute and blow up my world, one that I've been so careful with. As I open it and read the instructions, basically trying to figure out how many stripes mean what, I try to squash a flurry of eagerness trying to take over.

I think of anything I can except what I'm doing as I pee on the stick. Placing it on the counter while I wash my hands, I don't look at it. I know that whatever it shows in a few seconds will change my life one way or the other.

After I've dried my hands so that not a drop of water remains, flushed the toilet, dried off the counter, and fixed my hair in the mirror, I look.

Two. Pink. Stripes.

The gasp isn't completely out of my mouth when the door shoves open. I register it. I sense the movement of Vi and Heath coming in, but I don't move. I just stare at this little piece of plastic in front of me.

"I knew it," Violet gushes, pulling me in a hug. I don't hug her back. I don't even move my arms. I just hold the stick in front of my face and feel the hot tears slowly move down my cheeks.

Heath's arms wrap around the two of us as we stand in the middle of my bathroom. No one says a word.

All I can think about is telling Ford and his reaction. I wonder how it will mirror the first time I had to tell him I thought we were having a baby.

The tears come harder as I'm flooded with so many emotions I can't even begin to get them together. My friends hold me, rubbing my back, whispering things in my ear that I can't hear over the sound of my own thoughts.

Once I simmer down and they release me, I set the test on the counter and splash cool water on my face. It's only when I've pressed a towel to my eyes do I even try to speak.

"Well, there goes Wine Wednesday," I attempt to joke. "That wasn't funny, was it?"

"Do you have any idea how beautiful this child is going to be?" Heath gushes.

"She's not there yet, Heath. Give her a second."

Pulling the lavender cloth from my face, I look between my two best friends. "This is either a monumental fuck-up or the best thing that's ever happened to me. I'm not sure which."

I do know. I can feel it creeping into my heart, twisting itself around hopes and dreams that have scattered through my soul and binding them together. What comes with that? Blinding fear.

A family with a man like Ford is every woman's fantasy. Maybe I didn't want it now if I had the choice. Maybe I needed more time to get there. But the concept is something that has been the pinnacle of my wish-list for almost a decade, a pipedream I thought was unattainable. What happens if it gets ruined? What if it doesn't work out? What if—

"Easy," Violet laughs, bumping me with her hip. "I don't know where you just checked out to, but I'm going to need you to come back."

"I'm afraid to tell him."

"Why? He's going to be over the moon!" Violet looks at me like I'm crazy. "I kinda want to watch him find out."

The faces she makes usually make me laugh, but it doesn't even register now.

"What if I tell him . . . what if that's like jinxing it or something?" I wipe my eyes. "What if he comes at me like I know he will, wanting to put some plan into place to do everything the right way, and I . . ." I close my eyes, a sudden dizziness rocking me.

"You don't want to?" Heath crooks a brow. "I'd prepare myself for him going off the deep end in the sexiest way, my friend."

My phone dings in Heath's hand. He looks at it and then up to me. "You'd be smart to call your baby daddy back or it appears he'll be showing up here."

"What did he say?" I groan.

"The text reads, 'Either call me back or I'm coming to see you. I need to know you're okay. You have ten minutes, babe.' He called you 'babe,'" Heath gushes.

I roll my eyes. "Tell him . . . tell him I'm going into a meeting and I'll call him in a little bit."

"So don't say congratulations or anything?"

"Heath, don't you even joke about this!" I say, springing to my feet. My stomach flip-flops and I flash a look at Violet. "This sickness isn't going away, is it?"

She laughs, tossing an arm around my shoulders. "Not for nine months, friend."

Ford

"NO, I DIDN'T DO ANYTHING stupid," I sigh, pouring a glass of sweet tea. "You'd have been proud."

"Let's not get crazy," Mallory huffs through the phone. "You had to have done something to make her balk."

"Why is it always the guy's fault? Why can't it just be something in her head that caused this?"

"Because I live in reality."

Sighing, I try to get the edge off the ball of anxiety I'm dealing with. I might have been able to manage giving her actual space had she not gotten sick. I may have even been able to deal with just checking on her once or twice if I didn't know something was actually wrong. Without Heath, I probably wouldn't know.

Luckily for me, he gave me a heads-up this morning when I called her phone. Now I wait for her to show up at my house like she promised in a text an hour ago.

"She wasn't at yoga today," Mallory mentions.

"She's supposed to be here any minute. She's sick. Her dad is too. I swung by there this afternoon to check on him," I add quickly.

"I didn't realize you were so close with her dad."

"He likes me," I shrug before taking a drink of the tea. I think back to our conversation about his favorite fishing holes and the map he tried to make me to find the biggest ginseng patch in Georgia. "They don't make them like him anymore."

The doorbell rings in the front hall and I put my drink down. "Hey, Ellie is here. I gotta go. Tell Graham I'll call him later since you hogged the conversation."

"Will do. See ya, Ford."

Slipping my phone into my pocket, I jog to the front door. I don't even look, but I should've. Maybe it would've prepared me for what I was going to see.

Ellie is standing on the stoop, her face swollen and blotchy. Her eyes are glassy and it's obvious she's been crying. For a while. Not one or two tears, but enough to make the whites of her eyes almost pink.

"What's wrong?" I take her hand and pull her inside, positioning her under the chandelier so I can get a better look at her. "Are you okay? What happened?"

She seems unharmed. Physically, anyway. I don't know what to do as her bottom lip starts to tremble, so I pull her into a hug.

"Did someone hurt you? Is your dad okay?"

She nods against my shirt. I pull her in tighter, my heart in my throat. "You're scaring the shit out of me."

"I need to talk to you."

Her face is pressed against me, the words muffled, and I can barely make them out. She's stiff at first, as if she doesn't want held. But after a few seconds, her hands are dipping beneath my shirt and lying flat against my back.

"Ellie, I need you to explain this."

Her back begins to shake. The sound of muted sobs slips through her efforts to contain them. The combination causes my heart to lodge in my throat, adrenaline to spike.

I guide her backwards so I can see her face. She has red lines in her skin, her lips plumped from crying, I guess. Her hair is matted against her face. "What is going on?"

She still refuses to say anything, just looks at me with tear-filled puppy dog eyes. I have to laugh or I'm going to lose my cool.

"Come on." I take her hand and lead her into the kitchen. I get her situated at the island and hand her a glass of tea. "Tea fixes everything. Or that's what my mom says. I find it not to be true, but it's the best I have off the cuff."

She laughs, blinking back tears. "Thank you."

Rifling through drawers, I locate a cloth and dampen it. When I turn to hand it to her, I see her watching me. There's something in her eyes I can't pinpoint. Whatever it is, it stops me in my tracks.

"Babe, you're going to have to start explaining this because I'm struggling to stay calm."

Her head nods back and forth and I can almost see the words stuck in her throat.

"Is it your dad?"

"No." The word is strangled, thick in the air. She takes a shaky sip of the tea.

"Halcyon?" I offer, getting exasperated.

"No."

"Ellie," I sigh, taking a deep breath, "I—"

My phone rings in my pocket and with an irritated glance, I pull it out. "It's Barrett. He can wait."

"Get it," she says, her hand lying on the base of her throat. "Get it and give me a second, okay?"

"You sure? I'm happy to send him to voicemail."

"Please get it."

"Yeah?" I say into the receiver.

"Hey, Ford. You okay?" Barrett asks.

"Fine. What's up?"

He starts in about his possible next political move. All I want to do is to tell him how much of a fuck I don't give right now and turn back to Ellie. To what matters.

Instead, I turn away from her so she doesn't see the irritation in my eyes. I know that won't help her tell me what's happened. And I need to know. Now.

"Hey, Barrett," I say, rounding the corner into the dining room. "I don't mean to be a dick, but I have my hands full right now with some things, and I need to call you back."

"No problem," he says. "Take care of you first. Talk to you soon, man."

"See ya."

Ending the call, I turn the corner.

She's gone.

"DAMN IT, ELLIE!"

My truck roars to life as her phone goes to voicemail again. I have no idea where she went or why or what in the hell has happened to make her this shaken up.

I shouldn't have turned my back. I should've given her all my attention.

With one hand on the wheel and the other swiping across my contacts list, I call Violet. She picks up as the wheels hit the street.

"Hello?"

"Violet, it's Ford. Where's Ellie?"

"She's with you, isn't she?" There's a panic in her voice that almost sends me over the edge.

"No, she's not. She was and just walked out. She was a mess when she got there and I have no idea why."

"Where are you?"

"On the road. I'm . . . I don't even know where I'm going, Violet. I just need to find her."

A soft laugh wafts through the phone. I hear her click me to speakerphone. "First of all, calm down. Okay?"

"Calm down? And why are you laughing?" I boom. "This is not funny."

"No, it's not," she says. "But trust me when I tell you that it's going to be all right."

"So you know what she was upset about?" I ask, re-gripping the wheel.

"Yes."

My palm smacks off the console. "Great. Then tell me or tell me where to find her because I'm a nervous fucking wreck."

There's an extended silence that does nothing for my anxiety as I pull out onto the road taking me into Savannah. "Violet?"

"Okay. She's headed home. She just sent me a text."

I blow a U-turn in the middle of the highway, my tires squealing, and go the other direction.

"What the hell was that?" she shrieks.

"I had to go the other way."

"Nice."

I crack a turn to the south, my headlights bouncing off the street signs along the road. My heart is going even faster than my truck, neither of which are safe.

Ellie

MY HOUSE SEEMS SO COLD. And empty. I turn on every light I pass in hopes it will make me feel less alone.

I should've told him. I should've and I was wrong not to, and I'm sure he's upset I didn't.

I'm such a coward.

"Ellie?" Violet's voice rings down the hall. "Where are you? You have this place lit up like a Christmas tree!"

"In the kitchen."

I hear her come down the hall. "There you are." She tries not to smile, but I can see it coming. "What the hell happened?"

"I just needed you to come back," I say, referring to the text I sent her. "I didn't tell him. I couldn't."

Just thinking about it sends my pulse rate spiraling upwards.

"I need a drink," I say, leaping to my feet. "Shit! I can't have one."

The tears are back again, not as much from the lack of wine in my new life, but more for all the changes I'm going to be encountering. The fear of the unknown, as my dad would say. I hate the unknown.

Violet laughs. "You can't have wine. Or caffeine. Or some cheeses and fish."

I must give her the saddest look ever because her laughs just get louder. Before I can tell her to fuck right off, the doorbell rings.

Once.

Twice.

Three times. All in a space of probably two seconds.

My eyes go wide. "He found me quick."

"Well . . ." She sticks her hands in her pockets.

"You told him! You rat!"

"He called me, Ellie. What did you want me to do? Lie to him?"

"That's precisely what I wanted you to do! Give me some time. Cover for me."

"Sorry. Not really, but you know what I mean," she laughs. "Should I answer the door?"

I don't know what to say, so I just let out a low-key wail.

"I'll take that as a yes." She disappears down the hallway she just came through. My legs shake as I sit down, my hands wringing together.

He barges through the doorway before Violet could've had time to open it. "Seriously?" He looks at me with narrowed eyes.

"What?" I ask, the word sounding even more innocent than I thought I could muster.

"You don't get to just walk out like that."

"I needed some space."

He chuckles angrily. "You could've gone into the bathroom. The bedroom. Sat in your fucking car in the driveway, Ellie. But you don't show up at my house upset and then disappear."

"I'm sorry."

He looks at the ceiling and breathes, the tension in his shoulders settling only a little. "What the hell is going on?"

"What do you mean?"

"What do I mean? You're really asking me that?"

I don't move. I just focus on breathing.

"Why are you crying?" he asks, the question too composed. He's on the brink of anger, I can see it. Hear it. Feel it.

"Because of you."

"Because of me?" he almost booms. "You're crying because of me?

I haven't even fucking talked to you in what feels like days because you need space. Well, you know what, fuck your space."

I see Violet hidden in the darkness of the hallway, letting me know she's still around if I need her. Suddenly, I wish she weren't. I wish it was just Ford and I.

"Ford, I'm sorry."

"Me too. I should've put my foot down when you started this bullshit and gotten to the bottom of it then." He pulls out a chair but doesn't sit. "What. The. Fuck. Is. Going. On?"

"Violet is here," I say, like that explains everything. Of course it doesn't and he gives me a look telling me just that.

"Violet?" he calls, looking at me. "Will you leave? Please?"

I glance around him and make eye contact with her. She indicates she'll be outside until she hears from me and then the door closes softly.

That's followed by a stream of tears.

"Tell me how to fix you," he says quietly. "Tell me what I need to do. I hate this, Ellie. I hate it."

"You can't fix this. There is no fixing this."

He marches in a circle, running his hands down his face. I watch his body move, the concern on his face, the palpable misery he's in because he's worried about me.

"Answer a question for me," I say. "What did Barrett want?"

"What's that have to do with you?"

Everything. "Just answer me. Please."

"I honestly don't know because I wanted to talk to you. But I'm guessing it has something to do with his campaign."

"So he's running?"

"I think so."

Squeezing my eyes closed, I say a silent prayer that someone is watching over me.

"Ford," I say, clearing my throat. "I have to tell you something."

"What is it?"

"I want you to sit down."

He heaves a breath but does as instructed. His top button is undone on his work shirt, his tie and jacket both long gone. The blonde spikes of his hair are unruly, and I can see that he's been running his hand through it.

I wonder what it would look like in the middle of the night after he's gotten no sleep because of a crying baby. What his arms would look like, so big and strong, with an infant curled up in the crook of his elbow.

"You can tell me anything," he says right before I start to speak. "I mean it. Anything."

"Okay." I take a deep breath and just spill it. "I'm going to have a baby."

His face slowly changes as the words seep into his brain. His brows pull together, his mouth opening, then closing. His head cocking to the side as his eyes go wide inch-by-inch.

He shakes his head. "What did you say?"

"I said," I whisper, "that I . . . we . . . are having a baby."

"This is for real, right?"

"Yes," I nod. "I took a test earlier. I know the last time I said I thought I was having your baby I—"

His chair flies across the room, hitting the floor with a racket. He's in front of me, crouched down, his eyes level with mine. "Say it again."

"We're having a baby."

The intakes of breath are quick and shaky as his eyes start to sparkle with a joy I could have only dreamed of. It's not like before when he was staying calm for my edification. This time, all I see is an elation I couldn't describe if I tried.

"You're serious?" he asks, a laugh built into the words. "We're having a baby? You're sure?"

I nod, still not sure he's processed it all.

"Ellie," he breathes. He lays a hand on my stomach and just stares at it. "My God."

"I don't know how far along I am," I choke out. "I just found out a little while ago."

A quietness descends between us as he looks at me. There are a myriad of emotions playing out on his face and the longer the silence lasts, the more unnerved I become.

I force a swallow. "I don't want you to think this is something you have to do. I know this is a lot and very unplanned, but you can walk away. I don't need you."

"Maybe I need you."

As I begin to smile, beam, even, all seriousness leaves his face. It's replaced with a look of absolute joy. "I can't believe it."

"Believe it," I laugh, fighting tears.

His hand nearly covers my entire abdominal area, his fingers thick and calloused from work. I see the little star on his hand. I move my own to cover his, my thumb pressing against the mark of ink.

"I've never been happier in my life," he says, looking away. I can see the fight of emotion in his features as he struggles to stay composed.

He stands, bringing me to my feet and pulling me in to his chest. His arms wrap around my body, holding me close. There's so much to discuss, so much to figure out, but right now, letting him hold me is the preferred answer.

After a while, he leads me to the living room and sits on the sofa. He pulls me down beside him.

"I want to marry you."

"Wait," I say, shaking my head. "Let's hold up a second."

He just laughs.

"Ford, what I said the other day doesn't change."

"Everything's changed, Ellie."

"No, it hasn't."

"Oh, baby, it *so* has," he grins. "That space bullshit is over. I'm sorry. I can't. I'm going to be all over your shit like white on rice."

I press a finger to his lips. "We have a lot to talk about besides whatever ideas you're cooking up."

"Plans, Ellie. Not ideas. Plans."

I know this is a losing battle. There's no winning with him when he has that look in his eye. Still, I'm not ready to give in even if it means a fight. I'll be heard one way or the other.

"Just remember your plans are yours. They don't necessarily involve me."

"You are ridiculously adorable," he laughs. "So, I'll call G and have him get some moving trucks over—"

"Stop."

"This is happening."

I roll my eyes. "This is not happening. I'm not putting all my eggs in one basket."

"Clearly, I know what to do with eggs," he winks. I slap him on the shoulder and he laughs heartily. "Seriously, though—trust me, Ellie."

"I have a hard time trusting anyone," I whisper.

"I know you do. You're a smart girl. But you and I were brought together again, this time at a point in our lives where we can use the lessons we've learned and go forward. Together."

I look at the floor, my worry taking over the joy again. "Let's talk about the together part."

"Okay. Shoot."

"What about Barrett? Are you going to take off again?"

I look in his eyes. The way his soften shows me he sees the fear in mine. "Ellie, listen, I—"

My phone interrupts him, ringing like crazy on the coffee table in front of us. It's my dad's cell number. I hold up a finger and grab it.

"Hello?" I ask.

"Is this Ellie Pagan?"

"Yes. Who is this?"

"Honey, this is Shirley Templesman from Savannah General Hospital. Your father had an accident this evening. You need to come down here as quickly as you can."

Ellie

IGNORING THE LOOKS FROM THE people I whiz by, I fly around the corner to the Intensive Care Unit. My hand trembles as I press the button repeatedly to open the double doors. At an ant's pace, they break free.

The room numbers are on little blue panels hanging from each doorway. I try desperately not to run around the curved hallway until I find the one I'm searching for.

"I'm sorry, Miss. Can I help you?" A nurse stands from behind a counter. "Visiting hours are over."

"My father is Bill Pagan. Room 12E. The hospital called . . ."

I blink back tears, finding a small amount of relief when Ford's hand steadies me. "Can we see him? Even if it's just for a few minutes?" he asks.

She nods. "12E is right down there. I'll let the doctor know you're here."

"Thank you," I say, but I'm not sure she hears me considering I'm already halfway to the room.

The monitors chirp steadily, the room dark and cool, as we enter. He lies on a bed, a tube sticking out of his nose. With each haggard breath he takes, machines glow and blip all around him.

"Oh, my God," I breathe, dropping my purse on a chair. I try to make sense of the numbers glowing from the various instruments around him, but they all sort of meld together.

Dad's eyes are closed.

I step to the bed and take his hand in mine. It's cold and limp and it takes everything in me not to fall to the floor on my knees and weep.

"Daddy?" I say softly. "Can you hear me?"

His breaths turn into a cough, but he doesn't open his eyes.

"It's me. Ellie. Squeeze my hand if you can hear me."

I wait, silently pleading with him to give me some sort of indication that he can hear me. Placing my other one on top of his, I wait for some sign that he's still here.

The noise of a curtain being pulled sounds behind me. I don't turn around, but hear Ford greeting a doctor. In a few seconds, she appears on the other side of the bed.

"You're Ellie, correct?" she asks.

She has short, curly, red hair and bright green eyes. A stethoscope is around her neck and a chart in her hand.

"Yes."

"I'm Dr. Issac."

"What happened to him?" I ask, my voice starting to break. Ford is at my side in a second flat, but lets me do the talking for which I'm grateful. "How did this happen?"

"According to the report, your father fell in his front yard this evening. A neighbor called for an ambulance, and he was rushed here."

"What were you doing?" I ask, blinking back tears as I see him looking so lifeless in the bed. "Why didn't you call me?"

"Your father had some trauma to his abdomen. A couple of broken ribs and a lacerated kidney."

I squeeze his hand as I look at the doctor. "How long does that take to heal? I'll . . . I'll move him in with me," I sniffle. "I'll make sure he does exactly what he's supposed to."

The look she gives me pierces me to the core. It's one of those smiles that tells you she's trying to warm you up for the pain she's about to deliver. Like the alcohol swab before the injection, she's preparing to destroy me.

I grab Ford's arm.

"Did you know your father has cancer, Ms. Pagan?"

"He did," I say, confidently. "He's been in remission for a while now."

Dr. Issac looks at Ford, then back to me again. "It's in his lungs and lymph nodes, and by what I read in his chart, his liver too."

"What?" I breathe, swaying back and forth. "That can't be true."

"There's a report from his oncologist in his file dated six months ago. Maybe you didn't know, but your father certainly was aware."

"Is aware. He certainly is aware," I correct her.

She takes a deep breath and changes her line of sight to Ford. "His injuries are pretty severe for anyone. But adding his age and health to the mix, I'm afraid I don't have a very good outlook on Mr. Pagan's condition."

"Define that more conclusively," Ford asks.

She braces herself. "I don't have a lot of hope he will make it out of Intensive Care."

I hear the sob that escapes my soul. It echoes off the walls of the dimly lit room, no match for the pain I'm feeling.

Scrambling to the top of the bed, I lay my head next to his. He smells weird, not like my dad. Not the scent that has comforted me since I was a baby.

"Daddy," I cry, throwing an arm over his chest.

There are so many things I want to say, so much I want him to know and be told, but I can't find the words. They're hung up somewhere between my brain and my lips.

The sound of his laugh as I tangle my fishing line up in the trees trickles through my mind. The feel of his hand on my leg as he bandages a little scrape I'm sure is going to kill me after a bicycle wreck is as real as if it were happening. I can smell the scent of his famous deer jerky and see the smile that would accompany his, "Good morning, darlin'," when he'd wake me up for school.

The tears are relentless, dripping down my face and onto his neck. I wind my fist in his hospital gown as if it somehow will keep him here with me.

"Please don't leave me," I whisper in his ear. "Not yet. I'm not ready."

I hear Ford's voice intermingled with the doctor's as I cry silently. I don't care what they're saying or what it even means. None of it matters. I've heard all I need to hear.

Ford's hand rests on the small of my back. "Do you want me to give you a minute?"

"Stay. Please," I sniffle.

"Absolutely."

He gives me a gentle pat and then moves to the corner into a stiff plastic chair. I swipe a tissue off the bedside table and try to clean the snot off my face, one hand still holding my father's.

"Why didn't you tell me?" I ask him, fighting the tears. "If you knew you were sick, why didn't you let me know?"

He looks so peaceful, so much so, in fact, that I'm not sure he's even here.

"ELLIE."

"Ellie."

My hand moves and I jump. "Daddy!"

His head is turned to the side facing me. Ford is reclining in the chair in the corner. He fell asleep an hour or so ago, right before I must've dozed off.

"How are you, pumpkin?" he garbles.

"I'm fine. How are you? Do you hurt anywhere? Do you need any-thing?" I ask, searching his face for any sign of pain.

He doesn't answer me, just tries to squeeze my hand. It's a weak attempt, especially for a man that once had the strength of Bill Pagan.

"I saw Ford lying over there," he says, trying to nod towards the corner.

"He's worried about you."

"He came to see me today."

I kind of laugh, wondering how out of it he is. "You haven't been asleep that long."

"I know that," he sighs. His head pops back on his pillow and he winces.

I stand and help him get situated, but end up tangling myself up in his lines. He tries to laugh but can't quite make it happen.

"The doctor told me you have cancer," I say. "She said you knew it."

"I did."

"But why didn't you tell me?"

"What were you going to do about it?"

"I could've helped you!"

"There is no helping me," he whispers. "I'm ready to go, honey. I just wanted to stick around long enough to make sure you were in good hands."

I glance at Ford. He has a ball cap pulled down over his eyes, his feet hanging off the edge of the chair.

"I hope I am," I say softly.

His oxygen gets knocked off and the alarm begins to sound. I fasten it back under his nose again, and he takes a few long, deep breaths.

He closes his eyes, resting from the exertion of talking to me. I take his hand again and squeeze it, glad that it's a little warmer this time.

"Ellie," he whispers.

"Yes, Daddy?"

"Do you remember the time I took you camping? And that big storm rolled in out of nowhere."

"It about blew our tent into the trees," I recall. "Our cooler was toast. Everything was soaked."

"Yes." He takes a minute before he speaks again. "That was one of the worst storms I'd ever seen in my life. I didn't tell you that, of course, but I was pretty scared. I just held on to you and figured as long as I kept you with me, we could replace everything else."

"And we had to," I laugh softly. "Even my pink fishing pole was gone."

He reaches for my free hand. I scoop it up with mine and hold them as he struggles to talk and breathe. I want to tell him to relax, to sleep it off and we'll resume it later, but I can see it's important for him to continue.

"I want you to always remember that," he says. His eyes open and he looks at me, the greens of his irises as clear as a mountain stream. "And I want you to remember what happened when the rain stopped."

"The double rainbow."

His chest rises and falls harshly as the greens of his eyes start to dim.

"There's always a rainbow, Ellie. Wait for the rainbow."

His eyes flutter close and his hands go limp. I stand at his bedside, tears streaming down my face, and watch him slip away.

"No!" I cry. "Not yet. Please, don't leave me. I have something to tell you. Please! It's important," I sob.

One eye opens just a crack. "What's that?" His words are a rasp, barely audible through the heaviness of his breath.

"I'm pregnant. You're going to be a grandpa," I sniffle.

The struggle to open his eyes is painfully visible, but he does it. His deep, dark eyes look at me. It takes them a second to focus on my face, but when they do, I see a look in them I wish I could capture for an eternity.

"You are?" he asks. "A baby?"

"A baby, Daddy. I'm having a baby."

Tears flow down my face like an overflowing river. He smiles, a small curve of his lips that I know takes an effort to make. "Little pumpkin . . . So happy, Ellie . . ."

He gives in, his eyes fluttering closed, the alarms buzzing all around.

I feel Ford's hand clamp over mine as my body heaves. The buzzers now wailing, they shatter the silence of the night.

"Daddy," I say. "Daddy!"

The corner of his lip turns to the heavens as he sucks in what becomes his final breath.

"Daddy!"

I'm shoved out of the way by the flurry of doctors and nurses swarming in. They talk to me, explain why I have to step out like I don't already know. I let them push me into the hall as I watch through the glass as my father lies quietly on the hospital bed.

Ford's hand is on the small of my back as I watch as they do what they can.

"Don't leave me," I choke out, my body racking as the sobs come faster than I can keep up with. "Don't leave me, Daddy."

My palms are pressed against the window as I watch, hope, beg for some sign that he's still with me. Even as I pray that somehow a miracle will send him back to me, I know the truth: he's already gone.

Ford

I'VE LOOKED FOR HER EVERYWHERE.

"Ellie?" I call again as I enter the kitchen.

It's just like we left it. Everything in its place like Bill could walk back in and settle down in his chair, flipping on an old Western. She doesn't want to disturb it yet and that's fine with me. It's her call. But this disappearing act she has going on has to stop.

I'm about to head back into the living room when something catches my eye. Moving over to the window that overlooks the backyard, I see her. She's sitting on a makeshift bench overlooking a garden that was probably a productive scene a few weeks ago. Everything is sort of overgrown now, some vegetables clearly rotting as they hang on their vines.

She's sitting with her back to me, facing the setting sun.

The last day has been hard for her, harder than I can imagine. I've not lost a parent and she's lost both. Camilla suggested I just stick around, offering to help in any way I can. It feels like not enough. Especially as she cried herself to sleep, finally, in my arms this afternoon.

The door squeaks as I go through and make my way around the corner of the house. If she hears me coming, she doesn't move.

I give her shoulders a soft squeeze as she rests her head on my arm. "The sunset is pretty tonight."

"Yeah."

I take a seat beside her and watch the streaks of pink and purple blaze across the sky. "Are you okay?"

"I will be," she says resolutely. "He'd kill me if he knew I was sitting here crying."

"I think he'd understand."

Her shoulders lift and fall. She toes a rock with her shoe before looking at me. "A lot of people looked at him like he was just another old man," she says. "He didn't finish high school. I'm not sure how well he could read, really. He used to have me spell the words when he'd work the crossword puzzles in the papers."

She smiles to herself at the memory. "I get now why he was so chatty the last few months. He knew he was dying."

"I think he wanted you to keep living your life and not feel like you had to baby him."

"Probably." She kicks another rock. "Speaking of babies, what are we going to do about ours?" She looks at me out of the corner of her eye, a little grin sneaking up on her lips.

"I don't want you worrying about anything, Ellie."

"Fine." She turns to face me. "I'm scared you're going to leave me."

My laughter fills the garden. "There's no way I'm leaving you and you sure as hell aren't leaving me."

"But what about Barrett?"

"What about him?" I shrug. "If he needs my help, I'll give it to him. Of course I will. But . . ." I lean close to her. "I hope I find myself as a married man in the next nine months and can bail out on the travel arrangements because my wife needs me at home."

"Really? You would do that?"

"You think there's a chance I wouldn't?" I laugh. "Look, Barrett is my family and he always will be. That goes for all of my siblings. But, make no mistake, you and our baby are now the most important thing in my life, bar none. No one comes before you. Period."

She blinks back a fresh round of tears.

"Come here." I pull her into my side, kissing the top of head.

"I want to apologize to you," she whispers against my shirt.

"Stop."

"No, hear me out. I've told you I have trust issues and I've blamed them on you—right or wrong. I've pointed out all the things I want to do with my life."

"Things you *will* do with your life," I correct her.

"Will do. Yes," she whispers. "We've both done stupid things and said dumb things and gotten scared for various reasons. I want you to know I'm sorry for doubting you."

"Seriously, stop," I say, squeezing her.

"It's important for me to know you know that. That you know I recognize how amazing you are. You check off all my boxes."

"Your boxes?"

"Don't worry about it," she laughs. "Thank you, Ford, for sticking with me."

"Thank you for being so stick-with-able."

She laughs, planting a kiss to my sternum. "We should be celebrating right now."

"We will, but we have months to think about that. Right now we need to honor your father."

"He didn't want a funeral," she says, her voice cracking. "I hate that. He felt so alone the last few years, and he just expects me to just toss him in the dirt."

"I tell you what," I say, "if you want to do a funeral, you do a funeral. He can't tell you no."

"What if no one comes?"

"Does it matter?" I ask. "It's your way of showing him the respect he deserves."

"Will you go with me to plan it?" She looks at me through her thick lashes. "I can't go alone."

"Baby, you never have to go anywhere alone again. It's me and you."

She turns to me and buries her head in my shoulder. "I feel really alone right now, Ford. I know you are here and I appreciate that so much. But . . . it's just me. My parents are gone. I'm an only child. It's . . ."

Pulling back, she wipes her eyes with her hand. "I don't want our baby to be an only child," she whispers.

"So you're saying you want me to give you a houseful of children? Sold." I grin at her and am relieved to see her smile back. "I'll give you anything you want as long as you keep giving me those smiles."

Her cheeks turn a shade of pink, and she looks back at the garden. "I don't want you to think I'm just saying this because of what just happened with my dad . . ."

I'm almost afraid to ask. Almost. "What?"

Her looks at me with wide, hopeful eyes. "I'm sorry for not trusting you. For not trusting us."

"Hey. It's okay."

"I laid in bed last night and thought about things. I thought about us and things my dad said and how I feel and the baby . . ." She hesitates. "This is my rainbow."

I give her a confused look and she laughs.

"You and this baby are my rainbow, the pot of gold after all the rain," she explains. "After we get through this, I'm yours. Completely."

I chuckle. "Like you already aren't."

"You're right," she says, reaching out and touching my face. "I already am."

Footsteps make us look towards the house to see Violet and Heath coming around the corner. Both of their faces are wet. Ellie runs to them when she sees them and they stand in a circle, hugging and crying.

I pad across the lawn. "Hey," I say. Violet turns to me. "Are you going to be here a while?"

She nods.

"I'm going to go take care of a few things. Will you stay with her until I get back?"

"Absolutely."

I kiss Ellie's cheek and leave them to have some time together.

Ford

"HI, MAMA."

I walk around her island and give her a kiss on the cheek. She adjusts her pearls around her neck and gives me a quick once-over.

"Oh, my," she says, taking my chin in with her hand. "What's wrong?"

"I need to talk to you."

She sets the spoon in her hand down and heads to the breakfast nook. I slide into a seat beside her, the smells of some kind of soup floating around the kitchen.

I've had dinner in this kitchen thousands of times. Just walking in here, I feel at home. I hear my brothers' laughs, my sisters singing stupid songs, my father telling us to all quiet down from over the years. It's a room full of memories, but we have the ability to recreate those sometime. Ellie doesn't, and I can't begin to imagine how she feels right now.

"Ford?" Mom asks. "Talk to me."

I blow out a breath. "This is not how I want to tell you this, but I'm kind of in a bind right now."

"Go on."

"Brace yourself," I say, shaking my head. "Do you remember Ellie Pagan?"

"Of course. Your sisters tell me you're seeing her again. Lincoln says—"

"Just stop there," I laugh. "Whatever Linc says is probably not true."

"Well, in this case, I hope it is." She gives me a motherly smile. "You've seemed happier lately. And you've not been coming by for lunch. While I miss your handsome face, I think it's a good thing you're finding someone else to eat with."

"I have been seeing her again. Actually," I say, testing the waters, "I've been doing more than seeing her."

"Really?"

"Mom, Ellie and I are having a baby."

Her jaw almost hits the table.

"Look, whatever you're thinking, it's not," I ramble. "This isn't some random thing or a mistake that needs cleaned up somehow. I wasn't drinking or on drugs or—"

"Ford." She stops me with one word. "I only have one question."

"Yeah?"

"Do you love her?"

I slink back in my seat, smiling without meaning to. "She's the first thing I think about when I wake up and the last thing that crosses my mind before I go to sleep. When I think back on my day or the last week or the last month, it's like a highlight reel of the moments I got to spend with her. And, if I play that back over the course of my life, the sweetest memories all include her."

Mom bats her eyelashes quickly, one hand going to her chest.

"I can't imagine doing anything and not telling her about it or taking her with me to do it. There's nothing that could be as tempting as slipping in bed with her at the end of the day. And, the thing is, Mom, I've always known that. I just didn't know how to deal with it. Now, I know. And I'm not about to ever, ever give that up."

"That's all I need to know."

I wait for her to continue, but she doesn't. She just watches me with a smile that reflects mine.

"So . . . nothing else?" I ask.

"No." She shrugs her narrow shoulders. "When can I meet her again?

I'd love to get to know her and see if she needs anything for the baby." She places a hand on her heart. "I'm going to be a grandma again. Maybe I'll get to hold this one."

We laugh at her joke. I close my eyes and feel relief course through me. "Thank you, Mom."

"For what, son?"

I shrug as I blow out a breath. "No matter what we do, whether it's Barrett wrecking Dad's car or Lincoln getting written up in the tabloids or Sienna moving to Los Angeles—you always have our backs. I haven't always appreciated that about you."

She grins softly. "It's not always easy raising this brood. You're a bunch of headstrong, opinionated, capable people, and that sometimes gives me heart failure. But I have to sit back and remember a couple of things." She folds her hands on her lap, a gold bracelet twinkling in the light. "For one, that means we've raised healthy, intelligent children that aren't afraid to be themselves. And two, your father and I—more your father—aren't perfect either."

Chuckling, I nod. "None of us is perfect."

"No, we aren't. But a hallmark of a strong family, Ford, is one that allows its members to grow and learn. And not just when they're babies. Sometimes the hardest life lessons are learned when we're adults."

"I'll try to remember that."

"Yes, you should. Especially now that you're going to be a daddy," she smiles. "I can't believe it. I want to go buy all the babies things."

"Easy there," I laugh. "You know, I was afraid you were going to think it was some kind of setup or something. I haven't brought her around and after some of my brothers' shenanigans . . ."

"You are different from your brothers," she says. "You're level-headed. If you tell me this is what you want and what is right, I'm behind you one hundred percent. Besides," she laughs, "I'm going to be a grandma again!"

I watch her face light up, her cheeks matching the color of her dress.

"I have something else to tell you," I sigh. "Ellie's father died last night."

"What?" For the second time in as many minutes, she looks shocked.

"How? That poor girl. Where is she?"

"It's a long story, but he had cancer. Had an accident last night and didn't make it. She's at his house now with a couple of her friends."

"I need to make a casserole." She gets to her feet and is at the freezer before I can say anything. "What does she like to eat?"

"Mom," I chuckle, "give me a second."

One hand holding open the door, she looks at me.

"She doesn't need a casserole, although that's very nice of you. It's just her. He didn't really have any friends and she doesn't have siblings or family. I can handle feeding her."

The door closes with a thump. "I have to do something," she insists. "What does she need?"

I stand and look at her, my phone in my hand poised over Graham's name. "There is one thing . . ."

Ellie

THE SKY IS THREE SHADES of grey. Not a ray of sunshine to be found. Even the breeze has a chill to it that seems fitting for the day.

Sitting in a chair draped with black fabric, I watch as the hearse pulls slowly into the cemetery. I thought this was a compromise between me wanting to honor his life and Dad not wanting anything—a graveside service.

Sitting under the awning are Violet and Heath and a few of my father's friends. They give me tight, sad smiles, their faces showing the fondness they had for Dad. It eases the slightest bit of my pain knowing I'm not the only one that will miss him.

The entire Landry clan surrounds me. They're an overwhelming bunch in the best possible way. Ford mentioned a couple of days ago he told his mother, and ever since, they've all shown up at my house with food, drinks, and chitchat. I couldn't fit another slice of cheese in my refrigerator at this point. Even the Governor is here, sitting in the back with his girlfriend, Alison, and her son, Huxley. Dad would be amused.

The hearse crawls to a stop. As if on cue, the Landry men stand, each looking regal in their suits, and file to the long, black car. I watch in amazement that they took this time out of their day to help me pay tribute to a man they'll never know.

One by one, they form two lines. Ford, Graham, and Barrett on one side and Mr. Landry, Huxley, and Lincoln on the other. Faces somber, heads slightly bowed, they accept the duty they've been tasked with such grace it slays me.

I forgo the tissue and just let the tears roll down my face. There's no sense in trying to keep up with them. It's impossible.

I watch these people give me one of the greatest gifts they could ever give. None of them had to be here today. They all have lives running businesses and states and charities. Yet they're here because Ford asked them to be. They're here . . . for me.

The casket is brought to the tent and placed on the platform in front of me. Each of them stops and gives me a hug before taking their seats. By the time little Huxley comes through the line, I can't see for the tears.

"Ms. Ellie," he whispers.

"Yes?"

"I'm very sorry your dad passed away."

"Thank you, Huxley."

"Here." He takes my hand and presses a small coin in my palm. "This is a token that Lincoln gave me when I was scared to go to Atlanta. He said to keep it in my pocket so I'd remember that I'm not alone, even when I felt like it. I want you to have it now."

I clamp a hand over my mouth and pull the child into another hug. "Thank you, sweet boy."

He straightens his tie and disappears into the aisle behind us.

I lean against Ford's shoulder, holding the little pewter coin in my hand. "Your family is amazing," I whisper.

He looks down at me. "They're your family now too."

The pastor begins the service with an opening prayer. Ford's arm drapes across the back of my chair and the other lies on my lap.

As I listen to the words spoken for my father, I feel a peace settle over my soul. Ford squeezes my hand and I give it a tug back.

The sun peeks through the clouds, almost casting a glow over the tent. It's suddenly warm.

I look around and see the faces of Ford's family carefully listening to the pastor. If you were looking in from the outside, you would think someone important was being put to rest in the black coffin in front of me.

I smile, thinking how proud he would be. And then I smile a little wider when I remember his words, "Figure out what puts a smile on your face and give that a try."

"I figured it out, Daddy," I whisper, dabbing my eye with a hankie. "I finally figured it out."

Ellie

"IT'S LOOKING GOOD, HUH?" I spin in a circle, showcasing the final look of Halcyon before the doors open next week.

"It looks great!" Mallory looks at Camilla. "That green is amazing, don't you think?"

"I don't know. I'm looking at this shirt. Can I buy this now?" she laughs.

"I want that in purple," Danielle chimes in. "Now that I'm not so round I'd look like a grape."

"Don't talk about grapes," Alison blushes.

"Why not? You don't like grapes?" Mallory asks.

Danielle bursts out laughing. "I think it's quite the opposite, wouldn't you say, Ali?"

Alison giggles. "What I wouldn't give for some grape-age right now."

The girls laugh, parting ways, and all clamor about checking out Halcyon's inventory before we go live. I stand in the middle of them all, feeling incredibly blessed.

It's been two weeks since my father passed away. Each day gets a little easier, especially with my Huxley coin in my pocket and my father's words in my ears.

"I love that rainbow," Sienna breathes, checking out the hand-painted art Heath tucked in a corner for me. "It's gorgeous."

I don't tell her it's my ode to my father, my reminder that there's always a rainbow at the end of every storm. Violet doesn't even know why it's there, just that it was important for me to have.

Sienna comes up to me with a smile. "Everything looks fantastic. If you ever want to get some up-and-coming designers, let me know. I have some friends that would fit in well here, I think."

"Really? That would be awesome, Sienna. Thank you."

She tosses a lock of hair off her shoulder. "Yeah, you're welcome. Anything I can do, just let me know. I have contacts here and there."

"Ford said you were thinking of going back to Los Angeles soon?"

"I was. I probably won't though."

"I've always wanted to go there," I admit.

"It's amazing in a lot of ways. It's beautiful for sure and there's always something fun happening and lots of work opportunities. But I just don't feel like a California girl," she sighs. "I think what I want is to just . . . go. See. Do. Not necessarily in LA, just somewhere that's . . ."

"Not here?" I offer.

"Exactly!"

"Maybe you just want to travel and not necessarily put down roots," I suggest. "I can't imagine not seeing your family for months on end. That has to be hard. Even when I was in Florida, I could come home once a month or more, depending on my schedule."

"Sometimes. And sometimes it's not so hard," she laughs as the girls burst out in a fit of laughter. "I see what the boys are doing to Cam and her love life, and I don't want that."

"Ford was telling me about them trying to figure out who he is."

"Who who is?" Danielle asks as she and Alison join us. "Oh, are we talking about Camilla's mystery man again?"

"I can't believe Barrett went into The Gold Room," Alison sighs. "If one picture would've gotten out . . ."

Danielle takes her phone out, looks at the screen, and laughs. "Look at this. This is what I have to put up with."

Flipping the phone to face us, I see a picture of Ryan asleep in his crib with a miniature baseball glove on his hand.

"That's adorable," I laugh.

"Wait until it's Ford. He'll have your baby doing pushups," Danielle teases. She hip bumps Alison. "When are you joining the Landry baby factory?"

She looks at the ceiling. "I don't know. Do I want to do that all over again?"

"Yes," Danielle, Sienna, and I all say in unison.

Alison laughs. "Barrett wants one now. You all have given him baby fever."

"I'm not sorry," Dani shrugs.

"Me either. Besides, it would be nice going through it with someone else," I say. "I have no idea what to expect besides throwing up and gaining weight."

"Well, if Ford is anything like Lincoln, that won't bother him a bit, if you get what I'm saying."

"Ew," Sienna says, wrinkling her nose. "Let's move this conversation along."

We all laugh at her expense as Mallory joins us. "What are we laughing at?" she asks.

"Sienna," Alison says. "She doesn't like thinking about her brothers getting it on."

"I hate to tell you ladies, but I'm certain I snagged the best Landry," Mallory gushes, fanning her face. "And now that I have him doing yoga . . ."

They begin teasing Sienna again when I excuse myself. I wind through the racks of garments and accessories and find the pink sofa in the back.

My feet hurt. My back hurts. My stomach hates me.

I find a package of crackers on the table and nibble one as I try to rest a quick second. My eyes closed, I listen to the Landry women having fun in the front of the store.

Their camaraderie is so easy, their love for one another so apparent. They've done what many families cannot—they've accepted one another, seen the best in each other, and worked together to form a bond that's indelible.

And they've accepted me.

They're my rainbow after the storm.

I take out the coin Huxley gave me and hold it in my fingers. Twirling it around, I feel a warmth take over me.

"I'm going to be okay," I whisper, feeling what I can only describe as my father's presence. "You knew that though."

I put a hand on my stomach and yawn. "By the way, your zucchini plants have grown so much they died under their own weight. I'm pretty sure your garden is a goner."

My eyes are so heavy that I close them for just a few seconds to rest them. I must doze off because I awaken to Alison calling my name. Her head pokes around the corner. "I'm sorry! Were you sleeping?"

"I guess," I laugh, standing up and stretching. "I didn't mean to be."

"I remember those days." She walks into the room and takes me in. "Your phone has been going off like crazy out here, then Ford called Mallory to check on you. You should probably call him back. They can be unrelenting."

"Oh, don't I know it," I laugh.

"Did you get all your things moved in? Barrett said you were working on that last week."

"I did. Well, Ford did. He had a moving company come and pack my stuff and deliver it to his house," I shrug. "What do you say to that?"

"Nothing," she laughs. "You say nothing. Otherwise, it makes it a fight until they win because when it comes to things like protecting you, he will win."

"Now I just need to rent my house or something. I have no idea what to do with it. I just got it."

"Hey!" she says. "I have a friend looking for a house! Her name is Lola and she's moving in with this guy friend of hers that's never going to work out, but whatever. I used to work with her. You'd love her. I could give her your number if you're interested?"

"Really? That would be great."

"Perfect! Now, I'm taking off but I'll be back down for your grand opening. I'll make all of my friends come by," she winks. "In the meantime,

Barrett and I wanted to throw a giant celebration tomorrow night at the Farm. We hoped you'd come."

"What are we celebrating?"

She giggles. "First of all, this family doesn't need a reason to celebrate. Give them a half-assed reason to get together and they'll convene like seagulls to a picnic."

"Noted."

"But we're really just celebrating . . . life. Lincoln and Dani and Ryan. You and Ford and the baby. Sienna since she says she's heading back to LA. Mallory and Graham. Just all of the good things we have. We're so blessed."

"That we are." I slip the token back in my pocket. "That we are."

"So you guys can come? Tomorrow around seven?"

"As far as I know. I'll run it by Ford, but I don't see why not."

"Yay!" She turns to go. "I'll see you then, Ellie."

"Bye, Alison."

Ellie

"I HAVE NO IDEA WHAT I'm supposed to wear to this," I say, coming out of our bedroom. The pale yellow dress was pretty on the hanger, but I'm having major second thoughts about wearing it tonight.

Ford looks up from the floor where he's doing a set of push-ups . . . in a pair of khakis and a navy blue button-up shirt. He grins.

"Is that a yes? A no? A . . ."

He pumps out ten more in quick succession and springs to his feet. "That's a yes." He dips me, planting a hard, heavy kiss to my lips.

"You aren't taking me seriously," I laugh as he stands me straight again. "This is my first major Landry event."

"It's a dinner," he says, looking at me cock-eyed. "Not so much a 'major event.'"

"It feels like it," I moan. "I'm on their turf tonight. That's intimidating."

Ford bursts out laughing. "Their turf?"

"You know what I mean," I huff, going back to the bedroom. I find a pair of straw-colored heels that look cute with their embellished straps and put them on, figuring my days wearing heels are numbered. Thankfully.

"I love when you wear jeans and my t-shirts," Ford says from his spot leaning against the doorframe, "but I like you in dresses and heels too."

"I figured I should."

"Since it's a major Landry event and all," he cracks.

Ignoring him, I look in the mirror once again. With my hair down and curled and a pair of earrings glittering from my ears, I look much better than I feel.

My stomach is still a constant state of misery from morning sickness, a term that's an out-and-out lie. There's nothing "morning" about it at all. It's an around-the-clock ailment that I haven't worked out.

"You ready?" he asks.

I take his hand and let him lead me down the hallway. Pictures of me and my parents now join the images of him from his childhood in the frames between the bedrooms. My grandmother's vase joins the statue he picked up in Barcelona on a tour of duty. The house is now a mix of both of us. I love it.

Ford stops outside the first room at the top of the stairs. He looks at me and grins. His free hand turns the knob and we peer into the room we chose for the baby.

It sits mostly empty now, save for a few random things I've set inside. My old rocking horse that I found in my parents' attic. A giant strawberry toy box we found in an antique store last weekend that reminds me of the one I had growing up and a box of old toys that Vivian had saved from Ford's childhood.

"I was thinking," Ford says, leading me into the room, "we could go next weekend and pick out some paint samples and see what we like."

"But we won't know if it's a boy or a girl for a while yet."

"We can pick a color and if it's wrong, we'll paint it over," he grins.

"You're way too excited about this," I say, bumping him with my shoulder.

"Only because I've waited for this my entire life."

I step in front of him and look him in the eyes. "I know what color I'd like to use, actually."

"I'll go buy it tomorrow."

"I'd like it to look like a meadow with green grass and a sky the color of your eyes. Maybe a little lake in the corner over there that reminds me of the day we met, the moment that kicked off our story." I look around the room and point to another corner. "And a rainbow over there."

"You can have whatever you want," he whispers. "As long as I have you."

"You do."

"Swear?"

"Pinky swear," I wink. "Now come on. We have a celebration to attend."

"I CANNOT POSSIBLY EAT ANOTHER bite," Danielle says. "That was amazing, Vivian."

Ford's mother looks at her daughter-in-law and beams. "Thank you, sweetheart. It was my pleasure to fix food for you all. This makes me happy."

"Me too," Harris says. "You don't cook like this when it's just me at home."

"Oh, hush," she says, lightly smacking him on the shoulder. "What about you, Ellie. Do you need anything?"

"I'm great, Mrs. Landry. Thank you."

"It's Vivian," she insists with a kind smile. "Please, honey. Call me Vivian."

"Hey, Ellie," Alison calls from the far end of the table. "Dani needs a manicure bad."

"It's not that bad," Danielle interjects.

"It's bad," Alison giggles. "Want to go with us tomorrow? Mallory opted out because of some yoga thing."

"The other instructor called off so I have to go in," she pouts.

"Anyway," Alison continues, "want to go with us?"

"Um," I say, tucking a strand of hair behind my ear. "Sure."

Ford rests his hand on my thigh. When I look at him, I melt.

He grins a smile that he only uses when he feels at ease. That isn't often. He may feel relaxed a lot but I don't often see him like this—completely untroubled.

The long table in the dining room of the Farm erupts in laughter. Glasses are refilled, silverware clinking against plates, as the entire brood talks and enjoys one another.

I've never seen anything like this in my entire life. The love and respect in this room is incredible.

"Hey, Dad!" Lincoln calls. "Want to go golfing in the morning?"

"No one wants to go golfing with you," Graham says.

"Jealous, much?" Lincoln teases. "I can't help I'm the born athlete of the family."

"Hey, now," Ford interjects. "I beat your ass the last time we played."

"Language," Vivian warns. "There are little ears around here."

"I've heard worse, Grandma," Huxley says. "I did spend the afternoon with Lincoln and Ryan yesterday."

The noise level reaches an all-time high as everyone laughs and Vivian chastises her youngest son. When Barrett stands, the chatter begins to quiet. One by one, everyone looks at the Governor.

He's incredibly handsome in a more finessed way than Ford. Barrett has darker hair and smoother skin and a smile that, on cue, can light up a room. I'm sure he had every female vote in the last election based off that smile alone.

"I have something to tell you all," he says, looking down at Alison. He nearly beams. "Tonight is more than just a dinner party."

"What do you mean?" Mallory asks.

"Mom and Barrett are getting married!" Huxley shouts, springing up from his chair with a smile as wide as the table.

The room erupts into a mad frenzy as everyone processes Huxley's declaration. Shouts of delighted shock and confusion echo off the walls. Barrett waves his hands down, encouraging everyone to be quiet.

"He's right," he says once everyone settles some. "I've persuaded Alison to marry me tonight and we'd love for you to take part."

"Are you serious right now?" Dani stands, Ryan tucked into the crook of her arm. "You're getting married tonight?"

"Yes," Alison almost squeals. She too stands and wraps her arm around Barrett's elbow. "Vivian and I have been planning it for a week now." She looks at her soon-to-be mother-in-law. "Thank you, by the way."

"It's been my pleasure."

Huxley jumps up and dashes wildly into the living room. Ford takes my hand, pulling my chair back and tucking me close under his arm as we walk through the house and into the converted space.

"Your brother just decided to get married today? Who does that?" I laugh.

He looks at me curiously. "That's not so crazy, is it?"

"It's totally crazy," I laugh.

"Do you think it's a bad thing?"

"No," I gush. "I think it's seriously sweet. I just expected a big wedding or something. He's the Governor, after all."

While we were eating, it's obvious a team of people were transforming the living room into a mini-wedding chapel. There are flowers, all white, in vases around the room. A little podium has been brought in and a table placed behind it with two tall pink candles. The furniture has been pushed to the side for us to sit and watch Barrett and Alison say "I do."

I'm in shock at how laidback this is for a family as sophisticated as the Landry's. It's a simple elegance, an unassumingly beautiful backdrop to such a significant moment in this family's history.

As Ford and I sit on the couch beside Camilla, we watch the family get situated in two rows, both facing the center of the room.

Mallory catches my eye and smiles. There's something in the air tonight that's truly special and I know she feels it too. She takes Graham's hand in hers and places them on her lap. He turns and kisses her on the forehead, and I almost swoon.

"Hey," Ford whispers, nudging me gently with his shoulder. "Was this enough of an event for you?"

"Did you know about this?" I giggle.

"It's funny what people tell you when Lincoln liquors you up with tequila," he laughs. "This was one of Barrett's admissions on the way home from The Gold Room. They were trying to set it up then." He says the last two words a little more pointedly, glancing over my shoulder at Camilla.

"Don't go there," she says through clenched teeth.

"I wouldn't dream of it," he says, then turns to me and winks.

A man comes in from a doorway on the other side of the room and stands beside the podium. Barrett and Alison take their places in front of him with Huxley at his mother's side.

Hux bounces on the balls of his feet, a small box in each hand. He looks at Barrett with such adoration, it brings tears to my eyes.

In just a few minutes, the pastor asks who is giving Alison away. Huxley steps forward, clearing his throat, and accepts that responsibility. Barrett squats down, has a quiet, private conversation with Hux, a smile on both of their faces. They shake hands before Barrett stands and takes Alison's.

There's not a dry eye in the house. Vivian has a handkerchief dotting her eyes with Harris looking on with such pride I think he's going to burst. It's an incredible moment with an incredible family—a large, loving, remarkable family that is as simple as they are complicated.

Standard vows are read and Alison is declared to be Mrs. Barrett Landry in just a few short minutes. As Barrett lays a kiss heavier than I would expect on his new bride, the family erupts in cheers and hugs.

I lean my head against Ford, his muscled shoulder moving so he can wrap his arm around me. He glances down, his eyes filled with emotion. He doesn't speak, but he doesn't have to. I feel the same way I see in his eyes.

"That was beautiful," Vivian gushes, getting to her feet and swatting Barrett away. She takes Alison at arm's length. "I want to be the first to welcome you into the family, Alison."

"Thank you," Alison grins. "I know that was quick and to the point, but I already have everything I want. And I didn't want to have a stuffy event with a bunch of senators' wives," she cringes.

"Thank God for that," Vivian laughs.

"I have one more announcement," Barrett says, clearing his throat. "Hey, Hux. Where are you, buddy?"

His new step-son races in the room from the kitchen, a cookie hanging out of his mouth. "Yeah?"

Barrett stands in front of him, holding out a piece of paper. Alison steps to Barrett's side, this time her face awash with more emotion than ever before. Vivian hands her a tissue as Alison latches on to Barrett's arm.

"I want you to read this," Barrett says, handing the paper to the child.

Huxley takes it. The cookie falls from his lip as his head snaps up to Barrett's. "Really?"

"Really."

"Like, really, really?"

"Like, really, really," Barrett smiles.

Huxley launches himself into Barrett's arms. Alison embraces them both, her arms enclosing the two men in her life. It's a sight to see, even though I have no idea what was on that paper.

The family is quiet, watching something unfold in front of us. Vivian and Harris arrive in the center of the room and the five of them have a quiet conversation.

"What did the paper say?" I whisper to Ford.

"He's adopting him," Ford tells me. "His biological father signed his rights away."

My vision now blurs as I watch Harris come away with a smile reminiscent of Ford's. His eyes shine with pride, of course, but maybe something else. Maybe of a job well done. Harris Landry may have made millions of dollars in real estate over his lifetime, but his greatest accomplishment is his children.

Barrett looks at Ford. With a raise of his brow, he leads Alison and Huxley off to the side. Much to my surprise, Ford untangles my arm from around his waist and stands.

The room quiets again. I look at Mallory, then at Sienna, and they're both looking at me with huge smiles.

My heart starts to race as I realize Ford hasn't moved. He hasn't disappeared to the bathroom as I expected, nor has he ventured into the kitchen for a second slice of apple pie. Instead, he's standing in front of me, ignoring his family's whispers, and waiting for my reaction.

"Ford?" I ask.

His eyes are sober, his Adam's apple bobbing as he bends on one knee. I gasp, grabbing Camilla's hand and squeezing it for dear life.

"Ellie," he says, clearing his throat. "I've loved you since the day I first saw you. You were wearing jeans with the right knee out and a grey shirt that hung off your shoulder. You had mud everywhere and a fishing pole on the ground next to you."

I vaguely hear his family chuckle, but I'm too focused on the gorgeous man in front of me to mind. I take his hand and place my thumb over the star in the crook of his fingers.

"I swore to myself if God ever gave me another chance with you, I wouldn't blow it. That I'd do everything in my power to take care of you and love you the way you deserve to be loved."

My hand touches the side of his face as the heat of my tears slides down my cheeks.

"A few weeks ago, I talked to your father."

Just the mention of him causes my heart to flex in my chest. My bottom lip begins to tremble and I can barely see him through the on-slaught of waterworks.

"He gave me permission, and his blessing, to ask you to be my wife."

I hear gasps from around the room, but all I can do is watch the man in front of me, on his knee, telling me he did the one thing that matters. He thought of it all.

"It would be the biggest honor in the world if you would be Mrs. Ford Landry."

"Yes," I whisper. I don't think twice about it. I don't overthink it or reconsider. I just go with my gut, and that says to scoop this man up.

Ford brings a ring out of his pocket. A large but not gaudy diamond sits in a gold band encrusted with tiny diamonds. It's simple and elegant and something I'd pick myself if I had the choice and resources.

"The diamonds around the edges are from your mother's ring," he whispers just for me to hear. "Your father gave it to me."

I throw myself at him, telling him how much I love him and how happy he makes me. It's a ramble, a tear-filled slug of words that I'm not even sure is coherent.

He stands, pulling me with him. "I have one final question."

"What?" I laugh, wiping my eyes. "What else could you possibly ask me?"

"Will you marry me right now?"

I gasp. Mallory gasps. I think everyone might suck in a breath at Ford's unexpected question.

"If you don't want to, we can wait," he admits. "If you want a big wedding, I'll throw you the biggest damn wedding Savannah has ever seen. But we have a pastor here and he's in possession of a wedding license we can sign . . ."

I search his eyes. I have no fear, no second thoughts—nothing but a smile on my face. "Yes. Let's get married. Tonight."

We take our positions in front of the podium to the cheers of the Landry family behind us. We sign our names to the marriage application and then hold hands as he reads from the Bible.

Our vows are repeated simply, easily, just like our relationship. And in a few minutes, we, too, are pronounced husband and wife.

The family nearly attacks us with hugs, kisses, and tears of joy. I'm welcomed to the family by promises of love, offers of goodwill, and warnings to prepare to fight over pie at Thanksgiving.

It's simply one of the best moments of my entire life.

After everyone moves back into the kitchen, with Lincoln suggesting they break out the tequila, I finally make my way to Alison.

"I'm sorry we just butted in on your wedding," I say.

She tosses me a wink. "Ford ran it by us before he did it," she laughs. "We thought it would be fun to share an anniversary with you." Pulling me into a hug, she grins. "Congratulations, Mrs. Landry."

"Wow," I say, trying to wrap my head around that. "I mean, to you too. But doesn't that sound . . ."

"Amazing?" she offers.

"Amazing," I concur.

It's in this moment with this family, *my family*, that I realize I'm truly going to be okay. That the best things in life come when you take a chance and do things because they simply make you smile.

I look at Ford, my new husband, talking quietly with his father. It's a simple scene—two men talking with glasses in their hands. My cheeks split as I feel my chest warm in a happiness that I can barely contain.

"What are you thinking about?" Danielle asks, coming up beside me.

"You have a pretty serious look on your face."

I tear my eyes away from Ford and look at her. I shrug. "Just how I need to remember that when storms roll in, how beautiful the rainbow is going to be."

*E*pilogue

"YOU DID IT." FORD CAGES me into the corner of the back room of Halcyon, his lips hovering over the shell of my ear. "I am so proud of you, Ellie. You may have had to take a few extra weeks with everything that's happened, but you did it."

I haven't stopped smiling all day, the grand opening of the store I'm so incredibly proud of. Twisting in his arms, I see my happiness reflected on his face. "Thank you. I couldn't have done it without you."

"While I love that, it's a lie. You did do it without me." His eyes widen, as if to remind me it's a touchy subject.

I giggle. "I didn't do it without you! You've weighed in heavily on some aspects. I couldn't have finished painting the ceiling without you. Don't forget that," I say, tapping him on the nose.

"I'm so glad I was able to do that. Lord knows you couldn't have had that done by anyone else." He takes my hand and leads me towards the front.

"No one would've looked as good as you shirtless," I point out.

The crowd we've had all day has dwindled. We officially closed almost an hour ago, but how do you kick people out when you're so grateful they're there? You don't. You smile and chitchat and refill the cookie tray by the front door.

Violet left a few minutes ago, leaving me to enjoy a little time with Ford and his family.

Taking in the few faces still here, I'm overcome with emotion. That's been happening a lot lately. Everything makes me cry. Violet thinks I'm a lunatic, and Ford worries I'm unhappy, but in reality, it's the opposite: I'm just incredibly happy.

Ford drops my hand and heads off to see Sienna, one of the reasons why we had such a fantastic day. She and Camilla invited all their friends, all of their mother's friends—practically all of Savannah. With their charm and connections, they took my dreams and made them a reality.

Sienna reaches up and wipes at Ford's cheek. I watch his muscled shoulders rise and fall as if he couldn't care less that my lipstick was imprinted on his face.

"Hey."

I look to my right and see Camilla.

"Cam, I just wanted to thank you again for—"

"Will you stop it?" she laughs. "You're family, Ellie. We take care of our own."

I feel the burn in the bridge of my nose that tells me I'm going to be fighting tears any moment.

"You and the little one," she says, touching my stomach. "I'm pulling for you to be a girl."

"I'm not sure Ford can afford me if I have a girl," I laugh. "I'm not even a girly-girl, but if this one turns out to be . . ."

"Girl," Camilla says, putting a hand on her hip, "if I get a niece, you better watch out! Dani says we spoil Ryan, which might be true, but a girl? All the things, Ellie. All the things."

Her cheeks redden a bit, her eyes sparkling. A weird look flickers across her face as her smile just grows.

"Cam?" I ask curiously. I can't help but return her smile.

"You guys are giving me baby fever," she giggles. "I just want to hold a baby, cuddle it, breathe in that baby scent. I could hold Ryan all day if Lincoln would let me."

I yelp as someone bumps me from behind. Ford's arms go around my waist and pull me in to his chest. He rests his chin on the top of my head. "I'm going to pretend I didn't hear that."

"I—" Cam begins, but is interrupted by the husband of one of their mother's friends.

"Good to see you, Ford," he says. "How's life going?"

"She's pretty good."

The man looks confused and then down at me. With a slow nod, he gives Ford a small smile. "That's good. We are heading out. I just wanted to thank you, Mrs. Landry, for opening another business to take all of my money."

We all laugh as he and Ford bid their farewells and he exits, followed by the last two shoppers.

The sun begins to set outside, the sky lit up with a spectrum of pinks and purples. It's a beautiful evening, the perfect cap to a perfect day.

I twirl the coin in my pocket that Huxley gave me as I watch Sienna make her way across the room.

"That went over well," Sienna says. "What a day, Ellie!"

"I know. But my feet hurt," I wince.

"Let's get you home and in the bath." Ford grabs my hand and squeezes it. "You two need to hit the road."

"Gee, thanks," Camilla laughs.

I look up at my man and silently ask him if I can start the plan we've talked about since yesterday afternoon. He winks.

"I want to invite the two of you to our house this weekend," I say, trying to quell the burst of excitement in my belly. "I'm going to make dinner and would like you all to come."

"You do realize there are a bunch of us, right?" Sienna laughs. "You're cooking for us all?"

"Yup."

"Even Mom usually hires a caterer at this point," Camilla giggles.

"I want to do it," I say fervently. "And I'd love for you to be there."

"Only if I can come early and help." Camilla pulls me into a hug. "I don't want you stressing my little niece out."

"Wait," Sienna says, holding a hand up. "It's a girl?"

"We don't know," Ford says. I elbow him in the gut and he winces.

Sienna's brows pull together as she assesses the situation in front of her. "You guys know something. What is it?"

"It's a secret," I say, giving Ford a look to be quiet. "One that you can be in on if you come to dinner on Saturday."

"Count me in," Camilla says.

"You," Ford says, pointing at his blonde sister, "can only find out if you bring whoever it is you're seeing."

Cam sighs, rolling her eyes. "Stop it."

"I'm being serious."

"No, he's not," I say. "Of course, he's welcome, whoever he is. But you can come without him."

"Just bring him, Cam," Sienna gripes. "I'm tired of being in the middle about this."

"I can't." Camilla's voice is a clear warning to her twin to tread lightly. "You know I can't."

"You can. You just won't." Sienna gives Ford and I quick hugs and heads to the front door, Cam at her heels. "I'll see you Saturday, I guess."

"Bye, guys," I call out.

As the door closes, I nearly fall backwards into Ford's arms. I yelp as he picks me up, my legs dangling over one of his powerful arms, and look into his handsome face.

Just looking at him makes me smile. Not because he's my husband or so incredibly good-looking with his sun-kissed skin and rugged jawline, but because of what I see buried in those blue eyes.

It could be described as love. Maybe respect. There's a possibility it could be lust. But I think it's more than that. It's the look of forever.

"I love you," I whisper to him, my hand finding the side of his face. "I'll love you for the rest of my life."

He grins. "Pinky swear?"

"Pinky swear."

The End

Read more about the Landry family:

SWAY (Barrett)

SWING (Lincoln)

SWITCH (Graham)

SWINK (Camilla—coming summer 2017)

About the Author

USA TODAY AND AMAZON TOP 10 Bestselling author Adriana Locke lives and breathes books. After years of slightly obsessive relationships with the flawed bad boys created by other authors, Adriana has created her own.

She resides in the Midwest with her husband, sons, and two dogs. She spends a large amount of time playing with her kids, drinking coffee, and cooking. You can find her outside if the weather's nice and there's always a piece of candy in her pocket.

Adriana can be found on all social media platforms. Look for her on the ones you frequent most!

Her website is the place to go for up-to-date information, deleted scenes, and more. Check it out at *www.adrianalocke.com*. Don't forget to sign up for her newsletter, sent monthly, filled with news, pictures, fun and giveaways.

If you use Facebook or Goodreads, there's good news! Adriana has reader groups in both places. Join Books by Adriana Locke (Facebook) and All Locked Up (Goodreads) and chat with the author daily about all things bookish.

Acknowledgements

THANK YOU TO THE CREATOR above for blessing me with so many things, none of which I deserve.

To my family, Mr. Locke, the Littles, Mama, and Peggy and Rob: I love you. Always.

To my team Kari (Kari March Designs), Lisa (Adept Edits), Christine (Type A Formatting), Kylie (Give Me Books): I'm tempted to break out in song and dance! Ha! Number ten is in the books. Can you believe that? Ten! Thank you, thank you, thank you.

My PA, Tiffany, keep me organized, laughing, and on my toes. Thank you for always having my back and being two steps ahead. You're one of the best decisions I've ever made.

It's simply amazing some of my betas will even speak to me at this point. You all know who you are. Thank you for your patience. God knows I've tested it with this one.

To my admins, Jen C, Jade, Tiffany, and Stephanie: You four keep the wheels turning (and laughs coming!). Thank you for your time monitoring my groups and keeping things running like a well-oiled machine.

To Susan: Thank you for being such a good friend and an incredible inspiration. You astound me with your strength and energy and ability to keep a sunny disposition no matter what. I adore you.

To Mandi: Just because. All the things. You get it.

To Lisa, Jade, and Alexis: You know life, it's all about . . . people like you. I adore you all.

To Carleen: You saved me.

To Candace: May we endeavor to never go through this many revisions again. Ha!

Candi, my Locke Librarian, keeps the little details at my fingertips. Thank you for your diligence. You'll never know how often I have to use the library!

Ebbie: Your work with the FitBit Challenge in Books by Adriana Locke is changing lives. Whether you know it or not, you are a difference maker! Thank you for being so amazing and thoughtful and giving of your time and energy.

To bloggers: You blog for the love of it, yet we are always begging you for more. It takes a special person to do what you do and I want you to know it does not go unnoticed by me. Thank you, to each and every one of you, for choosing to support me and this book. I appreciate it from the bottom of my heart.

Books by Adriana Locke and All Locked Up: Your energy feeds me. Your love sustains me. Your support keeps me going. Thank you for being my friends.

CPSIA information can be obtained
at www.ICGtesting.com
Printed in the USA
LVHW080906280120
644930LV00013BA/1145